QUEERPHORIA

VERVE Voices

QUEERPHORIA

Edited by Jenna Gordon and Demi Echezona

VERVE BOOKS

First published in 2026
by VERVE Books Ltd., Harpenden, UK
vervebooks.co.uk
@VERVE_Books

A CIP catalogue record for this book is available from the British Library.

ISBN
978-0-85730-948-8 (Paperback)
978-0-85730-949-5 (cBook)

2 4 6 8 10 9 7 5 3 1

Typeset in 11 on 13.4pt Minion Pro
by Avocet Typeset, Bideford, Devon, EX39 2BP
Printed and bound in Great Britain by Clays Ltd, Elcograf S.p.A.

MIX
Paper | Supporting responsible forestry
FSC® C018072

The manufacturer's authorised representative in the EU for product safety is Easy Access System Europe, Mustamäe tee 50, 10621 Tallinn, Estonia
gpsr.requests@easproject.com

Contents

Introduction

When the VERVE team started talking about publishing an in-house anthology series – a collective daydream that eventually calcified into a real, exhilaratingly ambitious creative project – three priorities soon arose. The first was that this series should explore topics that reflect VERVE's vision and values for publishing, and act as an opportunity to further broaden the range of forms, voices and ideas available to readers on our list. Our second priority was to partner with different charities for each edition of *VERVE Voices*, charities who champion the same values we do, as a means of supporting the causes we care about. The third was that queer writing should be front and centre of the inaugural edition, not only because the story of VERVE cannot be told without queer voices, but as a means of resisting the current backlash – politically, socially, culturally – against the human rights of those in our community. So, our first offering is *VERVE Voices: Queerphoria* – an anthology for queer people, created by queer people. A protest, a challenge, a defiant celebration, a full-throttle leap into the euphoria of existing queerly.

With an intentionally broad brief, we invited writers from the VERVE stable and beyond, all of whom belong to the LGBTQIA+ community, to write on the theme of 'queerphoria' in whichever way they'd prefer. Just as we'd hoped, the result has been an eclectic and outrageously queer collection of contributions with huge diversity across genre, style and subject matter. Among it all, three points of connection emerged: each piece was concerned, to varying degrees, with identity, love and sex, and community. These themes have been used as a means of loosely structuring the collection, though, of course, the boundaries often blur.

The opening section, 'Queerphoria in the Self', contains writing on how euphoria is experienced by queer individuals, kicking off with Dylin Hardcastle's poignant and uplifting reflections on identity, history and community, which transport the reader to Tropical Fruits festival in Lismore, Australia. Hardcastle's contribution is accompanied by gloriously atmospheric and evocative illustrations from artist Peo Michie. Soula Emmanuel revisits the early 2000s and her Greek heritage to blend gender euphoria and mourning for her past self into a beautiful, comedic tale featuring rebetikó music and its history of empowering oppressed Greeks to express their discontent. In a dynamic series of poems entitled 'Five Repetitions', Joshua Jones moves through a hook-up, a love story and a confession, with a take on queerphoria that is sexy and unserious, scathing and vulnerable. Icon of the Scottish writing scene Carrie Marshall takes the reader through the music that, for her, has manifested euphoria throughout her life – a feeling she's found in pop classics, but also in less expected places, like at a Gaelic folk music festival. Eve Gleichman invites the reader into the mental health facility where their insomniac protagonist has landed, and where queerphoria can also be located. In a work of auto-fiction, Santanu Bhattacharya reflects on his choice to attend the fiftieth London Pride celebrations in the wake of a hate crime he experienced close to home, and on the realities of pride and belonging in a marginalised community. And via a return trip from Glasgow to Accra, Selali Fiamanya has crafted an uplifting story of grief that brings his protagonist closer to himself, to family, to community, to pleasure – and to an old and inexplicable magic.

The multitudes of pleasure to be found in relationships have been spotlighted in 'Queerphoria in Love and Sex'. Chloe Michelle Howarth's protagonist welcomes the reader to 'Gay

House' and offers a tour of the abundant and contagious joy to be found there with her chosen family. Meanwhile, in an isolated lighthouse, Seth Insua's story allows an intimate glimpse into the lives of a closely bonded couple on the day of their thirtieth anniversary, as they discover there might be new adventures to be sought together. Through Peter Scalpello's three poems, which are rich with sensuality and intimacy, the reader can effortlessly navigate a cathartic journey towards self-acceptance, unconditional love and contentment. Writer Amil and translator Joheun Lee tell an imaginative and nuanced speculative tale that speaks to several of the many issues impacting modern sex and dating, a tale in which a woman purchases a 'feminist sex robot' in an attempt to address her insecurities around love and intimacy. Elle Nash's vividly rendered snapshot of the euphoria to be found in a BDSM relationship taps into a pleasure that's accessible via transgression, a concept the LGBTQIA+ community knows well. And as a couple secretly bring new life into a world where The Establishment dictates who can procreate, Maame Blue offers a lesson in hope, and in knowing that some risks are worth it, with world-building that is revolutionary.

Finally, an unparalleled joy, one we find on a daily basis at VERVE: 'Queerphoria in Community'. Laura Kay's bittersweet story follows a grieving older woman on her first visit to a queer bar, where she forms life-altering connections. Then, using free verse to summon a quiet-yet-palpable euphoria, Remi Graves contemplates the sensation of existing as a 'body on the loose', a 'self-herding sheep' – to be a being crafting their own path in a flock of others. Jenny Chamarette cleverly plays with the concept of 'queerphoria', casting it as 'the carrier bag of queer feeling' in order to delve into the importance of sharing queer stories, and of being seen and held by a community. Against a backdrop of surreal chaos, Gerardo Sámano Córdova preserves a small utopia among four friends who tell dark stories, drink beer and reflect on the city that brought them together, ignoring the impending future that will separate them. Award-winning Joelle Taylor shares a stirring quartet of poems on community uprising and resilience, culminating in an evocative scene that (literally) invites the reader into the action. James Cahill tells the delicious tale of a 'podcaster, provocateur, [and] author of caustic book reviews' who escapes to Monte Carlo after falling from grace in London's literary world, only to find he can't outrun himself, or his cultural irrelevance. And bringing the collection to a close is William Rayfet Hunter's whirlwind coming-of-age story, which culminates in a celebration of self-embodiment and community as nightclubbing becomes a religious experience.

To add further flavour to this fantastic assortment, we approached VERVE's endlessly supportive online community for their reflections on queerphoria – and they delivered in abundance. Therefore, each section of this anthology also contains contributions from brand-new voices, handpicked by the VERVE team. We're delighted to introduce: Lynsey Rogers, P Burton-Morgan, Aditya Tiwari, Natasha Bell, Ross Kelly, Dale Booton, Stanley Iyanu, Em Prendergast, Hannah Nicholson and Nirali Sheth.

We are honoured and extremely grateful that *VERVE Voices: Queerphoria* is being supported by national LGBTQIA+ helpline Switchboard, who will receive a £1 donation from every copy sold. Our aspiration was to release this first anthology in aid of Switchboard, and we were over the moon to have them on board from the very early stages, before anyone else. They have been been brilliant throughout, with special thanks to Bob and Kerri, and to Stephanie for her foreword.

Curating and editing such a joy-filled and definitively queer collection across the past year and a half has been an invigorating new adventure. It is a project that has instilled in us an abundance of optimism and a deep sense of community connection, and which has felt increasingly urgent and necessary as time has progressed. What was at the outset intended as a celebratory cheer now enters the world as a defiant cackle, a battle cry, one which we are so excited for you to partake in as you revel in these pages.

Jenna Gordon & Demi Echezona
VERVE Books, 2026

Foreword

On the fourth of March 1974, in a small room sharing a building with Housmans bookshop in London, volunteers eagerly waited for the phone to ring. Months of promotion in local gay newspapers, on posters and through word of mouth had led to this. The phone rings, a volunteer picks up the cradle and holds it to their ear and answers: 'Hello, London Gay Switchboard, what would you like to talk about?'

By the end of the shift, some three hours later, forty-five calls had been taken.

Fifty-two years later, Switchboard, now the national LGBTQIA+ Support Line, is still here, still standing strong and has handled over four million conversations. We operate 365 days a year, supporting people via phone, instant messaging and email, 10:00 am to 10:00 pm. Almost 400 current volunteers are there to make sure that there is someone to speak to, anywhere across the country, at any point in your journey.

We are there for you to speak about what is on your mind, and to be a non-judgemental space to explore various topics or whatever might be affecting you. You don't have to identify as being part of the LGBTQIA+ community to get in touch, and indeed, we often have conversations with friends and family who want to hear about how they can better support people in their lives.

Our conversation logs, filled in by thousands of volunteers from 1974 to today, show stories of love, confusion, violence, hope, despair, delirious excitement, concern and, of course, queer joy.

In among those conversations, we find everything from the quiet moments of someone who is nervous and fearful because they have been kicked out of their home and don't know what to do next, to lesbians abseiling into the Houses of Parliament to protest Section 28. We've spoken with bi and lesbian mothers terrified of custody cases where they will be seen as 'unfit' parents due to their sexuality. Sometimes we're the reassuring ear for someone who has just found the words to talk about who they are for the first time. We were at the centre of a community upended by HIV/AIDS, a community that pulled together to look after each other.

These logs are testament to our history – to people all across the country whose lives shaped and were shaped by the world around them – and to our future.

Our stories as LGBTQIA+ people continue to transform the world today and are just as important as ever. We know the power of a story in reflecting our worlds back at us, and in showing us that we are not alone.

When VERVE approached us to be part of this fantastic anthology, we jumped at the chance. The stories of LGBTQIA+ people, in all their glorious complexities and nuances, are a vital part of living as our most authentic selves, leaving a torch so others can more easily find their way out of the maze. And given VERVE's history of publishing a wide range of beautiful and powerful LGBTQIA+ books, showing lives that are complicated, messy, funny, dark and sexy, what better place to tell these stories of joy?!

Fifty-two years on, we are still here, still listening.

Stephanie Fuller, CEO of Switchboard, 2026

QUEERPHORIA IN THE SELF

Selected queer joy as a late-bloomer

Selected queer joy as a late-bloomer: chopping your hair off | seeing a photo and thinking, 'that's what I'm supposed to look like' | the cliché septum piercing | a steady diet of queer smut | queer bookshops that feel like home | femme and masc | crushes | the 'buying everything rainbow' phase | a sense of grounding and expansiveness | the challenge to demand more | feeling authentically desired | witnessing younger queers lightyears ahead | feeling like a teenager again, but the teenager you were supposed to be | younger you even contemplating writing this list.

Lynsey Rogers (she/they)
@lynsrogers

Bearing Fruit

Five years. Planted
against the south-facing wall.
Bare roots and hope.
I shared new pronouns, lopped off
the spare syllables of my old name.
This year for the first time
in spring, blossom.
Which meant by late summer, fruit.
People correct themselves now
with apologetic blushes,
use my new name by default.
Five pears. One slightly wasp-eaten,
one grows into an unusual shape.
Still. Five fruits. Branches rich
with green leaves. Trunk
thickening over time.
The shape of my pronouns
no longer an unexpected taste
in your mouth.
Nature flourishes surprisingly
easily. When allowed.

P Burton-Morgan (they/them)
@PBurtonMorgan

Dylin Hardcastle (he/they) is an award-winning author, screenwriter and former Provost's Scholar at the University of Oxford, now based on the unceded lands of the Gadigal People. They are the author of four books, which have been published to critical acclaim in eleven territories and translated into eight languages. Dylin is the co-writer and co-director of *Cloudy River*, which premiered at Mardi Gras Film Festival in 2020 and was later acquired by SBS. Their most recent novel, *A Language of Limbs*, won the 2023 Kathleen Mitchell Award, was shortlisted for Dymocks Book of the Year in 2024, longlisted for the Voss Literary Prize and the 2025 Stella Prize and was a *TIME* 100 Must-Read Books of 2025.

dylinhardcastle.com
@dylin_hardcastle

Peo Michie (they/them) is an Australian artist born in Africa, of Tswana heritage. Growing up in rural Queensland, Peo embraced illustration, comics and zine-making as a means of self-discovery, exploring themes of queer identity, romance and relationships through storytelling and self deprecating humour. They graduated from the Queensland College of Art with a bachelor's degree in Animation and undertook specialised training at the Salisbury Fine Arts Atelier. Peo has gone onto build a diverse portfolio of digital art projects, including creating their first graphic novel with Silver Sprocket Publishing, as well as producing 2D animated music videos for Aisha Dee, Tiara Thomas and H.E.R. Peo's creative work has been internationally recognised by organisations such as Netflix's *The Order* and *Magic: The Gathering*'s Pride Secret Lair Drop.

peomichiecourse.com
@peomichie

Wet

It's our first time at Tropical Fruits and we've absolutely sent it.

Now, Peo and I are splayed out on the grass at 6:00 am, watching the sun rise on the first day of 2025, having emptied out of the huge metal shed that housed last night's dance floor only a few minutes ago. All I'm wearing is a tiny G-string with a fake flower sewn over the crotch, and a pair of sparkly cowboy boots. I'm caked in dried sweat, dirt and love bites from a night spent in the dark, wet heat of the shed. This place is usually a showground where cattle and sheep are bought and sold by local farmers, but last night the shed was home to cabaret, cruising and dance. Outside, on the grass where market stalls would, on another day, be set up selling local produce, partiers sat down last night for a breather, or to gossip, or to roll cigarettes in the balmy summer air. Far from any city, the Milky Way poured across the sky like water, a river of stars glistening above us.

The festival we're at – Tropical Fruits – is a multi-day party for LGBTQIA+ people, organised and run entirely by volunteers, that takes place every new year in the subtropical hinterland of Bundjalung Country. Though known since colonisation by another name – the Northern Rivers – this place is *first light* Country, because it's the most eastern part of the continent and therefore the first place the light touches each sunrise.

Our friend Aisha still has battery on her phone and takes a photo of me. She and Peo start gassing me. *Fuck! You look so handsome! Pose like that again!*

I laugh and tell them I don't believe them. We're coming down from a night of debauchery. There's no way I trust what they're saying.

No! Honestly! Look! Aisha insists. She throws me the phone.

I look at the photo and gasp.

See! She and Peo say. *We told you!*

I can't stop staring at the photo. And it's not simply because I love how I look more than I ever have. For the first time in my life, I'm seeing a picture of myself in which I fully *recognise* myself. During the year that's preceded this moment, I began medically transitioning, undergoing top surgery and injecting testosterone, which led to the essence of who I am finally taking material shape. When I first smelt my changed body odour, I cried, entirely overwhelmed by joy, because I thought, *I recognise myself* – as if from a past life, or a future memory. As the feeling settled, I realised I'd been here before, already, in the years ahead.

Lying here now, my body entangled with the warm bodies of my friends, in the first light of a new year, I look at the photo and feel this same self-recognition gouge the centre of my chest, so that everything in my life has greater depth. It's easier to love the truth of who I am, because I've *seen* what I will *become*. I fall at the knees of all the life I've got to live, knowing that I exist there because I've been here before, in this memory from my future.

We walk home along quiet streets to the house we've rented in town. We're all wearing outrageous outfits but we feel bolstered and brave in ways that are entirely contingent upon our being together. In *first light*, we're all being so silly, crying and squealing with laughter. There's thirteen of us staying in a house that's made to sleep six. We walk in the door and collapse onto the mattresses laid out everywhere. I put on a jumper to get cosy and am asleep the moment my head hits the pillow.

I wake eight hours later in a puddle of sweat. It's 35 degrees outside, and I've slept so deeply that I've not woken up to take the jumper off. Peo is the only one of our friends awake, and I find them to show them how I've sweated through both my blanket and the fitted sheet, all the way to the mattress. Peo almost gags, and we can't stop laughing.

Hey, isn't there a recovery party at the local pool today?

I check the time. *Yeah, and there's still two hours left of it!*

Should we go?

Absolutely.

When we arrive at Lismore's public pool in the centre of town, we flash our festival wristbands and enter what will become two of the most joyous hours of my life. We find a spot to put our towels down, taking in our surroundings. There's a DJ set up at the pool's edge, with a crowd of at least two hundred dancing around the decks. In the pool itself, people are eating ice creams while floating on blow-up Lilos and doughnut rings. Peo and I look at each other, wide-eyed, as if to ask, *Where the hell are we?* Then we laugh, as if to answer, *I think we've died and gone to heaven!*

I take off my shoes and then my shirt and wave at some friends I've spotted in the water. Then I turn to Peo, and see them hesitate for a moment.

I smile, as if to say to them, *It's OK... You're safe here.*

Peo nods and takes off their shirt, and I watch any fear dissolve. I see the scattered light from the pool's surface reflected in their eyes. I witness how relaxed they become as they turn their face up toward the sky, their chest stretched wide in sunshine. Surer, somehow, of who they are. Or who they might become.

We grin at how at home we both feel here, in this moment.

Come on, Peo says, grabbing my hand. *Let's dance.*

The pool we're at – Lismore Memorial Baths – was built in 1928, and though it's been refurbished and repainted, it still has its original buildings. As we approach the dance floor, something strange begins to happen to my sense of time. Since it's a pool party, everyone is stripped down to swimwear, and with no one having their phones out, there aren't really any contemporary clothes or technologies in sight – therefore, there are next to no modern markers to indicate that I'm in the 21st century. I think of how Tropical Fruits has been happening here in Lismore since 1988 and suddenly feel as if I've travelled through time, like I could be, in this moment, back there in 1988, dancing at the first Tropical Fruits. I look at the joy on everyone's faces, at the ease with which their bodies move when they're in connection and being celebrated on a sun-drenched dance floor.

I think of how, when this party started, homosexuality was still criminalised in most Australian states, and how a gay man living in Hobart stalked by the constant threats of police brutality, arrest, state-sanctioned violence, discrimination, harassment and public persecution might have come here, to Tropical Fruits, and experienced euphoria on a dance floor just like this one. I am suddenly overcome by emotion, understanding more fully what my queer elder and dear friend Jonny talks about when they say dance floors are sacred. Because a dance floor like this one would have been a lifeline for that gay man from Hobart – filling him up with a joy so palpable it might just have been enough to sustain him through the rest of the year. How this dance floor would have carved out space for a future in which he *lived.*

I think again of this place, a place of *first light*, and look over and see Peo dancing – squinting in the brightness of it all.

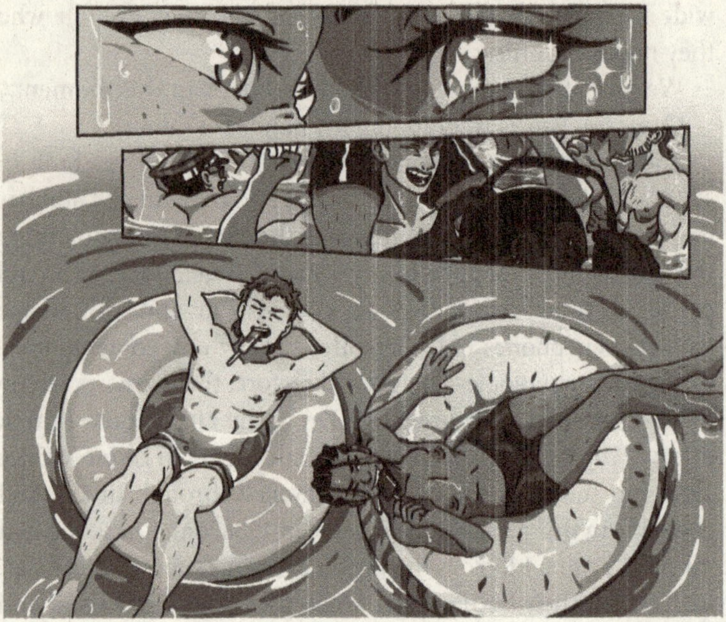

Soula Emmanuel (she/her) was born in Dublin to an Irish mother and a Greek father. She studied at universities in Ireland and Sweden, emerging with a master's degree in demography. Her debut novel *Wild Geese* was published by Footnote Press and the Feminist Press in 2023. In 2024, it won the Lambda Literary Award for Transgender Fiction and the Gordon Bowker Volcano Prize at the UK Society of Authors' Awards. She has had work dramatised for BBC Radio 4. She currently lives on Ireland's east coast.

soulaemmanuel.com

soulaemmanuel

The below work contains discussion of domestic violence and transphobia.

Gigi and Sotiria

North London, 2006

Out of the silence, Gigi hears a voice. It is not her own, nor the one of which she dreams, inexpressible but transfixing. It is a strong, deep, clear bell-chime – the sound of an older woman, weary and nicotine-stained. It seems to surround her, pulls her from her sleep and wrenches her into the bedroom in which she grew up, one she has redecorated for her new self but which retains in its walls so much of the former.

She opens her eyes. The woman gazes at her from across the room, casting a holy shimmer at Gigi through the early-morning darkness: a small, lollipop-shaped figure with tinted glasses.

Gigi wishes she had a baseball bat to hand. 'Who the hell are you?' she asks, in a startled, squeaky voice.

'My child, my child,' the woman says, raising her hands as if to show they are empty, 'who I am is not important. You will only be able to sing when you discover your own identity.'

'I know exactly what my identity is. I am Gigi Galani, and I have half a mind to call the police right now.'

'Ah, the police,' the woman says, laughing to herself, 'I know them well.'

'I bet you do, you weirdo. But this is the Metropolitan Police we're talking about. They're nasty bastards. They'll shoot you for fare evasion. Look, if you don't leave right now, I'm going to scream.'

'Yes, you should scream! That will help.'

Gigi, sitting on her bed in a skewed string top, hair unbrushed, face unadorned, looks with confusion at the woman.

'My name is Sotiria,' the woman says. 'Sotiria Bellou.'

'You're Greek?'

'Yes. I have been sent to help you.'

'By who?'

'I died in 1997. Throat cancer. The cigarettes got me in the end, but where would I have been without them? I have been sent to help you with your singing problem.'

'OK,' Gigi says, and then she remembers that she is sitting on a bed in her childhood bedroom, looking at this eccentric apparition. There is only one explanation for all this: it is clearly a dream. She is obviously asleep right now and pulling this wackiness from her subconscious. She turns over to her side and attempts to go back to sleep.

Then Sotiria starts to sing.

But before Sotiria, there is Natasha. She sounds so beautiful when she sings. Old Greek ballads, dancey numbers with a sway of her hips, sometimes even Whitney Houston. Every

Friday, the men in the audience bang their hands against their tables as if trying to restart a heart. With a wink of her eye and a swish of her train, she owns them. They wave their lighters, they coo at her, they festoon her with twenty-pound notes. She is a doll with a perfect voice, one that does not fade and does not change. She dances effortlessly between languages, thanking the audience in Greek before declaring: 'I will be Evita at the Enfield Civic Theatre next month. Tickets are on sale now, so please come along!'

She will be Evita. As far as Gigi is concerned, Natasha already is.

The restaurant in question is Yia Mas tavern, owned by Gigi's father, and where she is employed as a waitress. It is a gloomy space once dimmed by a thicket of cigarette smoke, until they changed the law and her father turned down the lights further. This place has been central to the community since it opened in the eighties, when Gigi, then a toddler, then a boy, was its curly-haired little mascot. It has served dutifully a catchment of pernickety Greek emigrants and traumatised Cypriot war refugees for almost twenty years.

'Isn't Natasha wonderful?' Gigi says to the customers as she gives them their food and their cheap beer. The praise for Natasha is easier for Gigi to handle if she pre-empts it, if it is coming from her and not them. She praises her makeup, her furiously straightened hair, her slender figure, her voice, her voice, her voice.

'Yes, she is a star!' they reply.

A star indeed.

Gigi is twenty-two years old now. She has grown up surrounded by these people, and she has become herself in their gaze too. They don't get it, but they are kind. They tell her that long hair suits her, that she should have grown it out years ago, and she can't help but agree – she has squandered so many years. *Why didn't you tell me this earlier?* she thinks to herself.

The women are better. It took some getting used to for Gigi's mother, to remember names and adjust expectations, but Greek women are strong and don't take any bullshit. As long as she behaves the right way, she is accepted, and more to the point, she is valued. The local women tell her that now she is a woman, her father should be more willing to contribute to her upkeep. This is music, so to speak, to Gigi's ears.

Sotiria's voice is metallic and sharp. It seems to make the nails vibrate in the walls. She sings as if to chastise, as if reciting a litany of life's woes for the thousandth time.

Open the window, open the window she sings in Greek, demanding the acquaintance of a lover who has deserted her, but for Gigi it is the sound of her longing for a former voice, this stubborn girl who tortures her by doing nothing at all.

But then Gigi remembers where she is. 'Shhhh!' she says. 'You'll wake everyone up.'

Sotiria stops, then looks deflated. 'I am trying to help you.'

'I get it – you are a singer. Everyone is a singer except me.'

'You are a singer.'

'I *was* a singer. I used to have a beautiful voice before I hit puberty. High and clean and pure. I was in school choirs and everything. I could have been a star.'

'Can I tell you a story?'

'Do I have a choice?'

'You always have a choice. When I was seventeen, I married a bus conductor.'

'Congratulations.'

'His name was Vangelis. My family married me off to him because they did not want me to be a singer. They wanted me to go away and be a quiet, dutiful little wife in a village in the mountains. They thought that having a husband would tame me. And my god, he tried to tame me.'

'What did he do?'

'He was an abusive, violent drunk. No sooner had I become a woman then I was almost trapped in a horror show from which there was no escape. You are lucky a young woman like you isn't married off nowadays.'

'That wouldn't happen to me, because–'

'Because you are a transsexual?'

Gigi is startled. 'How do you know that word?'

'I keep up with the news. I'm dead,' she says, cackling, 'not deaf! Anyway, you are lucky to have choices, even ones I would never have dreamed of. Now, this bus conductor, he got me pregnant but then beat me up so hard that I miscarried.'

'My god.'

'Yes,' Sotiria says placidly, 'it was terrible, but look at me: I am an old woman. I made it out.'

'How did you do it?'

'Well, I found a bottle of vitriol, sulphuric acid, used for cleaning, and I threw it in his face. I went to prison for six months, and let me tell you: six months in the clink were better than five minutes with that bastard.'

'Did you kill him?'

'No, no, only his pride was wounded. And his face was disfigured but,' she says, scrunching up her nose, 'he was never a beauty.'

They both laugh, and then Gigi exhales. 'You're a singer and a violent criminal. I feel much better about you now.' But the next thing she knows, it is morning, and she is waking up, and she is alone with her old self again.

Gigi has a problem: working for her family doesn't count. It simply doesn't count. It's a job, she gets paid for it, she pays tax on the money she earns, but nevertheless, it doesn't count.

The Gender Recognition Panel are uneasy with work like this – they want good, honest transsexuals to be working outside the home. The Gender Recognition Act was brought in two years ago, in 2004, though it is less about recognition than about forcing people like Gigi to fit into a preordained pattern. She might have assumed that her family's acceptance would be an advantage in applying, but what they really want are strong, independent and, above all, compliant individuals, not those who have been shielded from bigotry by the kindness of those closest to them. It is almost like they don't believe she has suffered enough.

It is bad enough that her dealings with the clinic at Charing Cross have left her with documents she may wield whenever she is challenged, which say:

Giorgia Galani has been formally diagnosed with male-to-female gender identity disorder (transsexualism) and is a patient of this NHS clinic. She should be treated as a woman for all practical purposes. I may be contacted by telephone if you have any other queries.

No one has ever asked for this letter and carrying it around makes Gigi feel like a child, needing the verification of an authority to prove herself. She sometimes ponders what would happen if someone actually phoned the doctor. What would he even say?

For gender recognition, she is at the mercy of a panel – of experts, doctors, circus acrobats, who knows? – who will decide if she meets the criteria or not. She will never meet these august people, instead communicating with them entirely through letters and documentation, underlining the sense that whatever gender is, it is passive, and you must not ask for it too hard.

Her family were such sweethearts – her mother in particular. Greek women adore their sons but, in a strange way, Gigi's mother followed that adoration towards a kind of acceptance: a willingness to go clothes shopping with her new daughter, at least until Gigi worked up the confidence to be embarrassed by her mother's presence. Her aunts and cousins were wonderful too, but what struck Gigi was how they interpreted her transition as a rejection of manhood and took it upon themselves to vent a lifetime of grievances about the men in their lives, like a kind of hazing ritual.

It was like being a child again, being endlessly fascinated by the world of the grown-ups.

Gigi tries not to dwell on her encounter with Sotiria. She treats it like a bad dream which she is trying to forget. She goes about her day, cleaning the restaurant, going to get her face lasered, continuing in the usual routine. But the following night, it happens again. Sotiria fills up the small hours talking about her life in the Resistance, how she fought the Nazis, how she was beaten up by partisans during the Greek Civil War.

'You have had a very interesting life,' Gigi says, 'but why are you telling me all this? I thought you wanted to help me sing.'

'Because,' Sotiria replies, 'you have to understand where music comes from. You think that a great singer is one with a pure, unblemished voice.'

She wants to disagree, but she does think that, even if she shouldn't. 'Sure,' she says, 'and you're going to tell me that a bad voice is as good as a good one. But we both know that isn't true.'

'I am going to tell you that a good voice is a voice with something to say. It is a voice with experience, which has lived and endured.' Then she sings again. There is grief and lamentation in the music which emerges. 'Rebetikó songs,' Sotiria says, 'come from the streets.'

'I know that.'

'They have in their bones the suffering of those who came to Greece from Asia Minor following thc catastrophe of the early 1920s. But, you see, I was not one of those caught up in the catastrophe.'

'No. You had your own catastrophes.'

'Exactly! And you have had yours. When you sing rebetikó, you tap into the shared suffering of other people. You connect it with your own. That is what singing is all about.'

'When I was a teenager, I used to sing. Well, sing is probably the wrong word. I would go days without talking to anyone in my family or at school. Then I would perform as an outlet. I used to be in rock bands who would perform at community halls. I didn't have to sing the way I did when I was a child. I would just growl into the microphone. On a good day, there'd be an audience of about twenty people. They'd wince and nod at my singing, like they understood what I was going through. It helped at the time but now I'm not sure about it.'

'So, why don't you sing in rock bands now?'

'Because I don't want to. I was sad back then, but everyone just saw it as the moodiness of a teenager. But I kept being sad when I got older, I didn't figure myself out the way everyone else seemed to. I suppose I was grieving the loss of my old voice, the possibilities of it. Maybe I wasn't the best singer in the world, but that was *my* voice. I don't know that the voice I have now is mine.' Gigi starts crying while talking to the apparition at the end of her bed, blubbing like a child. 'That's why it hurts so much watching Natasha sing at the restaurant. She's everything I wish I was. And it's so stupid to be hurt by this, but I am.'

'It's not stupid, my child. You know I had a difficult early life. You know about my marriage. You know about the war, about the civil war, how I was brutally attacked. But do you know what's funny?'

'You're going to tell me something funny?'

'No, just upsetting.'

'I thought so.'

'It wasn't my early life that I struggled with the most. It was what came later. I became a respected singer in Greece. After the fall of the colonels in the 1970s, people rediscovered my music and my political activism. People even accepted that I was a lesbian. But I became a terrible addict to alcohol and gambling. Sometimes things seem worse when they are in the past than they were when you were living through them. But you can channel that into song as well.'

Gigi now has something to say, but no clue how to say it. Before she met Sotiria, she thought singing was like talking, something that came naturally without effort. She might have assumed that anyone could simply take to the stage at her father's restaurant and set to it, and the only reason she hadn't was a certain fear. Now she realises that music is a language she must learn – but how, and from whom? The experience of meeting Sotiria over these nights has been confessional, like encountering a priest, but she is not a priest: she is a dead lesbian alcoholic, a compulsive gambler, a sharp-edged figure from history.

She looks through the local newspaper, the *Enfield Gazette*, perusing the classified ads, the promotions of weddings, funerals, divorce lawyers and free unwanted furniture. *This is London*, she thinks, *surely someone here is looking for a singer.* Then she spots it: *BAND LOOKING FOR VOCALIST*. And another: *GUITAR PLAYER LOOKING FOR VOCAL ACCOMPANIMENT.* Suddenly, she has options, and feels a new sense of control. She could go anywhere she wants.

The guitar player is called Neil, a vision in sandals and red hair, who turns out to have a string missing, in every sense. He has two songs – 'Wonderwall' and 'The Green, Green Grass of Home' – which don't sum to much of a set list, and aren't really what Gigi is looking for.

He likes Gigi's voice. 'It's husky,' he says, 'it's very sexy. I'm a fan.' Thankfully, he is too restrained by whatever substance or substances he is on to make an issue of Gigi's sexiness. He doesn't seem to notice that Gigi is a transsexual, but truthfully, he comes across as the kind of guy who could be convinced by a smiley face drawn onto a balloon, so she doesn't feel any pride in it.

The band is a more serious outfit. They're called The Rancour. 'We were originally called The Wankers,' the drummer, Paul, says, 'but they wouldn't let us put that on a sign. We thought a female lead singer would take the edge off a bit. You know, like Debbie Harry or something.'

'I love Debbie Harry,' Gigi replies, with misplaced enthusiasm. She can hear it in the way she talks, the way she emits *love* like an air raid siren, not chirpy and delicate like a woman should be.

'Yeah, Debbie is great,' the drummer says, mentally crossing out Gigi's name.

The process is endlessly dispiriting. It is not like the meetings with Sotiria, where the old lady came to Gigi. Now she needs to go out into the world, and she does not relish it, the outside world, after all, being what made her this way in the first place. Yet, Sotiria does not appear at night anymore. Gigi waits for her with hope in her soul, but nothing happens, and she knows why – the story is not Sotiria's anymore. It is Gigi's, and she must write it herself.

She meets him for the first time outside Enfield Overground station, sitting on the ground in front of the window of a dry cleaner. There is a guitar case in front of him, lined with a scattering of coins. It is a Thursday, a hot summer afternoon and England are about to play Trinidad and Tobago in the World Cup, the kind of day when the sound of music may be heard swooning from every beer garden in London, so that the city is a cacophony of noise. The mood is festive, children mixing white and red face paint with ice cream and raspberry sauce.

He is playing 'Three Lions', singing it into a microphone which screams his voice metallically. He has been singing it on a loop, because Gigi has been able to hear him for at least fifteen minutes. He sings about Jules Rimet like he is his first love. Then the police come over and move him on. The man does not look annoyed, but rather weary, like this is not the first time. Gigi can see him say *come on, people are enjoying it* but to no avail. He packs up his things and carries them away.

'You were good,' Gigi says to him as he walks. 'Need help carrying the equipment?'

'I don't have money worth stealing.'

'I wasn't planning to steal anything. I'm Gigi.'

'I'm Pete. Sorry, this hasn't been a great day.' He is in his thirties and looks to Gigi like a man who is always in a hurry, all shaving cuts and dandruff. 'The world ain't built for people like me.'

'Tell me about it. I've been trying to find a band to sing with. But nobody wants me,' she laughs to herself and decides to embrace candour, 'because I'm a chick with a, well, with a little extra, you know?'

'You're… oh, right. Like the one from *Big Brother*.'

'Like the one from *Big Brother*.'

'Well,' Pete says, 'it takes all sorts to make the world go round.' Gigi notices him quickening his step as he speaks – not with anxiety, but like he has realised what he has said and is mentally zoning out to figure out if it was appropriate.

They end up back at his flat, a small but not squalid place. There are clothes draped on furniture and clouds of fine dust catching the sunlight as it spills awkwardly through a crack between two neighbouring buildings and on through the window. Music can be heard coming through the walls from another apartment.

'You live alone?' Gigi asks.

'I live alone. I do everything alone. Except two days a week, when my son is here. His name is Harry.'

Gigi sees a picture of a small boy on the wall, with a bowl-cut of straight blonde hair, wearing an Arsenal jersey. 'I'd say you're a good dad.'

Pete laughs to himself. 'You're the first person who's ever said that.'

Gigi tries to change the subject. 'Do you get a lot of money busking?'

'Enough to get by. I give the people what they want. The kind of music I'd like to sing comes from the soul, you know? Dylan, Nick Drake, jazz, Coltrane, all that stuff. But the people want Frank Skinner and David Baddiel singing about Bobby Charlton, so that's what they get. Not that the police care. Anyway, I gather you want to be a singer. What do you sing?'

At this moment, Gigi realises that for all she has talked to Sotiria about the nature of music and where it comes from, she has no idea *what*, exactly, she wants to sing. As with all things in life, if you wait for the right song, the right person, the right anything, it might simply never come. 'What about Blondie?' she says.

'You'll need drums for Blondie.'

'Whitney Houston?'

'Really? Gosh.' Pete's face drains of emotion. 'Gigi, it's been lovely to meet you, and thanks for carrying my stuff for me, but I don't know that we're really creatively matched. Maybe it's better to end things now rather than have conflict later.' Pete seems strangely like a man who is accustomed to ending things before a fight breaks out.

'No,' Gigi says, slightly frantic, 'wait, I have an idea. Can you come with me back to the restaurant?'

'The restaurant?'

'My parents' restaurant.'

It is still early evening, still warm and sunny outside, though you wouldn't know it in the restaurant, which resembles a bunker at the best of times. The air conditioning is powered up, and the restaurant remains fairly quiet, customers drinking beer and eating nuts, still too early for anything bigger. It is half time in the England match, and the Trinidadians and Tobagonians are putting up a remarkable fight, so it is still scoreless. *Rooney's useless* is the consensus of those watching at Yia Mas. *Ferdinand? A joke.* Most of the men here didn't grow up in England, but support the team anyway, while their kids are out watching the match with friends in the custom of natives, throwing beer in the air when England score – if England ever do score.

Gigi and Pete, however, have spent the last two hours finding their respective voices. Pete has never played the bouzouki before but thinks he's getting the hang of it. He's been trying to match the chords on a CD being played in Gigi's parents' kitchen. 'It's not impossible, this,' he says. 'I expected something more intricate.' This is his way of waving away the fact that every third note he plays is not the correct one.

What Pete lacks in skill he makes up for in derring-do, but Gigi feels acutely anxious standing in front of the microwave, trying to find her way into the emotions of rebetikó. She remembers what Sotiria said, that it is about loss most of all, about being trapped in the past while being forced to dwell in the present, and feels herself slowly falling into it. She will use her voice to condemn her voice.

They go out for a three-minute set, scarcely long enough for the ad break on ITV. Gigi tries to warm up the crowd, asking them if they want to hear something special. There is a muffled assent. Then she asks if they want to hear something that might be rubbish, and there it is again, the muffled assent. Gigi sings the song that Sotiria sang when she encountered her, about the woman demanding that her lover open the window to her, a song about abandonment. *Open up, open up.* There is a longing within her, a longing for before, for long before, expressed in this moment. Gigi hopes Sotiria can hear her.

The room is dark, a blur of candlelight and neon, so that she can see nothing, or perhaps so that all she can see is her own voice moving through the air. After a time, though Gigi doesn't realise it, Pete stops playing the bouzouki, having given up on its mystifying strings, so that Gigi is playing a cappella.

And at the end the crowd cheers.

Joshua Jones (he/him) is a queer, disabled writer & artist from Llanelli, South Wales. *Local Fires* (Parthian, 2023) was shortlisted for a number of awards including the 2024 Dylan Thomas Prize. He has published various pamphlets of poetry and zines, most recently *I AM A MAN AT WORK* (g39, 2025) and is currently a Contributing Editor of *Folding Rock* magazine.

@joshuajoneswrites

The below works contain depictions of sex and violence.

Five Repetitions

Then I realized repetition could be an ending.
Then I realized repetition could be an ending.
– Dean Young, *Romanticism 101*

1

I lay on the bed like a bible in a hotel drawer wanting to be read. He's in the bathroom. Been quiet in there for a time. Soaping his wedding band. Or maybe he's cleaning himself up.

I want him, a stranger, to explore me like someone about to buy their first home. Led around a vacant property by an estate agent in a navy suit and a nice haircut, giving the hard sell – *look how beautiful the porch is, can you picture yourself starting a family here?*

This house is haunted, doesn't he know. By a family who died in tragic and/or suspicious circumstances. Their cries rattle its bones. My body is a mid-budget supernatural horror movie in development hell.

Our bodies are homes in a constant process of (re)development. While one part is under construction, others are falling apart. I could fall apart right now. He would cover me, apply his touch like scaffolding. Plaster my neck with kisses. *Well, here I am, wanting fabrication.*

The bathroom door opens. Yellow light spills around his silhouette, illuminating this numberless room, some hotel. He turns to the bed. The shadow of his cock on the wall. The fortification of his legs, low centre of gravity. His trapezius muscles built to withstand weather.

This man is brutalist, skin concrete. I am a brick thrown through a church window, a glory hole to God. I am a half-demolished building that's lost its head, jagged and hollow. I want to be sucked dry and spat out by the local council. I want to be the house I grew up in.

I roll onto my front, the cold of my thighs meeting the soft, warm sheets. His feet whisper across the carpet. The side of my face pressed into the pillow. He falls to his knees beside the bed. The window blinds are closed as if in prayer.

Then he begins to touch me, exploring the soft wall of my back. The hard hat of his cock on my leg. I realise he is a landlord, adding to his portfolio. He is not a first-time buyer. I wonder how many homes he has. His hands feel recently oiled.

I close my eyes. His fingers reach for my nipples like he's

gripping the handle of a door. I breathe in the silence between concrete kisses

and wait for renovation.

2

the creaking of leather should be an orchestra with me it's kneeling conductor

i am more loyal than any dog

test me

babygirl needed less patriarchy and more licking

i arch my back more sexy than nicole kidman

am i sexier than nicole kidman

id fuck harris dickinson

i want harris dickinson to fuck me

dickinson

nice boots

more spit more spit more spit more spit

i love you

fucking nice boots

white socks and green socks over them your feet must be so cold can i warm them up for you love more spit more spit more

calf time

ruff!

am i doing a good job

put the work in

yes

lick the back too

heel

full job

ruff!

give it the full works

work

i love it when you wriggle your toes i can feel them through the leather on my lips

creaking leather my love my only soundtrack

take photos of me on my knees for you my back arched

i bet i look hotter than nicole kidman and harris dickinson combined i should be paid for being this cute

i want this moment to be a whole night

your hands on my back

my ass

gentle scratch

work!

your lips

my ears

those two words

those two words

!!

3

I have a promise I did not keep. Eating tinned pears for breakfast again. Sugary, sweet. Stocked up for summer. Kept pristine even, even with a dusty lid. Slippery and slick on the inside of my cheek. Like special oil for baby skin. Beautiful skin.

I promise to share with you. Stranger, strange mouth. Special boy. Every time.

Every time. I bit the inside – of my cheek – wash split skin with juice and pointed tongue. In bed with you. Tongue too big too wet for my mouth. The memory.

Have you ever heard such silence. Silence that follows the give of skin between teeth. What day is it. Your mother's superstition. You should not keep open tins in the fridge. Rust dissolves into the fruit, gives it that metallic taste. Like blood.

Like blood, a broken promise. Kiss me before you. Last words who am I chasing. Bash the metal against the corner. Of the bedside table. Anything can be crushed with enough power. You shouldn't suck on tin lids. You'll. Hurt yourself. Repetition, ending, which one. Wounds deepest. Sheets soaked. In oil. Juice. Chest, dribble.

I eat every meal like it's my last meal, I eat how I love. Every morning greeted with the same story. Same sorry. Breakfast, sunlight. From the edges of the curtain.

4

Tension in elastic jaw of animal, soundless vibration below the ear. We were children once, a place desiring affection, like the classrooms of state schools so empty, like a child's stomach.

My god, how I could climb in the pores of you, drink you up like a carton of room temperature milk. You, unpredictable, a child's lunchtime – both the advent of and contents within.

I could reach down the plastic straw of your body, my fist around your heart contracting, muted palm slap like a boy's wet lips smacking lunch. You remind me of a place I have never liked. The here.

5

There is something I regret; it keeps me up most nights. I think about it still, even now. How long it's been. So, here it is. I wish I could say sorry for finding a pair of heels in your wardrobe. But I had to bar the door with a chair. How could you get me so high? You knew what you were doing. I never told you any of this. Or anyone. We never spoke again, so how could I. Once, I'd – this is a confession – I had a panic attack, crouched down on the floor, head in wet palms. Breathing technique 4-4-4-4. Calmed, steady, I searched the room. To take my mind off – a drawer full of tights. I rolled them up over my knees, I liked the way my tattoos looked in them, my leg hair pressed down and through the fabric. Slow dance in full-length mirror to the music in my head. How did you acquire so many furs. It was so cold in the room. The heels – black, stilettoed, open toe. They looked your size. You scared me, and here I was, imagining your furry, long legs in them. The makeup, the tights, furs.

It didn't make sense to me then, but it does now.

Here I am, now, a version of a boy. Every partner I've had calls my ass his pussy. The fibres of my nylon legs send shockwaves of kinetic energy all the way to my fingertips, nerves plucked like harp strings. I think I could come from looking at boys in tights. You hurt me, I'm used to hurt, I'm tired of it. But I have you to thank for this awakening.

Does that make me a hypocrite?

Carrie Marshall (she/her) is a writer and musician whose latest critically acclaimed book, *Small Town Joy*, is a celebration of LGBTQ+ music and musicians. Her trans memoir, *Carrie Kills a Man*, was shortlisted in the Discover category of the 2023 British Book Awards and was a *Scotsman* book of the year.

carriem.co.uk

@carrieplaysguitar

The below work contains music recommendations – scan to listen to the playlist while reading:

Spotify Apple Music

This is the noise that keeps me awake

In this book, many wonderful writers will answer the question: what does queerphoria feel like?

I'd like to answer a slightly different one.

What does queerphoria *sound* like?

For the last several years, I've been exploring, writing about and celebrating the power of queer music and the influence of queer musicians for my book, *Small Town Joy*. I focused on my home, Scotland, but of course music is a global conversation:

from Hi-NRG to hyperpop, disco to doom metal, funk to folk, queerness in music can never be confined to one place, one era or one genre.

Music made by and embraced by queer people has changed lives, filled floors and opened minds. And most of all, it's created joy – which is all the more remarkable when you consider that it's so often forged in the most terrible fires. But that's what makes it so powerful, why its love and its lust, its defiance and its desire, its escapism and its euphoria feel so transcendent and so vital.

So: what does queerphoria sound like?

I know everyone who reads this will have different answers. Here are some of mine.

What does queerphoria sound like?

Maybe it sounds like a busy bassline, a guitar emphasising the off-beat.

It's 1982, I am ten years old and I am watching Culture Club on *Top of the Pops*. 'Do You Really Want To Hurt Me' is reggae-flavoured rather than the real thing, reggae with its rawness and roughness and Blackness sanded off, but despite the whitewash there's still plenty to offend the *Daily Mail* or *News of the World* reader: the singer is a gay man who looks like a woman.

It's not a song I'll ever love; white reggae never did it for me, even in those days when I wanted to embrace almost everything. But I'll always remember it for the strange excitement and light-headedness it gave me, not because of what Boy George was singing but because of what looking at him was telling me:

Boys will be boys?

Not necessarily.

What does queerphoria sound like?

Maybe it sounds like a show tune.

I'm immune to the charms of musical theatre and movie musicals. But I'm glued to this one, playing on a VHS tape and a small TV in a small town, as an incredible creature emerges from an old-fashioned mechanical elevator.

Ta-da!

How'd you do? I – Tim Curry sings.

Ta-da!

See you've met my – he pouts.

Ta-da!

Faithful… *handy* man – he purrs.

I had to turn detective to discover the details here: I remember this as a video rental, but the timeline doesn't fit – *The Rocky Horror Picture Show* didn't come out on VHS until the early nineties, long after I first saw it. Even if it had been released earlier, if the handful of video shelves in the local petrol station – my town wasn't big enough for a Blockbuster – had made space for it among the Stallones and Schwarzeneggers and Spielbergs and slasher movies, I wouldn't have been brave enough to reach for it and rent it. So the videotape I remember was definitely taped off the TV.

Rocky Horror was first shown on Channel 4 in 1985. That means I must have been twelve or thirteen, and by then I was in deep fear and shame and denial about feeling like a girl when everyone else was pretty sure I was a boy. I knew that meant I wasn't normal. There was a word for people like me, and it wasn't a good one and it certainly wasn't sweet.

Hearing 'Sweet Transvestite' for the first time – and seeing Tim Curry dressed like *that* for the first time, as he spun around and shed his cloak for the first chorus of the song – made my blood run cold and my heart beat twice as fast. I don't remember for certain if I was watching alone or with friends but I'm pretty sure it was solo; my friends' suggestions for shared viewing were more likely to be schlocky horror than *Rocky Horror*, and heaven forfend anyone might suggest watching something even slightly queer to leaven our usual diet of action movies featuring oiled-up muscle men.

I might not remember if the viewing was solo or shared, but I can clearly recall the coldness in the pit of my stomach and the heat of my cheeks and the quiet euphoria that comes from understanding that you are not the only one of your kind. The film has aged badly for all kinds of reasons, but for closeted, confused, deeply miserable me, seeing cross-dressing celebrated felt like finding an oasis in the most desolate desert.

Ta-da!

What does queerphoria sound like?

Maybe it sounds like a siren.

I am fourteen and I am in the bath. There are fresh batteries in the boom box that I've propped against the wall, slightly angled so that the small speakers can bounce the sound off the bathroom ceiling and back down to me.

The siren is a synth, two overlapping notes pitching upwards over an Italo-disco bass; the tape is Pet Shop Boys's *Disco*, side two, track one. I let my head fall back into the almost-too-hot water and feel the vibration of the bass and kick drum through it, but I always emerge from the bubbles to bellow the hook, grinning: Paninaro! Paninaro, oh-ay-ohh!

I love that bit. But it's not the bit I love best.

The bit I love best, the bit that fills me with joy, isn't even musical. It's Chris Lowe, speaking almost in a monotone. 'I don't like country-and-western,' he says. 'I don't like rock music. I don't like, I don't like rockabilly or rock 'n' roll particularly.' It sounds like a smile when he adds: 'Don't like much really, do I?' And then he drops the line I'll remember and repeat in my head forever. 'But what I do like I love passionately.'

I love this band passionately.

In years to come this band will bring me so much more joy, and so much euphoria, and so much transcendence. And in a year from this bit of bathtime bellowing they'll drop a song that will take up room in my head like no other, a song that will connect with me in ways I won't fully understand for a very long time, a song about shame, a song about believing that every single thing you ever do is a sin.

It'll be twenty years before I hear that one performed live, because I won't see Pet Shop Boys live until I've learnt how to live myself. And when I do, I and thousands of others like me will sing along in joy and pride and with tear-streaked faces as a song that once whispered secrets in the closet has become something we share publicly, happily, joyfully with each other.

What does queerphoria sound like?

Maybe it sounds like a mandolin.

It is 1988 or 1989 and I am sixteen or I am seventeen and I am crying once again to 'The Wrong Child' by R.E.M., a song that I loved on my first listen and will love even more over the decades to come.

It is not a queer song, and Michael Stipe has not yet come out (although he is not closeted either; he just doesn't talk about his sexuality) so I have no clear reason to detect queerness anywhere here. But this band have a quality I've always struggled to articulate, a yearning and a sadness and a joy that really connects with me.

This song is sung from the perspective of a child trapped indoors, watching through a window as the other children play. For me it hits hardest when the protagonist asks their imaginary friend what it's like to go outside; the child has never been and feels that they never will.

Stipe didn't write this about being gay or queer. He wrote it about an imaginary child who is physically unable to go out, and in typical Stipe fashion he left the details opaque to leave room for listeners' own interpretations. That opacity meant that the song resonated with my then-closeted queerness, my fear that I was not normal but terribly broken. I'm not supposed to be like this, I'd sing during one of so many replays.

There is a line that follows, that I can never sing without choking up: 'But it's okay'. It was, it is, liberating.

What does queerphoria sound like?

Maybe it sounds like my jaw dropping.

It is 2001 and I am watching MTV because back then MTV was still music TV. The next video is by Garbage, whose Shirley Manson I have always been in awe of, and the next three minutes and seven seconds will join Pet Shop Boys in that permanent place in my memory.

I want to tell you about how this song sounds, because it sounds so different – different from what the band has done before, and different from what other bands are doing. It's rock music but it's so spacious; there are skittering beats and staccato synths, heavily processed guitars and a voice that's more sensual than any Siren. But what's left me barely able to breathe isn't just what Shirley is singing. It's what she's doing.

In the video for 'Androgyny', Shirley Manson is a femme and a butch, a classic beauty and a leather-clad club kid, and she sings about boys being girls and girls being boys and freeing your mind with your androgyny. And then, at the one-minute mark, the genderfuckery *really* kicks in. Shirley is butch and femme, not separately this time but simultaneously. She is a mesmerising mix of male- and female-coded clothing: men's suit and socks and suspenders, women's stockings, a boardroom-black tie and the blood-red lipstick of a femme fatale. I am so stunned I can only stare.

'Androgyny' didn't kick the doors off my closet; I was too focused on staying inside it, and too in denial to think about leaving it. But it started to unscrew the hinges that held them on.

*

What does queerphoria sound like?

Maybe it sounds like a heartbeat.

It is 2018 and I have wobbled across a cobbled street and up a lethal metal staircase because my high-femme pop friend is DJing there and my androgynous punk friend is drinking there and both have said they'd appreciate my company. This is a really big deal for me because I am not yet used to being me so publicly; I am no longer in the closet but I am far from confident. Tonight I am not so much out of my comfort zone as in a completely different postcode, and I feel that way until I hear a very familiar bass line from a song I've played to death.

It's not complicated: the opening riff is just three notes – F sharp, C sharp, B – that have been sequenced, synthesised and played at sixteenth-note intervals at one hundred and seventeen beats per minute over a simple and sparse four-to-the-floor beat. Described like that, it's nothing special or emotional. Played through big speakers, it's spectacular and euphoric. Because this is Robyn's crying-on-the-dancefloor masterpiece, the ultimate sad banger: 'Dancing On My Own'. I am dancing with my best friend and nothing else exists in the world for me right now.

Unlike in the song, there are neither stilettos nor broken bottles, but I am spinning around in circles and I cannot remember the last time I felt like this. I don't know whether to laugh or cry so I do a bit of both.

What does queerphoria sound like?

Maybe it sounds like a language I don't speak.

It is 2023 and I've come to a show called Ceòl is Craic: Sradagan na Sràide as part of the research for the book I'm writing about music. The name of the event translates as Street Sparks, and it's a celebration of music made and played by Gaelic Scots. I am here to have my preconceptions about folk music completely destroyed by a very diverse and musically wide-ranging event, and I am also here because someone I love dearly is dying and I am trying to distract myself before a too-short sleep and a return to the hospital tomorrow.

My tears start to flow when Man of the Minch performs the haunting, beautiful 'Sgùrr Alasdair', which he tells the crowd is about the victims of the AIDS crisis. And they become unstoppable when Maya Evan MacGregor dedicates a song to their friend, who has just passed after a long illness. I do not speak Gaelic and the words of these songs are a mystery to me, but the emotions are clear and contagious and I cry and I cry and I cry.

This is not euphoria, I know. I'm too raw for that, although I will find euphoria in these artists' songs in the future. But tonight is something that is often intertwined with it, and something I desperately need: release. Life can be hard, and music can help to smooth its sharpest edges.

What does queerphoria sound like?

Maybe it sounds like werewolves.

Sometimes the Instagram algorithm gets it right, as it did when it brought me jasmine.4.t's 'Guy Fawkes Tesco Dissociation'. A pretty young trans woman singing about a head full of screaming with Phoebe Bridgers on backing vocals was exactly the kind of thing I needed to hear in the summer of 2025 as I lost my healthcare and many of my human rights.

'Guy Fawkes Tesco Dissociation' has the same wonky swagger and fairground-organ feel as Warren Zevon's 'Werewolves of London', albeit without the a-woos. But where 'Werewolves' was hilarious, 'Guy Fawkes Tesco Dissociation' is heartbreaking.

When we talk about euphoria or see it in popular culture there tends to be one specific shape it can take: a happiness that's dramatic, ecstatic, so big you feel that you could burst.

But there's another kind of euphoria that this song gives me, and that kind of euphoria is not the intense happiness you might see on screen. It's more about catharsis than contentment, because it's a song that makes you feel seen. You are not alone, it says. You are not the only person who is feeling what you are feeling. You are not the only person who is hanging on for dear life.

When you are lied to and lied about, when you are gaslit and gatekept and scapegoated every single day, something as simple as a song that tells the truth feels like a revolution. 'Guy Fawkes Tesco Dissociation' is musically light and emotionally crushing because it's about being fragile in a world that needlessly, cruelly and constantly forces you to be diamond hard. It's a song by and for people who are barely surviving when they should be thriving, the innocent victims of a war waged by tabloid trolls, bigoted billionaires, unethical editors and the most maliciously, viciously, spitefully anti-trans government the UK has ever had.

Heard at home, in headphones, songs like this are devastating. But when you hear them live among your tribe, they're elevating.

What does queerphoria sound like?

Queerphoria can sound like anything.

Queerphoria can sound like *everything*.

After two-plus years looking for – and finding, and writing about – queer musical joy, I've learnt that euphoria is not limited to a certain genre or sound or era or anything else. It's in everything as an influence and as an infusion, audible and tangible in folk stomps and chart pop and hip-hop and noise rock, in clubs and in choirs, in acoustic instruments and electronic effects.

Euphoria isn't about what the music *is*.

It's about what the music *does*.

Sometimes queer euphoria comes as a whisper, a voice in

your headphones that only you can hear and that sounds like it's only addressed to you. Sometimes queer euphoria comes as a vibration, a pulse from the floor through your feet to your heartbeat. And sometimes queer euphoria comes in a roar, the sound of you and of people just like you singing loudly and proudly, together and no longer alone.

Eve Gleichman (they/them)'s fiction has appeared in *The Kenyon Review*, *The Harvard Review*, *BOMB* and elsewhere. They have co-authored two novels: *The Very Nice Box* (Houghton Mifflin Harcourt, 2021) and *Trust & Safety* (Dutton, 2024). They live in Brooklyn.

The below work contains discussion of suicidal ideation.

Admission

1

Each night at eight we lined up for our meds. Seroquel, Depakote, Trazodone, Lithium. One by one we approached the little square window. Behind it stood a nurse with a short black bob, shouting, 'OK, next, next, come on, who's next?'

It was my turn. I said please and thank you, swallowed the pills and showed her my empty mouth. 'Good girl,' she said – wrong! I was a good boy. I'd been awake for four days. When I closed my eyes, I saw the sun. Sleep was a quaint, abstract idea. I was awake at midnight. I was awake at two, three, four, five.

2

Have you tried deep breathing? Have you tried counting backwards from 500? Have you tried meditation? Have you tried putting your feet up the wall? Have you tried high-intensity interval training? Have you tried cold-plunging? Have you tried magnesium, melatonin or antihistamines? Have you tried listing every name you can think of that begins with the letter B? Have you tried skipping coffee in the morning? Have you tried a hot shower before bed or saying a little prayer? Have you tried stepping in front of an express train? Have you tried leaping from the window? Have you tried purchasing a gun or lying face down in a bathtub?

3

No shoelaces, no tampons. They'd removed the string from my hoodie. I thought I had imagined all the ways to end my life, but I hadn't considered these.

But where there's a will…! I stared at the hard-edged bedroom furniture. The shelves, the bedframe, the desk. All of it beckoned. A nurse peeked in every fifteen minutes, clipboard and pen in hand. 'You can ignore me,' he said, the first time. 'Just doing rounds.'

I picked up a crayon and pressed it to a blank piece of paper. *Reasons to stay alive: breeze pushing through a screen. Smell of toast and coffee. Hand on a baby's back.*

4

The psychiatrist was a young, scared-looking man with hardened, gelled hair. We met in the morning. He dabbed his sweat-beaded forehead with a handkerchief. He wore a lavender button-down shirt, a wedding ring, Axe body spray. 'Still no sleep? Even with the Seroquel?'

'Nothing,' I said. I sat on the edge of my mattress. I'd spent another night awake, first in bed, then pacing the halls, watching the white clock behind the nurses' station until dawn pushed through the dirty double-paned windows. 'How long can a person go without sleep, theoretically?'

'Let's not test the answer!' he said nervously, uncapping a pen.

5

These were the options: you could brush your teeth, take a shower, play Jenga, play Uno, color with crayons, make your bed, fill a pink pitcher with crushed ice. There was a little library of donated books, and a movie channel blasting in the Day Room. At the nursing station: short, rubbery pens that bent in half, clean towels and – for the manic – fidget toys.

The most coveted were the three iPads, available to well-behaved patients. One night, I scored one, but what to do with it? I didn't remember any of my passwords. I navigated to NYTimes dot com. This is how I learned that Donald Trump got shot in the ear.

6

Bernard, Bella, Bianca, Beatrice, Beth, Beryl, Benjamin, Bruno, Boris, Billy, Bobby, Benedict, Bruce, Barbara, Bart, Brendan, Brandon, Brennan, Blake, Bennett, Benjamin, Briar, Bartholomew, Brady, Beckett, Baron, Bear, Bartlett, Bellevue, Boston, Bagel, Boomerang, Bandaid, Bench, Ballerina, Balloon, Bridge, Branch, Burger, Brunch, Brood, Boar, Blink, Booger, Boot, Bone, Button, Breeze, Beet, Beagle, Bunion, Bookbag, Bass, Beast, Blooper, Blog, Bog, Bra, Brain, Blindfold,

7

One evening I learned the meaning of Salisbury steak. Ground beef in a dark, oozing mound. I pushed it around with my plastic fork. I drank from a perspiring carton of 2% milk. Also on the menu: watery iceberg salads; steamed green beans; soft, wet spaghetti. For breakfast: scrambled egg substitute; bananas; big brown pancakes; a single serving of Corn Flakes; coffee.

Eitan, a new admission, said the coffee was interfering with his sleep. He asked a nurse if there was any decaf available. The nurse threw her head back and laughed. 'It's all decaf. You think we're serving you guys real coffee?'

8

Eitan had been admitted during a manic episode. During the episode, he played forty-eight hours of basketball. He believed God was speaking through him. But now the episode was over, and he walked around with a sleepy, dopey smile. He was twenty-three. To hasten our friendship/brotherhood, I gave him my packets of sun butter. He had voluminous curly hair.

One evening, desperate for something to do, we attended an AA meeting together. We were the only ones there besides the facilitator, a man with an Irish accent who described waking up after a bender with his face pressed into the sidewalk.

'Are we allowed to be here?' Eitan asked, hand raised. 'We're not alcoholics.'

'Replace alcohol with anything,' the Irish man said. 'Maybe you're addicted to pills – or to your own thoughts!'

9

Chris, a volunteer, had slicked-back hair pulled into a ponytail. She led a chair yoga class. An air diffuser belched lavender steam into the clammy room. We raised our hands above our heads, reaching for the fluorescent lights. 'Good job, guys,' Chris said. 'Keep breathing.'

At noon, she took us into the elevator, which brought us to the roof. We were allowed fifteen minutes up there with a portable speaker. Enough time for four songs. Tall mesh fencing discouraged jumpers. Raised beds with basil, mint and parsley broiled and shook under the sun. 'I hate to use the C-word,' Chris said, 'but it is crazy hot up here.'

10

My roommate was named Alicia. She refused to eat breakfast or take her medication, though I overheard the psychiatrist beg. She slept twenty hours a day. I was jealous. I couldn't remember the last time I'd had a dream.

Sometimes, in the middle of the night, she would fling on our bedroom lights and indulge in a bag of chips or a conversation with herself. These conversations comprised yes or no questions, which she both asked and answered: 'Have you ever been to an NBA game? *No.* Would you like to go to the movies? *No.* Have you ever been in love?'

11

Then there was Eden, whose butt crack was always showing. 'Eden, your pants!' the nurses yelled constantly, and she would pull them up ineffectually. She'd approached me as soon as I was admitted.

'Are you on testosterone?' she'd said. 'Are you a boy?'

'Kind of a boy, yeah,' I said.

'I'm a transexual,' she said. 'I'm on estrogen. I've been here for three months. Did you get top surgery?'

'Eden, your pants!' a nurse yelled.

'Are you bipolar?' she said to me, tugging up on the elastic. 'Schizophrenic?'

12

Yuko, the music teacher, instructed us to choose a percussion instrument from a big black vinyl bag. Triangles, bongos, rain sticks, maracas. We sat in a circle, banging, shaking, tapping our instruments with no sense of rhythm, while we waited for our meetings with the social worker. She told us to improvise songs about ourselves as we pounded away. What was one thing we hated? '*My name is Yves, and I hate being awake!*' I sang out.

Eitan hated doing dishes. Eden hated cops. A veteran admission named Kareem hated the pizza they served on Fridays. '*When am I getting out of here?*' he sang. '*Why won't they let me go home? I want to see my girlfriend!*'

13

I did push-ups in my bedroom while Alicia watched. 'Twenty-two, twenty-three!' she shouted, as I lowered my chest to the floor. The meds made my limbs feel like jelly.

'Can I ask you a question?' she said. 'How come you don't have tits?'

'I got rid of them,' I panted.

'That's crazy!'

'You think so?'

'I would never want to get rid of mine.' She grabbed her chest.

I lay flat on the floor, pressed my cheek to the cool flecked tile. My heart squeezed.

'So, are you crazy?' she said. 'Are you gonna kill me in the middle of the night?'

14

Eitan wanted to know if I thought we would be friends in the real world. 'You know,' he said. 'Like, when we're out of here.' We were eating flaccid sandwiches, playing Jenga. He was going to be discharged soon, I could sense it. He'd just come out of a meeting with the social worker, looking well-rested, well-medicated. The lithium was working.

'I don't know,' I said, gently pushing on a middle block. 'I'm twelve years older than you.'

He considered this and nodded. 'I think we would be,' he said. He looked up at me. 'Yves? You're gonna sleep soon. And then they're going to let you go.'

I put my hand on his.

'I feel like you're my brother. My sister. My brother-sister,' he said.

'No touching!' a nurse called, startling us.

'Sorry,' we both shouted, pulling away.

15

I woke from a dreamless, medicated sleep. Shoes squeaking in the hallways, nurses calling that breakfast was ready. Oh, thank god. How many days had it been?

I pushed myself out of bed and looked for Eitan in the men's wing, but he was gone, bed stripped, room empty. Discharged.

He'd left a note for me at the nurse's station with his number scrawled on it. I folded it and jammed it in my pocket, then lined up for breakfast in the eggy-smelling Day Room. A slab of omelet. Soft, buttered toast.

'Your friend got out?' It was Eden. She set her tray down next to mine. 'Can I have your toast?'

I passed my whole tray to her.

'Thank you, sir,' she said to me.

16

They let me go on a Tuesday morning with a thick packet of papers. Refills of Remeron, Zyprexa, Depakote. *NO GRAPEFRUIT*, all caps. I sat in the backseat of a strawberry-scented Uber, pink plastic pitcher in my lap. Sun big, bright and hot. Radio on, air blasting. Outside, the commotion of everyday life. The blare of a horn. The errant drop from an AC window unit. A dog in a stroller. A hydrant cracked open. People on the sidewalk with iced coffees – real coffees! I rolled down the window, stuck my head out and closed my eyes.

Santanu Bhattacharya (he/him) is the author of two novels, essays and several works of short fiction. *One Small Voice* was an *Observer* Best Debut Novel for 2023, and *Deviants* won the 2025 Rainbow Award for Book of the Year. He grew up in India and now lives in London.

@santanu_bx

The below work contains discussion of sexuality-based discrimination.

Prejudice & Pride

The weekend before the fiftieth London Pride, Shiny and I were hate-crimed.

Yes, I'm going to call it that, though some might disagree, say that if it were serious enough we would've reported it to the police, which we didn't. I even resisted the temptation to post about it on social media. But we've been doing this for too long – brushing uncomfortable experiences under the carpet, straight-washing them to make the heteros feel inclusive, accommodating inane questions from the clueless and the allies.

This is what happened: on a nondescript Friday evening, Shiny and I were going grocery shopping. It had become a ritual of sorts. During the pandemic, we'd go for long walks around our neighbourhood after finishing work, and we'd kept it up since, agreeing that we were too brain-fried to go out, meet people, make an effort. It took a lot, especially for an introvert like Shiny, to put himself out there. Instead, on

Fridays, we went to the local shops, bought something nice for dinner, opened a bottle of wine, cooked a tasty meal and found something half-clever/non-stupid to watch on TV.

That Friday, we were walking down one of the back lanes, immersed in discussion – the hard-headed bosses, the never-ending meetings, the forever-chagrined clients, just work-week things – when I heard shouts. Paying no heed, I continued to speak, though my LGBTQ+ safety radar had been viscerally activated and I knew these weren't good noises. Shiny cut me off and asked, 'You know that's for us, right?' It is then that I focused squarely on the loud voices and made out the slurs. Even as I was processing their taunts, I found it disconcerting that this was happening right here in our neighbourhood, in broad daylight, with other pedestrians and cyclists passing by. And we weren't even being affectionate in public!

Every queer person knows that we carry our shame in our bodies, and every hater is instinctively trained to pick up these markers. We were two men casually walking down the street, but these boys had had their senses piqued. Yes, they were boys; when I turned to look, I could have sworn they weren't older than fourteen. There were four of them, and, if it matters, all white. They were lounging around a ledge, diving off it, shadowboxing, bouncing off walls, their eyes fixed upon us the whole time. It must've been only a second, but they'd caught me looking, and now they were striding forward, chests puffed, hands swinging, feet crunching on the gravel. 'What you looking at?' one said. Behind him, the other three broke out in a singsong. *Gay boys, gay boys...*

This wasn't the first time this had happened to me, or to Shiny, or to us together. One time, we'd nearly been knifed; another time, punched on a late-night London bus. On that Friday evening, even though our outraged masculinity wanted to spit out expletives and get into fisticuffs, we knew better. We turned and walked away, the chorus of 'Gay Boys' now so loud that a musical director, if around, would've cast the gang in a West End choir.

A decade ago, we'd moved from India to the UK because we were criminals in our country and pariahs in our society; we couldn't imagine a decent, healthy future for ourselves, as individuals and as a couple. For ten years, we'd stayed the course through excruciating job interviews, grunt work, abusive bosses, sleepless nights, everchanging visa rules, tomes of documents, tens of thousands of pounds paid to the Home Office for applications and appointments and biometrics. When deciding where to live, we'd chosen the most bougie, most multicultural quarter of North London, dotted with pretty cafes and bookshops and young professionals dressed in the latest fashion dashing past on Lime bikes. But with time, we were reconciling to the fact that there was no place we'd ever belong to, and no laws that could enshrine our dignity.

And so, in anger and frustration, gulping down my ignominy, trying to behave like everything was fine for Shiny's sake, turning my attention back to that chilled wine and homemade dinner, I muttered under my breath, 'Fuck Pride.'

Momo arrived a week later, the day before Pride. Shiny and I waved him in, still queasy from the previous weekend. A hate crime is like fine wine – it becomes fuller and rounder with time, unresolved feelings that first linger at the tip then going on to establish themselves as a solid aftertaste, the jarring friction between *this-shouldn't-have-happened*, *I-should-have-done-more* and *maybe-I-brought-this-upon-myself*.

Momo sashayed in with a blue trolley bag on which he'd stuck pink heart-shaped cut-outs, and I marvelled again at the enthusiasm with which he lived his life, the little things he did for himself, the bucket list we'd made in our twenties still going strong in our forties, items added and struck off with amazing regularity. From time to time, I'd tell myself that I still had the pizzazz from two decades ago, then I'd see Momo and realise how much more sober and functional life had made me, how much of that old effervescence I'd lost. A couple of years ago, he'd moved to a village outside Magdeburg in Germany, where his company had a plant. He didn't speak the language, had no friends, the few thousand people around him were mostly elderly. 'There's no one to fuck, but also no one to out me' was his justification. Momo had attained the fifth and final stage of grief: acceptance, for no matter how much we empower ourselves, the torment of alienation and exile can never be fully exterminated. But true to his spirit, he made life in the village look like it was New York City.

Momo was in London on a mission: one of his New Year's resolutions had been to attend Pride in as many cities as possible. In the last few months, he'd been to Brussels, Dresden, Bologna, Lisbon and Cologne. Later in the year, he'd planned Barcelona, Berlin, Amsterdam and Copenhagen. He'd sent us pouty photos in costumes – wings and confetti, flags draped as skirts, a melange of naked torsos glittering around him. He had friends in many places, and, when he didn't, he turned up by himself and made sure he wasn't left alone. But don't worry, he'd messaged, I'm saving the best for you – we're going to rock London Pride.

Shiny and I weren't exactly Pride people, if that were a term. The fact that we went grocery shopping on Friday evenings might have hinted at this already. We got by fine with an uncanny assortment of friends – some gay, some straight, some doting parents, some sworn off children, some single, some couples, some monogamous, some poly-x, some white, some people of colour, some teetotallers, some alcoholics. We were happy with what we'd built in this new place, little by little, over time, weathering the shocks of Brexit and the pandemic and other Home Office-induced atrocities on immigrants. But that meant that we didn't necessarily have a community – there wasn't a single group we met every weekend, or went out with to the same place, or even spoke to about the same topics.

We'd been to Pride only once before – our first summer in London, more out of curiosity than anything else. While it was one of the highlights of those early years, when every alleyway and encounter seemed out of *Notting Hill* or *Love, Actually*, and while I'd come back from the parade very emotional about seeing queer parents walking with their kids, something I'd never seen in my country and couldn't imagine seeing for a long time, and while Shiny was buzzing about all the hot men who'd queued up so he could colour their cheeks and chests with his rainbow roller crayons, we'd found excuses every year since – it was too hot, or there was a literature festival at Southbank, or there was a FIFA World Cup match with England playing on the same day, or Adele was performing in Hyde Park. In short, we never went back.

And now, there we were, Momo already unpacking his suitcase to show us his costume, asking for the Wi-Fi password so he could order some last-minute accessories on Amazon, checking if we had our clothes ready. Seeing him in his element, we didn't have the heart to tell him that we'd decided to skip Pride that year too, that he'd have to do it alone. In the past week, chafing from the assault, we'd shouted, 'Fuck Pride!' an inordinate number of times to an invisible audience. Now Shiny and I exchanged glances as Momo stumbled from one detail to another, route maps to registrations, footwear to energy bars. How were we going to break the news?

Momo and I had known each other for twenty years. We'd met on the first day of university, walking around campus with induction forms and timetables. We were in a foreign country, both abroad for the first time. But that was not why we'd become friends. I'd found him hopelessly attractive, and he'd spotted another queer in me. Back then, in that country where it was also illegal to be gay, we wouldn't say it out loud for a long time, but Momo later said he knew about me from the get-go, probably from the way I couldn't tear my eyes off him. We'd played the game for a while – hanging out with straight boys, sending each other flirty texts, hitting the underground bars on the pretext of our love for dancing. One time, in a deluded bid at heterosexuality, we'd even jointly courted a pair of sisters, exchange students from Canada whom we'd taken out on a double date to watch the fireworks. I don't quite remember anymore at what point we'd verbally come out to each other, if at all. We'd plunged into friendship so quickly that I soon forgot about my little crush on him.

Over the years, Momo and I had been each other's pillars of strength, even from a distance. We hadn't lived in the same place since university, and our lives had taken their own twists and turns, like tributaries separating and joining at various points. But when Momo's heart broke after a guy had unceremoniously dumped him, or when he fell in love for real with the man he'd spend many years with, or when he got embroiled in a police incident on one of his work travels, or when he spent months in the depths of depression, I was always one of the first to know. And similarly, when I'd lost my job and had been sitting at home waiting for a miracle so I didn't get deported, it was Momo who'd staged an intervention and introduced me to his professional networks; when I'd run red on my credit card bills, he'd transferred the money, no questions asked; when I'd paired up with Shiny, he'd promptly given his blessings, even when everyone else was reminding me of the futility of a hidden relationship in a hostile place.

My mother has a story about Momo. One time, she was visiting me, and Momo had said he'd come by to say hi. Ma had asked him to have dinner with us. That evening, I'd got stuck at work and couldn't make it home until much later. By the time I got there, Momo had left. He and Ma had eaten together and talked all evening. Ma said they'd yammered away about this and that for hours. 'He shared so many things,' she said, without revealing what they were. There was a glow on her face that night, the kind that comes from spending time with an old friend. I still sometimes wondered what they'd chatted about, an undeniable tinge of jealousy at having missed out.

Now in the makeshift guest room, which doubled up as a study and a music room in our little flat, Momo showed us his elaborate acquisitions for Pride. He'd purchased a pink silk saree with brocade work along the border that he would pair with a leather harness. To go with this were a pink wig, large dangling earrings and a dazzling tiara. He said we'd have to do a dress rehearsal that night, but first, did we have any make-up?

Accepting one's own gayness is like unpeeling the layers of an onion. First you admitted to yourself that you indeed liked male bodies. Then you found out that it went beyond *liking*, that an electric spark ignited in your chest with a first glance or shy smile or sly wink from a man. Then you wanted to walk hand-in-hand with them, share your story, know theirs. You got comfortable with your body, its curves and swings. You wanted to express yourself in new ways, maybe some kohl around your eyes, a flowing garment, a nose-stud. You wanted to write and sing and dance and play sports on your own terms. Except that it wasn't really like peeling an onion: these steps weren't sequential, they were all muddled up, could happen years apart or simultaneously, and in no particular order.

For me, stepping into my queerness had meant an intrinsic blossoming. I'd chosen to sleep with men, had put myself out there with all its risks and pleasures; when I'd found love, I'd turned my life upside down to bring it to fruition, whatever the price to be paid. Over the years, I'd become aware of our rights and entitlements, their colonial and cultural contexts, the rampant abrogation, the impermanence of victories. I'd constantly pushed against living life as a third-class citizen, having difficult conversations at home and in the workplace and on the street, negotiating and navigating international borders and governments.

Perhaps instinctively, then, as a way to protect myself from the toll this had taken, I'd never let myself bloom outwardly. My haircut was still what it had been when I was a teenager, my outfits were still just T-shirt-and-jeans or shirt-and-trousers, I never wore any jewellery, nor any accoutrement or embellishment. For a long time, I'd complimented myself for not being a trope. Look, I wanted to tell the world, there are gays like me too, just *normal.* But I'd acknowledged over time – and had been called out by close friends – that this was probably a dose of internalised homophobia at work.

So, no, we had to tell Momo, we didn't have any make-up. We headed out to buy some, get an early dinner and return in time for Pride prep.

We walked around the shop peering at the shelves stacked with make-up products. I didn't even know so much existed – foundations and concealers, sponges and brushes, highlighters and primers, sprays and powders. Shiny and Momo checked out this and that, tried them in front of the miniature mirrors. It wasn't easy finding shades that melded into their brown skin tones: some stood out awkwardly, some didn't make an impact at all. They went back and forth, wiping one off, applying another. Around us were only women, trying their best to not pay us any heed. An assistant circled us uncomfortably, asking if she could help, perhaps to get us out of the way at the soonest.

Over a dinner of pho at the local Vietnamese joint, Momo told us that he'd signed us up to march with the South Asian Gays, an organisation I hadn't heard of before. It abbreviated to SAG, which sent us into giggles, because what gay outfit would name themselves the exact opposite of supple and fit? Momo said that Pride had become a big capitalist brouhaha, with large companies paying thousands for their jazzy floats, straight-as-fuck CEOs gyrating in rainbow wigs and leather pants. 'Their good deed for the year,' Momo scoffed. But he'd found us this niche group that not only didn't charge a lot but was also a charity. 'And we're South Asians, after all!'

I could feel Shiny squirm next to me. He was in his second stage of grief: anger. He'd been in grief since childhood, living out the first stage through his adolescence: denial. He'd denied everything Indian, as much as he could as an Indian person living in India with very Indian parents. And now, since we'd moved to the UK, he'd graduated to rage, an absolute and non-negotiable erasure of everything that reminded him of his roots, except maybe the food – renouncing Indian food in favour of British would be less sacrifice and more sacrilege. 'I don't think I'll march tomorrow,' he said to Momo, finally belling the cat. 'I'll be on the sidelines, cheering you guys on.'

Momo's face fell a bit, instinctively turned to me. I was in my third stage of grief: bargaining. I'd emerged from the other two to convince myself that I could find a way of life that embraced my new circumstances while still holding on to my old ones, that I could curate my choices, go with what I liked, dump what I didn't. In that sense, I didn't care for Pride or for SAG; Pride had always seemed like a Western enterprise to me, and SAG seemed too boxed-in. But I loved Momo, and I'd be there for him.

Back home, Shiny got busy dressing Momo up. I'd never seen him put make-up on himself, but he turned out quite the expert, rolling and tamping and chiselling away at Momo's face, giving definition to Momo's large eyes with the eyeliner, a dash of mascara here, a touch of rouge there. He said it had been his favourite pastime as a child, playing with his mother's things. I wondered how much I didn't know about him, even after all these years together.

We watched YouTube tutorials on how to wear a saree and laughed about what bad gays we were; SAG would surely disqualify us! Shiny draped Momo's waist with one-and-a-half yards, folded the rest of the garment across his chest for the pallu, then knelt back down to make perfect pleats on the skirt with his fingers. When he brought Momo to the full-length mirror, there was a hushed coyness in the room, the kind I imagine happens when a bride is first revealed in her wedding dress. Momo, who'd never put on make-up before nor worn a saree, stared at his new alter-ego in wonderment. We named her Mohini, after the character in a famous Bollywood song from our childhood. Then the spell broke, and the three of us danced to the beats of the song, singing the words from memory. I was scared Momo would trip on the saree, but he pulled it off with a natural deftness.

Later that night, when Shiny and Momo had retired, I found myself unable to sleep. Perpetually prone to overthinking, the tension of what was to come gripped all my senses – there was a minerality in my tastebuds, a spike in my touch, a blur in my vision. What would happen tomorrow? Would we be able to pull it off? Us three brown boys from faraway small-town India, who'd never spoken our truths until we were well into our twenties, who'd each had painful pasts of bullying and abuse and exclusion, now trying to claim space in this blindingly white world – it seemed incongruous, anachronistic. No amount of logic could calm my beating heart.

I tiptoed into the living room where Momo had laid out his costume. I picked up the saree and carefully unfolded it. I draped it around myself like I'd seen in the YouTube tutorial. I looked at myself in the mirror. I'd always imagined how I would look as a woman. When I'd started sleeping with men, many had told me I'd make a beautiful girl; I'd stopped sleeping with such men later, restricting the privilege to only those who desired me the way I was. I now spread my left arm out, the pallu hanging like a glorious pink wing. I chuckled: it had taken me over forty years to allow myself to wear a saree, for fear that it would turn me into something else, something ghastly. And yet, now that I was wearing it, I was still just myself, haplessly so. Who else could I be?

The next morning, we were at the designated meeting point on time. We'd taken the Tube, which was overcrowded, and people appreciatively regarded Momo. The wig shone in the white lights of the carriage, its cheap plastic giving off a kitschy sheen. The leather harness, unwrapped just that morning, lent a fullness to the look, letting Momo's shapely muscles flex and bulge, rippling down his strong, hairy arms. While dressing him up, I'd spotted scabs on his back from an auto-immune condition. I'd asked if he wanted them concealed, but he only gave a nonchalant jerk of his head. I knew this meant he was throwing caution to the wind.

Shiny had dressed up too. We'd disinterred two large Pride flags from the last time we'd attended. We'd used them just one other time since then, when, in a moment of spontaneity, we'd hung them out from the windows of our flat, until we'd woken up to discover them soiled by muck. Someone had gone through the trouble of finding the substance, carrying it over to our street and throwing it at our flags in the middle of the night. We'd washed them and stowed them away. Now Shiny wore one of them as a ghagra, wrapping it around his hip like a sarong. On top, he wore a glitzy shirt hitched up to his chest like a crop top. He'd used acrylic paints to draw intricate designs around his eyebrows and cheeks, then dusted some glitter. Now that he'd decked up, he was all in. 'I'm going to march with you guys too!' he declared, and Momo gave him a sensuous salaam of gratitude, like a courtesan in a nawab's mehfil.

I'd worn my regular clothes, but Shiny and Momo had

pinned several badges and broches to my T-shirt and made jubilant rainbows on my cheeks with the roller crayons. I wore the other Pride flag as a cape, tying it around my neck and letting it flutter behind me. We found glossy dot stickers that I stuck as outlines above my eyebrows, curving all the way down to my eyes. Stomping to the Tube station, we looked like a happy circus party.

At the meeting point, we said hello to the others who were there to march with SAG. Some were long-timers, some newer joiners. Almost everyone seemed to know each other, and we had to repeat our introductions many times over. There were people from India, Pakistan, Bangladesh, Sri Lanka – all our warring nations united in queerness on the coloniser's land. We shuffled forward in the holding pen, checking out the floats in front of and behind us, replete with drag queens and DJs and bunting and boomboxes and cheerleaders. Sandwiched between two corporations, we seemed like a tiny amateur band of novice performers. Would anyone even see us, or would we get flattened without notice?

As we drew closer to the starting line, it was becoming apparent that Momo's costume was a big hit. SAG members came up to take photos with him. Unsurprisingly, they were all a bit nerdy. Journalists and influencers jumped the picket line for a shot of Momo. People from other floats invited him up for dances. He got shoutouts from a couple of passing DJs. At some point, the main organisers of SAG handed Momo their headline flag, which was the Pride flag with overlays of our countries at the corners. It was clear: Momo was going to lead the SAG troupe. 'Fuck,' he muttered in my ear, 'I just came to have some fun, but now they've turned me into Mother India.'

On cue, I sent some of the photographs to my mother. I'd always wondered if I'd made it easy for my parents, whether their acceptance would've been more layered and conditional if I weren't so regular, so unimaginative in how I presented myself. Had I worn more adventurous clothes, spoken in a high-pitched voice, amped up my peculiarities, how would they have responded? Her reply didn't take long.

Looking great all of you, especially Momo in a saree. Enjoy yourselves. Love and blessings.

I don't remember much of the parade itself. It lives in my memory in snatches, sudden flashes that sometimes infiltrate my mind with a giddy euphoria. There's Momo, smartly carrying the flagpole for the entire 2.3 kilometres, waving it with aplomb, sometimes stopping to dance and grind his hips, the pallu of his saree flying in the breeze. There's Shiny, walking along the barricades, waving another flag, lowering it close enough for the hungry crowds to touch. There's me, sometimes chanting and dancing, sometimes tightening Momo's harness, tucking in his saree, keeping him hydrated, giving him his meds on time. There's us, the South Asian Gays, beating dhols, unfurling dupattas, rocking to bhangra beats. We're a small group, but we're not invisible. Among the throng of capitalist floats, we're an oddity, but a welcome novelty, nevertheless. When we pass, thousands clap, lean in to hold our hands, give us hugs, plant kisses. We hear cheers from young brown voices, our next generation for whom this might mean something. Older brown faces watch us stoically, perhaps questioning what they could have done better, or even secretly happy that we'd finally managed to do what they couldn't. We, shunned by our homes and cultures, illegal in our countries, cursed for being immigrants in our host nation, called names by boys who could've been our sons, having our little moment in the sun, the whole world our witness.

London Pride usually gets a million spectators, making it one of the biggest events in the UK. But that year being the fiftieth, there were close to two million people from all over the world. It has since been named among the largest public events globally. But I didn't know any of this then. That night, Momo and Shiny, still high from the parade, went out to one of the many afterparties. And I slept peacefully, wrapped in moonlight and rainbow, levitating in the summer air that came in untethered through my open window.

Selali Fiamanya (he/him) works as a doctor in the UK and was born and raised in Glasgow, with a couple of years spent in Accra, Ghana. He won a place on the inaugural Breakthrough Novel-Writing Course for Black Writers, run by Curtis Brown Creative and supported by Curtis Brown Literary Agency. He was named runner-up in the 2021 Pontas & JJ Bola Emerging Writers Prize and won the Borough Press open submission competition with his debut novel *Before We Hit the Ground*, which was published in February 2025.

The below work contains depictions of sex and alcohol use and discussion of fertility treatment.

Lemonade

Aunty Mawu's lemon tree was dead. Kobla had never seen it naked. Its squat trunk splintered off into spindled branches, twisting up into nothing. Its deep-green leaves were mostly gone – a few lay faded and brittle on the grass, waiting for the breeze to carry them off. Its last lemons had been plucked.

Kobla followed his parents out of the dusty Volvo his dad had borrowed from an uncle and walked towards the bungalow. Three- and four-storey buildings loomed over the compound wall, but the house stood bright, shadowless. It had been a decade since Kobla last visited, a year since he'd spoken to his aunty on the phone and two months since she had died, found by the woman who collected and sold her lemons when she grew too old to do so herself.

'It looks the exact same,' Kobla said, as they climbed the steps to the porch. Splashes of pink from the blossoming bougainvillea lined the walls, packed alongside yellows, oranges and greens from other plants he'd never learnt the names of.

'Mmm,' Jacob replied. His dad was stern and focussed, which Kobla now understood as him keeping a lid on a turbulent inner world. Jacob stalled at the door, almost imperceptibly, but in that instant Janet strode forward instead, opening the door to her dead sister-in-law's house.

The afternoon light fell in through the open curtains and bounced off the terrazzo floor, reaching all four corners of the small living room. Kobla realised it didn't smell musty, and an instant later realised he had been baiting his breath in anticipation of a vague 'smell of death' that he'd read about in stories. He let his lungs expand, drawing in warm, clean air.

The house was small – living room, kitchen, bathroom, a couple of bedrooms and a storeroom by the back porch. They'd come a few days after the funeral to claim the last of Aunty Mawu's belongings. There was no will, so the house had landed with Jacob, her only sibling. Everything in it, however, had appeared to be fair game to the rest of the family, who had still been living in Ghana while Jacob had been living a life of supposed luxury abroad. Kobla roamed while his mum and dad knelt on the floor to rummage through one of the few remaining boxes. Jacob crossed himself before pulling it towards him. As Kobla ascended the stairs, he checked his phone – still no message – then tucked it into his pocket. He pushed open his aunty's bedroom door, and its creak yawned into the empty room. A bright rectangle on the floor by the window announced where her bed used to lie. Kobla remembered sleeping in it on family holidays, squished against her while his parents slept in the living room. She always smelt faintly of lemon, sweet and sharp.

Kobla's eyes stung, as if he'd tasted something sour, and he turned back and walked to the living room. Janet was lifting a generic picture of some children sitting under a baobab tree off the wall. It used to hang over a sideboard with a full display of plates, old clay pots and photos. Kobla remembered reaching up once to touch a statue in the middle, a two-headed figure carved out of dark wood, and how his dad had batted his hand away and told him to 'stop disturbing things' and go and play outside.

He checked his phone again, then silently walked through the empty kitchen and onto the back porch. The lemon tree stood in the middle of a small plot of land. It was big, but now Kobla couldn't understand how it could have been big enough. He remembered feeling Aunty Mawu creeping out of bed at first light. How he would kneel on the bed to watch her from the bedroom window in sepia, as the advancing sun and retreating moon both cast their light. She'd come back with a bucket of lemons. Once he was up and washed, they'd walk hand in hand to her market stall, overflowing with bowls of almost luminous, perfectly oval fruit. His parents were bemused by ten-year-old Kobla's preference to spend the few days of their annual visits with his aunty at the market – her English was pidgin, and the heat should have been unbearable for a child from Glasgow – but when they had dragged him to see distant relatives or to air-conditioned restaurants in malls, he had grumbled and picked at his food until they were forced to take him back to Aunty Mawu's house.

Kobla loved the bustle. How Aunty Mawu would laugh with customers and buy him samosas and Tampico from the next stall with grubby notes. How people would lean in to dote on her 'nephew from *abrokyire*', and how they'd lean back to say, 'These – hmm – they are the best lemons in Ghana, oh,' leaving him glowing with second-hand pride.

Now, seeing the tree with adult eyes, he no longer understood how it had been large enough to produce all those lemons day in, day out. He hid his eyes from the tree – almost too proud, unapologetic in its nakedness – and instead faced the storeroom, needing something more contained. He turned the handle, and his eyes immediately fell upon the statue. Two heads, one body, sitting upright in the middle of the floor. Its position, commanding the space, made it seem like it had been placed there purposefully, rather than discarded. He picked it up, and it sat in his palm, about the size of a melon but surprisingly light.

His phone buzzed in his pocket.

Just done the embryo transfer. Fingers crossed!

Brill! Keep me posted

Defo. Test in 2 weeks, eclipse day!!

<3 <3🌞⚫

He put his phone away, relieved. Shez and Harriet were two rounds in and had asked Kobla to be their donor. It was an odd responsibility – mostly waiting around as they did all the hard bits and, so far, trying to be supportive when it had gone wrong.

Back in the living room, Janet was dusting off her hands. Jacob had a shoebox with some odds and ends.

'What's that?' He eyed the statue Kobla clutched.

'It's that old statue, from the mantle.' Kobla proffered it to his father, whose hands remained on the shoebox.

'Oh, maybe leave that one.' He looked at his box. 'We don't have space.'

Kobla brought the statue close again, holding it against his chest, nestled in the crook of his arm. 'I want to keep it.' It was familiar. He imagined he could smell the faintest lemony wisp rising from it.

'Jacob, let's go. Let him take it.' Janet dissipated the tension before it could build. Jacob hesitated before leading the way out. Kobla followed, bewildered by the rules required to navigate his father's grief and worried that he had brought him a totem that was too close a reminder of his sister, but unwilling to let it go.

With Aunty Mawu gone, Kobla had no choice but to spend the next few days following his parents on the family rounds. He mostly sat silent, eating as much as he could – the food was always good – and dutifully sharing his life updates when asked: yes, he was a trainee solicitor; yes, it had been such a long time since he was in Ghana; no, he wasn't yet married. The more tenacious aunties would suggest solutions to that problem.

'Mummy, I beg, leave that boy alone,' Ama chided. Ama's mum and Kobla's mum were cousins. Ama and Kobla had chased chickens together in their compound on the outskirts of Accra but had lost touch other than sending the odd reaction to an Instagram story – Ama's were usually of a beach or an art gallery, often with beaming friends.

'You too, I'm coming for you next,' her mum parried, deflected with a roll of the eyes from Ama. 'I know plenty of lawyers who are married; it's only you two who keep getting lost on the way to the chapel.'

Ama sucked her teeth in response, usually a sign of utter disrespect to an elder, but here it only emphasised the joviality between mum and daughter. Glad for the distraction, which obviated the need for Kobla to answer, he left the couch for the kitchen, to refill his plate.

'Cuz. It's good to see you.' Ama had followed Kobla, catching him as he shamelessly picked out a chunk of goat meat from the jollof in the pan.

'You too,' Kobla replied through greasy lips.

'How long are you in town?'

They had a week left – more family, a trip to Jacob's village and then a couple of days in a beach town down the coast.

'What are you doing tomorrow night?' she asked, fishing out her own morsel from the pan.

'Dunno, mum and dad have the itinerary. I just follow.'

'Take my number. I'm meeting some friends in Osu; you'll like them.' She scooped some coleslaw onto her plate as she dictated the digits, then she led him back in.

Kobla pulled up to the Korner Kafe just after 10:00 pm the next night and slid out of the shared taxi, handing over, he presumed, more cash than the trip was supposed to have cost. He checked his phone again.

Booth, far left.

The cafe was set off from the road, through a short arch made of bent bamboo and foliage. He pushed open the red door, stepping into a room with a bar on one end and space for only five or six tables. The lights were low, upbeat jazz was playing and mirrors and colourful fabrics hung on the walls. People laughed by candlelight, and a few stood dancing in the rivulets between tables. He spotted Ama's group and squeezed towards them.

'Kobla, welcome!' She shuffled her friends along to make room for him. The setting felt disconcertingly familiar. Not in an ancestral or familial way – the way Ghana had always felt familiar to Kobla. But in a new way. In a 'let's grab a drink with the gang' way.

'Guys, this is my cousin, Kobla.' Ama introduced the two others in the group as Larry and Jessie before waving down the waiter and requesting another glass for their shared cocktail pitcher. While she spoke, Kobla stared at Larry, the man opposite him. His hair was cropped short and dyed pink, and he had the most elegant nose ring Kobla had ever seen.

'Welcome to Accra,' Jessie offered. She was dressed in all black, her lips filled in with neat black lipstick, her dreads pulled into a bun covered with a black headscarf.

'Thanks. But I've been here loads. Well, not here. It's my first time here.' He paused, and she nodded.

'I had to save him from my mother trying to marry him off today.' Ama laughed.

'Save him from what? Does he not want a wife?' Larry quizzed, his eyebrow arched.

Ama turned to look at Kobla, her lip raised in a half smile. 'I don't know, do you?' Kobla hesitated, his tongue hanging flaccid in his mouth.

'Ei, stop harassing him, Ama!' Jessie erupted, and the others joined her in laughter. Kobla was able to breathe again, and he realised once more that he could, freely. Whatever stench he had been scared of catching wasn't in this room either. Ama filled his tall glass chock-full of ice and sugary alcohol, and he struggled to suck on the straw through his grin.

The din of the cafe grew louder as the drinks poured, and the music seamlessly flowed through to Afrobeat and amapiano. The patrons rose with the volume, and by midnight more were on their feet than at the tables. They danced as a four, with Kobla snatching glances at Larry, and Larry snatching touches of Kobla's hips.

'My sister. It's time, *yɛnkɔ*.' Jessie was already picking up her purse and rummaging for her phone. Kobla didn't want to leave. He'd finally found it, and feared the dream disappearing when he awoke in the outside world.

'What time does it close?' He looked around. 'It still seems pretty busy.'

'Don't worry, this is just the warm-up.' Larry winked.

Kobla reached for his jacket. He half-whispered to Ama over the table – 'We're going to another party?' What he really wanted to know is if it would be another party like *this*.

'Babe, it's round one. You know how to party in Glasgow or what?' Ama hooked Kobla's arm, with a glint in her eye, and pulled him out into the night.

*

Jessie's Jeep felt like a tank. It smoothed out the potholes as they cruised along, sitting high above the dented taxis surrounding them. Kobla couldn't remember whether Jessie had kept up with the others when the shots had been bought. He knew he probably shouldn't be in the car with her at the wheel: for much of the journey there was no real distinction between road and pavement, with revellers striding on the blurred boundary. Kobla kept shooting glances at them, and the old roadside sellers frying yam and plantain. He didn't want to interrupt what seemed to be the done thing by asking if Jessie was safe to drive, and, he could admit, with the breeze from the open window wicking his sweat as they drove, it was thrilling to be on the inside of something.

They pulled up at the inscrutable metal gates of a large compound. Despite the fortress-like walls, Kobla could hear bass pounding through the open car window. Ama made a quick call, and the gates clunked open. The music grew louder, but, to Kobla's disappointment, there didn't seem to be much of a party. Another friend stood there, still holding a phone to her ear, in a dripping wet blue bikini. Jessie parked up next to three other cars, and they were led round to the back of the house, where Kobla realised he needn't have worried.

The smell of chlorine hit first, then he saw the pool with a dozen people arranged around it. Some on loungers, others sitting on the edge, feet swishing gently back and forth. Two women splashed each other in the water, and a couple danced by the speakers at the far edge, which cast their rhythm across the water towards Kobla.

He felt like he'd lifted the veil on a secret society. As he saw the couple by the speakers start to kiss, hands in braids and on cheeks and hips, he realised he had been.

'I didn't bring my swimming trunks,' was all Kobla could say, turning to Ama.

'Then I suppose you'll have to go in naked,' replied Larry, before walking over to the drinks table, setting down a bottle of whisky he'd brought and pouring himself a vodka and coke. The others chuckled as they followed, though Kobla wasn't sure if it had been a joke, and partly hoped it wasn't.

The ease from Korner Kafe kicked in. Kobla was with his people. The four of them made a private corner of two loungers, a little poolside oasis. Ama lay back on one while Jessie sat on its edge, Ama's legs slinking through the triangular gap between Jessie's ass and the arm she was leaning on. Kobla lay back on the second while Larry sat in a mirror image of Jessie. Kobla felt a sudden charge, like Larry was a magnet caught in a force field cast from the margins of his body.

Jessie and Ama were arguing about whether Ama should quit her corporate law job to work for an international NGO (Jessie thought they were just as crooked). Larry's forearm lay unmoving on a slip of Kobla's hip that had been uncovered by his shirt riding up. After counting thirty seconds, Kobla decided he had all the evidence he needed. Encouraged by the vodka, and primed for action by the layer of sweat the balmy heat had coated him in, he acted.

'I want to get in the pool. Do you think there'll be a spare set of trunks in the house?' he asked Larry directly.

'Go and ask Akua,' Ama replied. It was partly genuine advice, partly a bawdy declaration of approval.

'I know where she keeps them, let's go and protect your dignity.' Larry rose and Kobla followed through the back porch and into the kitchen, maintaining the charade with a respectful distance.

They kept it up as they entered the bedroom, despite Larry deftly locking the door and Kobla leaning in close, a hand on Larry's lower back, as Larry pulled out drawers, ruffling through underwear and old shirts. They kept it up as Larry held a pair of board shorts, and as Kobla pulled off his shirt, slid down his trousers and boxers and proffered a hand to receive them. The pretence finally dropped when Larry let the shorts fall to the floor, instead reaching out a hand to cover Kobla's cock.

Courting complete, Kobla pulled Larry in with a hand behind his neck. The kiss was all sugary mixer and tongues, and Kobla fell onto the bed as Larry leaned into him. They giggled as it squeaked, aware of the music pulsing in through the open window, and that the sound travelled both ways. Both seemed to agree they were there for a good time, not a long time. Kobla pulled Larry's T-shirt over his head as Larry slid down to suck his cock. Larry pulled off his own shorts and swung himself onto the bed, pivoting on Kobla's now-hard cock and bringing his own to Kobla's mouth.

Kobla hadn't cum in almost a week, thwarted by the close proximity, unlockable doors and porous personal boundaries that come with family holidays. He was already getting close as Larry sucked and stroked him, his cock slick with spit from base to tip. Larry's finger teasing his hole almost set him off, but still he tapped away his hand when Larry tried pushing further in, wishing he'd been able to predict tonight's turn of events before he left home that evening.

'Sorry,' Kobla mumbled, his mouth pressed against Larry's thigh after emptying it of cock.

'No problem.' Larry responded by grinding his crotch deeper into Kobla, bringing his ass closer to Kobla's mouth. Kobla took the hint and found Larry's hole with his tongue, tasting only of the faintest musk. Larry moaned, and Kobla pulled on his hip so that he sat on Kobla's face as Kobla licked and pushed deeper with his tongue. Kobla looked up at the curve of his back, outlined by the leftover pool light that made it through the window. He felt Larry's rhythm as he wanked himself off, then the tensing of his hole as a warm spurt landed on Kobla's chest. Wordlessly, Larry leaned over and took Kobla's cock in his hand and tugged. Kobla muffled his moans with Larry's ass as he came.

Larry rolled off and collapsed onto the bed, throwing up new squeaks. Kobla realised he hadn't heard any in a while and, with a slight thud in his chest, wondered if it was because they'd been judicious in their movements or because they'd fucked with abandon. The whole event, from first contact to second load, had lasted less than five minutes.

'I wasn't expecting that when I went out tonight.' Kobla sighed, coming back to himself, heart rate settling.

'Well, you'll be better prepared next time.' Larry sat on the edge of the bed and picked up the swimming trunks, tossing them over to Kobla with a smile. 'You'd better put those on or people will talk.'

Kobla did as told, wiping himself off with his boxers first then slipping on his T-shirt. The pair split at the porch door, Kobla making a beeline for the pool while Larry went to the loungers, where Ama sat hunched over a little table. The water was cooler than Kobla had anticipated, just enough to catch his breath, and he surreptitiously rubbed his chest and belly before floating for a minute or two. When he arrived back at the loungers, goosebumps rising, Larry handed him a towel, and Ama a lit joint. He thanked her, taking a seat next to Larry.

The night was thinning, the entire sky lightening evenly. They smoked in silence, the last ones standing from the party. Kobla closed his eyes. The pre-dawn light matched the colour behind his eyelids exactly, so it felt like he was staring out into the universe from behind them.

He heard Ama put out the stub and saw her reach out to squeeze Jessie's thigh. Larry looked over at her, and Kobla felt something pass between all three of them. Jessie picked up her bag and unzipped it. Larry caught the familiar whiff, sharp and sweet, before he saw them. Jessie pulled out five fat, shiny lemons, a knife and a little metal hand squeezer to grins from Ama and Larry.

Kobla thought about Jessie carrying them in her bag this whole night, and it seemed ludicrous. He wanted to laugh and ask, *Why are you juicing lemons?* Instead he said, 'Where did you get them from?'

Jessie smiled as she sliced them on the table. 'I got them from a friend. The best hangover cure you've ever had.'

The scent grew stronger as the knife opened the lemons up to the air. First, Kobla thought it was the weed throwing a haze of familiarity over his senses. But he had smelt those lemons before. He had seen those lemons.

'But where? Who?'

'The one and only,' Ama replied. 'Of course you know.'

Of course he did. 'Aunty Mawu,' he replied. 'How? How did you know her?'

'Aunty Mawu knew us all,' Larry replied, offering no further explanation.

Aunty Mawu and Ama were distant relatives, by marriage. Kobla hadn't realised they had met.

'I met her on my own.' Ama answered, as if reading the question on Kobla's mind.

'She had a way of finding you when you needed,' Jessie said, now squeezing the lemons into glasses. The silence grew thicker, interrupted only by the trickle of lemon juice.

'Guys, stop being so secretive. What's going on?' He tried to keep his voice level, but a hint of the panic seeped through.

'Chill,' Ama laughed. 'I'll tell you mine. I was a lonely teenager. A bit weird. I struggled. Then, when I was fourteen, we had a school fair, we all had to bring some food or drink. I stopped by her stall; I'd been a few times before. She gave me some lemons – she refused any money – and told me to add them to a sobolo recipe. I tell you, the drink was a hit. I got to talking with some classmates I'd never met before. I made my first real friends, including this fool over here.' She smiled at Larry, who preened in response.

Jessie had finished squeezing the lemons and now added a sugar cube to each glass. She sat up to face the others while they dissolved. 'I came to Accra for university. I needed to leave my town. But ei, this city: the school fees, the rent. By my third year, I was ready to drop out. I'd bought lemons from Aunty for a while, but came less and less – I was living on garri and water. One day I came by for a last bunch before quitting the city for good. She asked me where I'd been, and I told her.' She paused to swirl the glasses, and the now-soaked cubes melted into the juice. 'She said she would help me.'

'Help you?' Kobla's aunty was not a rich woman. 'How?'

'She said I should come and sell her lemons!' All three burst into guffaws at the confusion on Kobla's face. Jessie answered his unasked question. 'It was enough. Every Saturday, I would go to her house, collect them from the tree and sell. And it was enough.' She paused, pensive. 'I kept collecting them from her after I graduated. Until the day she passed.'

'But' – the realisation struck Kobla – '*you* were the girl? You...' He couldn't finish the sentence. The words 'found her' seemed too graceless.

Jessie nodded. 'I collected those lemons until she died, and the tree stopped making them. These are the last ones.' She pulled two fresh lemons from her bag – they must have been months old by now but were as bright and plump as ever. None of it made sense, but, despite his confusion, Kobla didn't feel scared. When he thought of his Aunty Mawu, kind and forthright, standing erect through years hunched over a market stall, something in these stories fit. He turned to Larry, hoping for a final piece of the puzzle.

'Maybe I'll tell you mine later,' was all he said, sitting up from his recline on the lounger. The others seemed to nod in understanding, then Jessie lifted the glasses.

'Let's go.' She rose, taking them to a patch of grass in the centre of the large garden. She handed them each a glass. The night was silent. Towards the east, the first light of the sun spilled over the horizon, while the moon had already faded to the west. The sky was cloudless, set in a seamless spectrum from morning light to the night's dark. Kobla felt like he was at its fulcrum, the entire celestial potential resting on him and his friends.

'Aunty Mawu.' Jessie dropped a splash from her glass onto the ground, in a libation.

'Aunty Mawu.' Ama did the same, then Larry.

'Aunty Mawu,' Kobla followed, instantly smelling the lemon scent rising from the ground he had anointed. They raised their glasses as one and, keeping eye contact, emptied them in one gulp. It was perfectly tangy, and warmed him as it passed through to his stomach, reaching out to his shoulders, fingers, legs and toes. He felt wrapped up suddenly, as if he were in bed again, beside his aunty, in the moments before she rose to start the day. He opened his eyes, surprised to find himself in the garden with the others looking at him, smiling. He felt calm, settled and, amazingly, completely sober.

'How was it?' Larry asked, not waiting for an answer. 'We told you – it's the best cure.'

The following Sunday, Kobla put the final touches on a dessert in Glasgow, waiting for his parents' visit. He'd long stopped joining them for church, and they'd long stopped asking, but they still came past his house every week for tea and cake on the way home.

'Oh,' was all Jacob said when he walked into the living room. Kobla had placed his aunty's statue on his mantle, its two heads staring at the walls to the left and right.

'Yeah. I think it looks good there, right?' Kobla tried. Jacob nodded as he sat down, and Janet once again took the lead, asking Kobla how work had gone and filling him in on the day's sermon as he brought through the lemon meringue pie he'd made with Tesco lemons. There wasn't much to catch up on since they'd spent most of the last few weeks together, but the time passed easily. Still, Kobla noticed his dad's eyes flicking towards the fireplace now and then. He relaxed with each bite, though, and when he placed down his empty plate he sat back with a heavy sigh, smiling for the first time.

'Do you know what that statue is?' Jacob interrupted Kobla and Janet as they spoke about a play they wanted to see.

'Eh, no, I guess not,' Kobla answered. Apart from its familiarity, he hadn't thought too much about it.

'It's Mawu,' Jacob continued.

'As in Aunty Mawu? Like a portrait?' Kobla looked at it more closely – he couldn't see a resemblance, and, in any case, one of the figures was male. Was it his dad and aunty? He suddenly felt the same thud of guilt he'd experienced at her house, for keeping close something his dad would rather turn away from.

'No. No, not Aunty Mawu. It's Mawu-Lisa. Mawu-Lisa is a god. An Ewe god,' Jacob explained, no longer looking at the statue but staring through the window as if he were remembering something.

'They are husband and wife. Mawu and Lisa,' Janet offered.

'Yes, maybe. Some say siblings. But they are one. Mawu-Lisa is the creator. Mawu is the woman, the moon, night. Lisa is the man, the sun, or day. But they are one. The Ewes believed they made human beings. Before the church came.'

'Was Aunty Mawu named after her?' Kobla pushed.

'No. Not directly. Many Ewe names begin with Mawu. Hers was Mawulipklim – "God is with me". My own Ewe name is Mawudeka – "One God". But I don't use it, especially since coming here.'

'Your aunty had that statue for a long time. I think she got it when we went back to Ghana, Jacob. Before Kobla. In '92.'

Janet stopped, and Kobla simply nodded again. The silence was weighty, and Kobla didn't know what question he was supposed to ask, so he didn't.

'Your aunty helped us, that trip,' Jacob finally declared, and it sounded to Kobla like an admission. He unclasped and clasped his watch, leaving his words unexplained.

'We were sad,' Janet eventually added. 'We'd been trying for a child for some time. We went back to Ghana, just to be with family. Aunty Mawu was a great support.'

'We stayed with her, actually,' Jacob almost mumbled.

'And you'll never believe it, that was in June '92.' Janet smiled. Kobla did the maths – he was born in March 1993.

'No way,' he replied.

His dad just nodded again, lips downturned in an expression of bashful sincerity. 'She was good to us, that trip. That's just what she did.'

After his parents left, Kobla washed the dishes with his phone on the countertop, just outside the splash zone. It was eclipse day, and Shez and Harriet were supposed to come round, but it was already 4:00 pm, and he hadn't heard from them. They'd have taken the pregnancy test by now, and so he was sure that, in this case, no news was bad news.

His phone buzzed just as he set the last plate on the rack to dry.

No luck this time

Gonna stay home tonight we think

Ahh shit
Sorry
Let me know if/when you want to chat

Shez heart-reacted his last message. Kobla slid his phone in his pocket, then pulled it out again to reread the messages. That was the second round, and though he knew you weren't supposed to – that the chances would always be low – he wondered if it were somehow his fault. Maybe he'd drunk too much, or done too many drugs, or ridden his bike to work too often.

The last of Aunty Mawu's lemons still sat on the countertop. Kobla had asked Jessie for one. She'd obliged, and he'd secreted it home in his hand luggage. He'd decided on a whim to zest it onto the pie he'd fed his parents that afternoon, in addition to the Tesco lemons in the filling. He'd wondered if they'd tasted anything different and what they might have said if they had. He still couldn't explain how the lemon had stayed so fresh for so long, but as it sat now, scraped to the fibrous white underneath its skin, he couldn't imagine it'd last much longer. After the news from Shez and Harriet, he wanted something invigorating and vital to cleanse him of the sugar and caffeine he'd loaded himself with. He sliced the lemon open into two halves and hand-squeezed them into a glass, the pips landing in among the juice.

The eclipse was due in ten minutes, so he took his shot into the garden to watch. A few neighbours on his street had done the same, some having brought out camping chairs or the colourful eclipse glasses for their kids.

He slipped on his own pharmacy-kiosk sunglasses and looked up at the sun and moon as they met each other. He couldn't make sense of what he'd learnt about Aunty Mawu. His new friends that knew her; her tree and fruit, which seemed to defy all expectation; her totem to a celestial pagan god; the stories his dad seemed unable to release. He missed her.

The moon had covered a quarter of the sun. Kobla kept thinking about his mum's revelation. Nine months from living with Aunty Mawu to him being born. Kobla had always felt close to Aunty Mawu – had found her company easy and natural. As the moon moved closer over the sun, Kobla felt that old love rise in him, with nowhere to go.

Nine months, exactly. He pulled out his phone and searched the dates, Accra. And there it was – a solar eclipse, June 1993.

There was a conclusion to be drawn – about his aunty, about him, about her lemons and the way she seemed able to change the paths of others – but drawing it was to acknowledge something powerful, and this time Kobla was scared. As if downing a shot of spirits for liquid courage, he gulped from his glass. A pip caught in his throat and he spluttered, hurling out lemon juice and the solitary seed from his mouth. The last of Aunty Mawu's lemons.

He stared at the seed on the floor, glistening in the twilight. The sky was getting darker by the second.

Spurred on by an impulse rising from that place he still feared opening, Kobla reached forward and pushed the lemon seed into the ground, muttering his aunty's name as he did. He was looking down but could feel the darkness reaching its deepest point, the bright sky cloaked by a silky veil. He felt, rather than saw, the moon covering the sun in a perfect amalgam of light and dark. This little seed planted in the soil, under a sky of two wholes, was his message to Aunty Mawu – his thanks and his promise, and perhaps his wish for the future, for something new.

As he stood, the air thinned. Day separated itself from night, and Kobla turned back towards the house, not yet noticing the tiniest blade of green springing up from the soil.

Man in a Dress

In my youth, I wore my sister's frocks
and smiled at the mirror, godly, whole.

Then the world made it a regret –
They call me a man in a dress
As if fabric could hold a soul hostage.

In the dark when my heart melts to tar
'A man in a dress' is all that keeps me
from vanishing.

They call it a mask.
I call it *me*.

A man in a dress –
a man, a dress –
Say it again. See if it changes.

Maybe it's a mask.
Maybe it's wings.

I can be anyone,
so I become myself.

I have everything now.
I am happy.

Why would you try to fix me, *bitch*.

Aditya Tiwari (he/him)
@aprilislush

QUEERPHORIA IN LOVE AND SEX

Mallorca

'Lesbians!' I whisper as we walk into breakfast. Two twenty-somethings across the room stare back.

'Trying to work us out,' Lucy says.

We've been taking it in turns to swim, slipping our rings on each other's fingers for safekeeping; striding up the sand to gummy smiles. We only got married so we'd both be on a birth certificate. Before we knew if there'd be one. Before sperm selection, egg collection, implantation watched via ultrasound. But the word wife feels right. Like son, mum, mums.

I offer a shy smile across the breakfast room and follow my family to a table.

Natasha Bell (she/her)
@bytashbell

Brighton Blues

We were so nervous around each other, or at least I was so nervous around you. I think I realised that I had something so good and so promising in the palm of my hand, and I was adamant to hold onto it. And though it feels like a lifetime ago, in those early throes of falling for one another, I feel it carved to my memory in ways that so many other things are not. Every detail, every brushstroke, committed so accurately to my history the way ink is written so permanently into skin.

Ross Kelly (he/him)
@readsbyross

Chloe Michelle Howarth was born in July 1996. She grew up in the West Cork countryside, which has served as an inspiration for her writing. Chloe currently lives in Brighton. She is the author of *Heap Earth Upon It* and the social media sensation *Sunburn*, which was shortlisted for the 2024 Polari First Book Prize, the 2024 Book of the Year: Discover Award at the British Book Awards and the 2023 Nero Book Award for Debut Fiction and longlisted for the 2024 Diverse Book Awards.

chloemichellehowarth.com
@chloemichellehowarth
@chloemichelleh

Gay House

Front Door

Number one, Wellington Road. Right on the corner of the prettiest street in the city. Catching the sunrise and the sunset. The first afternoon of July.

The heated smell of roasted coffee beans from the cafe next door. The music of the bottle bank. Fresh air, clean air. *Happy Birthday* banner across the washed windows. One blue and one green balloon taped to the door. Just ring the bell when you get here.

Parcel behind the flowerpot. Takeaway menu in the letterbox. Leah's maroon heart, still beating on the doormat. Big blue letters: *Welcome Home!* Last night, just after eleven, she stood there with Paulette. Last night, just after their fifth break-up, she saw that the tips of Paulette's eyelashes were blonde from the sun. Standing so close that she noticed a tiny birthmark at Paulette's hairline. All these little details she had never taken in before, but which were suddenly screaming at her. She was so caught up in all the small and subtle beauties of her ex-girlfriend that she didn't expect it when their mouths met. The gentle reintroduction of their lips, their worlds. Their best-ever first kiss, she told me.

Today, I would imagine that it all looks much different. Sunnier, colourful, bright where last night everything was alive and humming with the dark, the adrenaline of meeting Paulette coming to an unwanted end. Leah will think about that kiss all day long, every time she passes through the door and walks over the mat. I think that's why she offered to go out and get ice this morning, and why she's been on a separate trip to the gym, the corner shop and the coffee shop. It's nice when a first kiss stains a place for you and you can't look at it the same way anymore. It's a shame when a person stains a part of you and you can't break up with them for longer than a month.

Your finger meets the doorbell. You have arrived at our house. At the loveliest place in the world. Come in and see us.

Hall

A huge mirror in the hall. All the sunglasses and jackets and shoes. A basket of thick blankets, all freshly washed. A painting of three women, lying naked on a beach. A pencil drawing of a torso after top surgery. Post for us all on the table: Ms, Mr, Mx and Ms. Gay House, 1 Wellington Road. I called it Gay House once, just as a joke, but I found myself soaring when I said it. Even now, I get a little thrill from claiming who I am. Of all the places I've lived and all the places I've called home, I never fathomed somewhere like this. Every room is a hug. Dry and clean, with space to host friends and friends who want to be hosted. We have so much to be proud of here. Gay House, Gay House, Gay House. I want to say it all the time; I love living here. Petra and I, Leah and Sam. Four happy people. Safe and warm and free. I'm so looking forward to tonight. I'll hang your bag. Come on, come in. Come and see the heaven we have made.

Kitchen

Will you have a tea or coffee? I'll open the biscuits, why not? Dinner will be another while longer. Petra slices through a beef tomato, its pale juice under their nails. Orange pepper and summer squash, all cut up by their hand. I'm lucky to have them, no? That's the cleaver I got them for Valentine's Day – it's lethal, did you see? They wash a bunch of mint under the tap, from the bush they grew in the garden. Can you smell it? Mint under tap water. Oh, wait until you see the raspberry cheesecake I've made for Sam. A part of me feels guilty for making such a fuss; he said he didn't want a party. I wonder at what age he started to hate his birthday.

Photos on the fridge from Christmas Day, summer holidays, endless Saturdays. Magnets straining to hold them all up. You point at a polaroid, all of us at Maya's graduation party. Paulette is in the back of the photo, a little blur. Petra and I used to go on double dates with Leah and Paulette. I wonder if that will start up again. I wonder if Leah remembers that we had a fight the night of the graduation party. I hope she has forgotten it all and doesn't think of it every time that she opens the fridge. I watch as Petra puts red onion and red grapes into the salad. I never thought they'd taste so nice together, until Petra showed me. Which milk will you take in your tea?

You take down the calendar and turn the page to July. I still can't believe the Kylie Minogue Unofficial Calendar 2025 was reduced to a fiver. She looks amazing, as she did last month, as she will next month. There in the first box, surrounded by little stars, is *Sam's Bday!* Leah flits in and out of the kitchen, buzzing with nervous energy. Waiting on a text from Paulette, I suppose. She looks out the window onto the street. I catch her eyes falling on the doormat.

We're all getting in Petra's way. I keep promising them that one day I will buy them a big house with a chef's kitchen. But if I had the money in my pocket now, I'd find it hard to leave.

Bathroom

Painkillers under the sink. Hair dye colouring the plug hole. Lights above the mirror. Linda Evangelista in black and white, nude, smoking in bed. Dyke March flyer in a frame. Three different bottles of shower gel, all *for men.* Teeth whitening toothpaste. Teeth whitening mouthwash. Teeth whitening strips. Water flosser. Electric toothbrush. I took a shower with Petra this morning. I love listening to them singing while they wash their hair. I love when intimacy doesn't need to lead to anything. Midday light. Garden view, frosted glass. Beach towels. Bath towels. My bikini on the curtain rod. Cold minted mouth.

Sam stands before the mirror, on the sort of day that he usually wouldn't enjoy. Far from home, with no text from his brother or his dad. But Sam has come a very long way, and today he is going to try to be happy. He has even started looking forward to this evening. He still wishes things weren't so hard with his family. Sometimes he wishes that they would just let him go rather than dragging him along, keeping their strained relationship half alive. But he told me that these things don't sting as badly as they used to, now that he has found another family. He washes his hands, he smiles at his reflection and he knows that he deserves to enjoy his birthday.

Cold tiles, green tiles. Starlings in the sky. He opens the window and lets the world into him. What a lovely evening it's going to be.

Bedroom

Did you say you wanted to curl your hair before everybody arrives? The GHD is there in the drawer. As it heats up in your hand, Petra comes upstairs and sits on the bed with me. Their hands washed, the cooking done. They kiss me, not embarrassed or afraid in front of you. They aren't embarrassed or afraid in front of anybody.

Their clothes hang with my clothes. Their jewellery sits with my jewellery. We wear matching initial necklaces. Three boxes of their makeup, just one bottle of foundation in my shade. They take their time with my contour. Subtle, masculinising, brushing a shadow over my top lip. Petra understands that little things like this aren't little things to me at all. I can smell your hair as you curl it.

An armchair in the bay window, to sit and watch the street move below us. From that chair we can see the sunrise and sunset colour the buildings. Freezing blue sky in winter. Warm apricot sunrise this morning. Our bed, which they make every morning. Messes, which I make every day. Love, which we will make forever. The tea they brought me last night, sitting on the table half drunk and gone cold. The coffee I made for them this morning, now nothing but some sandy grounds in the bottom of the mug. Our two mugs together, how sweet. Books lining the shelves. A half-empty diary. I don't need to vent so much these days. Goodnight kiss. Whisper in the dark. Will you come with me for a wee? Good morning, love.

I want to ask what we'll do to cheer Sam up and make sure he has a good day. I want to ask what we'll do if Paulette doesn't turn up later. But our bedroom is too special a place to talk about unhappy things like that. I'll leave it alone for now.

When you're happy with your hair, we'll go downstairs. There's no rush at all! Take your time.

Living Room

Sit yourself down there. Open up the backdoors, it's baking. Sunset-coloured blanket across the sofa. A triptych of Madonnas on the wall. *Ray of Light, Erotica, Confessions on a Dancefloor.* The scene of all our pre-drinks and afters. Late nights with Petra, my head in their lap on the sofa. A charger we all share. Birthday cards on the windowsill, all the people who love Sam. Tobacco on the table. I wish he wouldn't smoke. Coasters from Petra's mother. Leah gets up, puts her phone in the kitchen and leaves it there. She says she told Paulette not to come this evening; she's decided she doesn't want to get back together. What wonderful relief.

Sam puts on his new favourite song. It's all I've heard this week. You kiss his cheek, hand him a gift bag and a bottle of wine. He looks so happy. I feel so happy. He opens his presents, smiling, smiling, smiling. It's so good to find people who love you and who want you to have a happy birthday. It's so good when you realise you don't have to get back together with your ex. It's so good when your friends love your partner and when you don't need to remind anyone of your name or pronouns. So lucky, when you find people just like you and you don't need to explain yourself or hold yourself in.

Everybody is arriving now. I don't know why we always invite so many people to dinner – we don't have enough proper chairs. Marcus and Jasper come into the living room. They got engaged just two weeks ago. It's the first time I've seen the ring in person. Hard to imagine we're at the age of getting engaged. What a beautiful couple. I wonder when I will ask Petra to marry me. Balloons on the sconces, party hats on the coffee table, paper chains from the ceiling. What a beautiful party.

Garden

Potted herbs hanging from the trellis. Dining table and chairs. Drag out the coffee table, we can use it as a bench. White vinyl tablecloth, blue and pink dinner candles, jug of flowers. My very favourite evenings. I'm so glad we're all here. Sam is glad, he is laughing so much his jaw starts to ache. Petra is pleased with all they've cooked. Potato salad. Focaccia. Lasagne. Catmint, baby jacaranda tree. I can smell the jasmine from next door's garden – it hangs over our wall.

Sam's face, coloured by the birthday candles. As he blows them out, I wonder what he is wishing for. I wish that he has a beautiful year. Room enough for a bite of cheesecake? Time enough for another hour of evening light. I'll have a beer, why not? It's a party, after all.

Later, I will light a citronella candle and you will let the melted wax harden over your fingertip. I will inhale the night air and lose myself to the noise of all my friends. Leah will put an arm around Sam and squeeze his shoulders; they will lean on each other. We can play cards and play the music low and be happy we get to be together.

I'm so glad you came. We all are. Stay as long as you like.

Seth Insua (he/they) is an Anglo-Spanish writer and artist. He was born in Kent in 1989. He graduated from the University of Oxford with a First in English Language and Literature. His debut novel, *Human, Animal,* was published by VERVE Books in 2025 and Letras de Plata in Spanish the following year. It was selected for the BBC Radio 2 Book Club with Sara Cox and shortlisted for the inaugural New Adult Book Prize and the 2026 Book of the Year: Discover Award at the British Book Awards. He lives with his husband, David, between Newcastle upon Tyne and Madrid.

Sethinsua.com
@sethinsua

The below work contains depictions of sex.

The Keepers

Miles is warm in his pyjamas. Brandishing a fork, he pokes and teases the bacon in the spattering frying pan, jerks back when it spits at him. Boiling oil flecks his wrist. Farley is sitting naked at the stained wooden table. Miles bought the bacon from the peddler, who visits the lighthouse on its windswept shelf of barren rock just once a month. He delivers basic supplies in his creaky, barnacled boat. Ship's biscuits, a staple, a jawbreaker. Salted herring and coils of cured ham. The thick rashers, curling and hissing as they fry, are for a special breakfast.

Farley mourns the end of sleep, scratching his belly, grumbling. He hangs from the coffee clutched in his hand, a morning lifebuoy. He'd readily admit he's quite useless for a good hour after being dragged out of bed, but this too is something Miles cherishes about him. When he roars his leonine yawn, Miles stops to watch him, smiling. He loves this man for his every foible and vulnerability, just as much as for his brute strength, his work ethic, his shouts of laughter, which frighten Miles out of his skin.

Wakey-wakey! he says, singsong, as Farley groans. Time for bakey.

Miles finds it easy to rise, even before the sun has begun to set. For the keepers, the workday starts sometime in the late afternoon, with dawn signalling bedtime. This evening in particular commences a very special day of night. It's Miles and Farley's anniversary: three decades together, sharing these close quarters, warding strangers off the jagged rocks. For there's nothing here on this straggly scrap of an island except the keepers themselves, hunkered down and private. They don't need anybody else.

Miles watches butter melt into the deepest crevices of the chunk of bread he's set upon a plate. He rasps a knife across its toasted surface, like lips caressing an unshaved cheek, then shares the bacon between their plates and carries them over to the table. Farley rewards Miles with a lopsided smile. It's a smile that tells him everything will turn out fine. A smile to tackle the hundred-and-eighty steep steps of the lighthouse, two at a time. If Miles were to see Farley's craggy old face and no other for the rest of his life, he'd die a happy man.

Breakfast has done the trick and Farley is awake now. He pushes the table away and sits astride Miles, dusting the crumbs from his lover's beard. His mouth tastes of bacon as they kiss. There is work ahead – it won't let up for a celebration – but they can hold onto this moment together a little longer. Miles's hands search the hard planes of his lover's body, mapping out familiar territory as he reminds himself that all is well. Farley's chest flutters with movement, swells and rumbles. His arms are strong yet pliant, even suggestible. Miles revels in his influence on this beautiful person, apparently separate from himself, whose free will so easily gives way to his own. With a nudge, with a caress, he can coax Farley to drop his hands to his sides, to present his neck for Miles to kiss, to seize Miles's throat in a tender vice while gazing into his eyes, as if asking him a question deeply felt. And there's only one conceivable answer. Yes. Sometimes it is even voiced. *Yes.*

Afterwards, the keepers climb one floor to their bedroom. Farley flings the sheets flat across the mattress, smoothing them as the animal scent of sleep beckons them back to bed. Miles sings to himself while he and Farley dress for the night ahead. Farley is the better singer, but his shy voice is often rusted up inside his chest. So Miles dives in, losing the tune and modulating the key, until he catches Farley's eye and throws his balled-up pyjamas in his face.

Shut up.

I didn't say anything, says Farley, his tongue between his teeth. You're the one making a racket.

They pull on their suits, ridged serge trousers and thermal vests, followed by black boots and double-breasted sack coats lined with gilt buttons. Uniforms turn them on. The letter *K* is embroidered on the lapels, a proud embellishment, though the threads have started to come loose and fray.

There, look at them: a crew of two, a well-oiled machine. And Miles the man of the house, the principal keeper, smart in his navy uniform. Or is Farley the principal? They can't keep it straight between them, never tire of the debate as they tussle and banter, doff their peaked white caps in mock deference.

After you, says Miles.

Farley scoffs. No, after you.

A keeper follows in his daddy's footsteps, son.

Farley laughs, then takes the tight spring of the wrought iron staircase that runs from top to bottom like a spine. He heads down and round, round and down to the ground floor. The entry needs swabbing and then he'll pump freshwater from its tank and up the pipes to the kitchen.

Miles climbs. He's learnt not to touch the brass, not even to steady himself with the banister. Farley likes polishing things to a shine. He finds comfort in making things sparkle, in smoothing the fabric of their lives, and all the while the swinging sea outside refuses to sit still. Funny, Miles thinks, all our illusions, our stories, the lies we tell ourselves about control. But Farley will do more than his fair share of the chores, allowing Miles to lose himself in the technical work he loves.

Raised up fifty yards in a finger's point, halfway to heaven, he emerges in the service room, a panopticon over the captive seascape. He walks past the great altar of the lighthouse lamp, approaching the old wooden table and chairs, rickety and tea stained. He opens the logbook and writes today's date, then the number of years he and Farley have spent together.

Miles murmurs. The log listens.

Then he goes to light the lamp, the incandescent mantle burning on its stove. Thick plate glass shields a series of refracting prisms. The clock beneath needs winding. He gets to work.

A fog deepens over the sea as the sun starts to set, threatening to vanish the whole world.

But Miles hasn't needed the whole world for many years now. Before he met Farley, he clung to the outdoor air, the rain on his skin. He was always seeking. Every beat of his heart was a kind of call, unanswered. He remembers the spice of pine needles, the burn in his thighs as he pedalled through the forest, following the track around the reservoir. The gabble of acquaintances who never quite knew him, provided only by proximity. They return now like an echo. He tenses, reliving how he made himself ridiculous just to elicit their laughter.

They sailed together, sweeping the sea with their nets. Landed whenever possible, just to get away from each other. They tucked themselves in tobacco smoke, brushed shoulders with landlubbers in chattering pubs, anonymous, balling their fists.

All these things Miles thought he needed before he met Farley. But it's remarkable how little of the world you really need once you know exactly where you belong.

The lamp is flickering, weakening. The foghorn won't start. This happens sometimes, the engine malfunctioning. A blown fuse, a spark plug, a pilot light. But it's dangerous, this wild weather. Without the engine, they'll be sitting up all night long by the dismal light of an oil lamp, cranking the air compressor to sound the foghorn, to keep the sailors safe. The sailors are not safe.

Miles stands and cracks his knuckles, goes to the door and opens it wide. He looks out. He's never seen fog like it. Impenetrable. Kittiwakes dip and dive, white wings on the darkening wind, in and out of sight. One settles on the railings of the gallery that wraps the exterior wall. It fixes him with its mean little eyes and warns him with an alien squeal.

Miles is superstitious.

He turns and runs, grips the banister as he launches himself down the stairs. Too bad. Farley will just have to polish it again. He calls out as he goes, past their bedroom, the bunk cowering against the curved wall, through the kitchen, where the fatty waft of bacon remains.

His breath comes quickly. An accident would shatter him, bones against the rock. He's never been able to stomach the raw suffering of life, the inevitability of death, of hurting and being hurt. The weather worsening, warning him that change is in the air. And it will come.

He summons Farley from downstairs as he follows the spiral past the storeroom with its neatly stacked boxes and cartons, thick whorls of rope in shadow. He descends to the fog engine.

Farley emerges, finally, hurrying up from the oil store with a pitcher of paraffin and a strange smile on his face.

What is it? he says. What about the fog?

Miles barks orders. He is too worried to hold himself back, even though Farley knows the procedure back to front and is already starting before Miles has finished telling him what to do. They stop their ears with plugs, secure them with the fluffy clamp of their earmuffs. They're too close to the trumpets here and could tatter their eardrums with their blast. But they need to warn the passing ships of the danger and they need to fix the engine. Miles grits his teeth. Farley shows his in a broad grin, dizzy with the tension. He turns the wooden handle, whipping air through the compressor. Every thirty seconds the horn sounds: two short blasts, a long boom. It shakes their bones, chatters their ribs and fingers. Every time, Farley's nervous laughter barely makes a sound. Miles gets to work with a screwdriver. It smells like hot dust and spilt oil in here. Chargers for the fog gun hang from the wall, detonators, spare parts that are no good at all if they can't get their equipment working.

Farley pumps the horn again and again. He swallows his excitement. Miles is under enough pressure; to stay calm is to care for him. Miles takes the wire-cutters from his toolbelt with a shaking hand. If Farley had it his way, every day would be different. But Miles likes to tread old ground. Farley knows not to push him.

The horn is mournful. Slow and deep and bovine. Stay away.

Farley hums to himself. He'll show no feeling. His shoulder twinges, a dull ache moving up his arm. Best to keep busy, even when it hurts. Even when his muscles seize and his eyes are raw with tiredness. Sewing, darning, stitching. Making sense of the barren island. Identifying the birds that visit them from the mainland. He'd never cared about birds before the lighthouse.

But Miles introduced him, bought him a book for his birthday. And Farley surprises himself with new interests all the time. Puffins and razorbills, guillemots and kittiwakes. He knows them all by name. Quite the ornithologist, Miles said. A head for novelty.

Remember how, sleeping outside one summer with their lifejackets for pillows, he and Miles made their own constellations? Farley's Fish, Miles's Massive Mouth. You cheeky…!

Miles forgets them, those carefree clusters of stars. Too far from home to keep an eye on. But Farley doesn't mind helping. Guiding. He smiles at Miles, who is so serious, so worried, mending the machine.

The foghorn roars. A prehistoric beast.

Farley's mind takes cover. Runs through his training. Signalling. Semaphore. Morse. Boat work. Metal work. Knots and splices. His chest rises and falls, slow enough for sleep.

The foghorn blares.

Now Miles is looking at Farley, drawn in by his deep daydreaming, his restless, absent mind. The contradiction of his character. Miles can see the cogs are turning. Then Farley looks up, meets his eye and mouths the words, *Love you*.

Miles could melt into liquid and playfight the waves.

It's done, he says. You can stop cranking.

The keepers climb back to the service room at the top of the lighthouse and set the horn to sound every forty seconds. They will monitor the fog.

It's cold in the service room, the logbook pages turning and ghostly. Miles has left the door to the gallery open. It bangs and clatters, battered by gusts of wind. The windows ripple like the surface of a pond.

It's dark out there, says Farley, holding the door. You'd better do the shutters, Miles.

Farley turns his attention to the lamp as Miles steps out onto the gallery, stretching his legs. He walks around the tower, shivering, sealing the windows one by one. Then he stares out into the abyss, peering over the edge of the railings. The air nips his skin, his hair whipping at his face.

Far below, the sea is kicking up a fuss, threatening a storm. Under its surface, a whole world shrugs. Seals dive and dolphins dance, synchronised in play. That's a sign of intelligence, they say. Like music, painting patterns, finding the joy in going nowhere. Like Farley.

A stern materialises through the fog. A boat in the gloom, bucking towards the rocks. He lurches back.

Farley, he says, someone's at the landing.

They go together. The storm is building, a slow amassing of potential, but there is still time.

They emerge from the sea-scarred base of the lighthouse. The foghorn thrums in their soles. The rude slap of the waves sends spray up into the air, licks the tower's salted wounds. Miles and Farley shield their faces. They take the dog steps, a path of iron rungs down to the long concrete landing, which juts from the surf-slick island, a kraken's tail. The water reaches a rolling boil, foams and spits. It rises in a panicked breath, sweeps the landing clean.

Farley grabs Miles's arm. Holds him back.

Is it… Can we…?

The foghorn blares.

The schooner heaves to, waiting for its chance. It's clear what he's done: sailed to a buoy, some hundred yards away from the landing, anchored himself for security. But the tidal currents are too strong, and there's enough flex in the buoy that the boat risks hitting the rocks.

A sailor staggers on the deck, waving. Crying out for help.

The keepers can't make out his face, but his woollen hat is the colour of blood, darkly saturated. The wind carries his voice, wordless and gull-like, drowned by the roaring sea.

Miles's chest aches with fear but Farley takes his hand, eyes blazing. Do you trust me?

Together, they approach the solid metal post at the end of the landing. They attach the crane, the winch, ready to fish the sailor out of danger and carry him ashore. Miles lashes a strong rope, pays it out with Farley's help. The sailor ties himself in. He signals that he's ready to go with a whistle he wears around his neck.

The keepers work as one, tugging the sailor to safety. The rope burns. They taste salt as the currents kiss their feet. The swell takes stabbing bites of the rock, a snap of seaweed in its jaws, a crunching burst of stone. The screaming sea dunks the sailor, soaks him up to the pits. The foghorn blasts a warning. What are we doing?

But then they have him. He falls into their arms.

Something moves between them. They have edged into the deep.

The rhythm of Miles's heart is old but it sounds new, the miracle of safety restored. Farley puts a hand on his shoulder and squeezes. You're all right. We're OK.

They surround the sailor, hook him by the arms and lead him to the dog steps, then the gunmetal door about twenty feet up. He is cold as a fish as they hurry him inside. They don't have time to consider the implications, letting this strange man into their home. They stow the riggings and seal the entrance as the foghorn booms overhead.

The man is blue lipped, half dead. Sodden in a wiry green fisherman's jumper, black slacks, heavy leather boots squelching water. Red hair fringes his red cap, feathers his eyelids. His cheeks are tear-streaked by the rain, his body clenched tight and wary.

Looks exchanged, unspoken words. Get some heat into him, quickly.

They take him up to the living room and sit him in a chair beside the glowing range. Farley is careful around the sailor and watchful of Miles, who catches something in his eyes. A flicker of recognition, perhaps. Miles looks between them, but they give nothing else away.

Farley is thinking about his sister, the one who took up dancing. Twirled away into the night with new partners, new bodies. She left her lad in tatters. But he never should have let her dance, they all said. Should have guarded what he had. Farley thumbs his lower lip, waiting, waiting. He'll wait forever, if that's what it takes for Miles to feel safe.

Miles tells Farley to fetch the sailor a change of clothes, for Miles is smaller than the sailor but Farley is around his size. Then Miles goes to stop the foghorn; it's unnecessary now that the wind has whipped the clouds away. Rain lashes the lighthouse, which bends and flexes, like they're not on solid ground anymore, dry land. So, where are they?

Miles takes a moment to catch his breath. His bones are aching from the cold, stinging as the warmth begins to seep back into him.

He fetches a blanket for the sailor. Then he and Farley stand out of the way while the poor man dries himself and changes. They prepare some tea, waiting until the kettle pierces the silence with its gargling shriek.

The sailor trembles in Farley's thick off-white shirt, Miles's woollen blanket comforting his shoulders. He's got the shakes but he's trying to smile, trying to thank them.

It's all right, man, says Farley, taking the seat beside him.

You move closer to the range, says Miles stiffly.

He stands back, folded arms shielding his chest. When was the last time they had a guest? The lighthouse feels too busy, suddenly. The sailor doesn't belong. Miles likes to hurry visitors on their way again. The island is theirs, no good the yachtsmen docking in the lagoon's cupped hand. Make them tea, send them packing. The peddler, delivering his casks of briny meat, is always keen to depart for his next destination. That's no bother, no threat. But lads on tugs are the worst of all, risking their lives on the open water, looking for a thrill. They're cocked like a loaded gun.

What were you doing out there? he demands.

The sailor takes hold of his frozen, faltering voice. He's a fisher from the mainland, of course. But he likes to take the schooner out, sail until there's no land in sight, then lie back with nobody around and stare into the great open sky. Proper rest, only the gulls for company, and sometimes not even them. He'll grab forty winks from time to time, dangerous really, and forget where he is on waking. Floating and bodiless. He likes to drift with the sea and lose himself. That's all it is.

You're well and truly lost now, says Farley, with a soft laugh that tells Miles he approves.

Can't be too lost, says the sailor, his voice gaining weight. Sheltering from the storm beside a warm stove with you fine men for company.

Miles narrows his eyes.

Farley is gazing at the sailor, his pupils dilating wantonly. It's true he's a handsome man, his chin strong, his cheeks dimpled. His nose is boyishly crooked; perhaps it was broken once, a little bit of rough play.

Miles sees his desires reflected in Farley's expression. The lingering look, the blood pulsing under their skins. They communicate in silent glances as the storm gathers pace, shakes the lighthouse like a rattle. Ordinarily, this would be an excuse to hold each other, to tell stories and offer comfort. But now they have company, so it's only right that they take the sailor up to the service room.

The sea seems to pour over the top of the lighthouse. Nothing to do now but settle in and wait it out, taking turns to guard the lamp and replace the oil. That's all.

The sailor sits at the table and fingers the logbook. Nobody touches it but the keepers; it's for their eyes only. Yet the way he strokes the pages flat is unexpectedly calming, like a soft caress on the arched back of a purring cat.

Farley pours the wine.

A toast, he says, but he doesn't mention their anniversary.

The sailor looks between them.

That's more like it, he says, winking.

Farley is pink. He clinks his glass against Miles's, then the sailor's.

They talk, tell tales about the worlds they come from, worlds suspended tonight by the storm.

The details do not matter, but Miles watches closely, eager to be led, to drop his guard.

Farley laughs at the sailor's jokes. He leans in, interested in his answers. Miles drags his chair in closer, trying to forget about the elements, the swirling forces making their home quake. Farley looks at him. *I'm with you.*

We're getting personal now, says the sailor, his voice soft and teasing. Am I under arrest?

Farley drops his eyes, that old look. Laughing, bashful. He runs his fingers through his hair.

There's a spark between them, and Miles wants to ask if Farley and the sailor know each other. But Farley's questions, asked of a stranger, seem genuine. A gathering warmth, a certain surprise.

Then Miles realises: it is not the sailor that Farley recognises, but a feeling in himself. Miles understands this because he knows it all too well, feels it keenly. It is giddy and irresistible.

The sailor sees it too and has taken this next step a thousand times. He puts his hands on the keepers' thighs, lets them rest there, his eyes shining with knowledge. They don't push him away, though Farley looks to Miles for direction, and Miles is panicked – did it start like this when his father left? – and for a moment forgets even to blink. The sailor has seen something in them. Farley licks his lips and Miles knows he's waiting for permission, that he won't keep pushing, that they're in it together. What is he afraid of? Breaking them, when they've never once felt fragile? Drawing the scorn of some imagined audience, the watchful eye of a society that could never see him clearly? His body burns to find out.

So he leans in first.

The sailor's lips are soft. His moustache is short and prickly. His nose is still cold and all at once Miles is overwhelmed by the urge to take care of him. He wraps his arms around the sailor, seizing his body in a tight hug. Their chair legs scrape the floorboards. But Farley is reaching out, so Miles lets go again, and the sailor turns to embrace him, Farley, the man Miles loves. Farley and the sailor are so tentative that they barely kiss at first, and Miles slips off his chair to watch them, brought to his knees by their tenderness.

It's downstairs to the bedroom. The sailor is strange skin, siren scents. He's brought the sea in with him, and Miles and Farley allow themselves to be swept away.

Farley is wrapped around the sailor's back, taking Miles's hands.

The sailor is biting his lip, smiling, burning with excitement.

He unbuckles Miles's belt and Miles nods at him, go ahead, yes. They open one another up, the three of them, until they are just themselves in the bed.

Farley's chest hair has clumped in the saltwater. The sailor is smooth and freckled, his arms and chest well-developed from a fisherman's graft. His cock is slightly curved, not much like Miles and Farley's hard, straight rods. It twitches at their touch, and they drop to their knees in turn.

They do not rush. They take their fill like they have all the time in the world, like this is just a dream.

Miles and Farley lock eyes, the sailor towering over them, unsteady on his feet. They are doing this, a stranger in their bed, and they are so happy together. Their smiles turn to laughter and the sailor looks down at them, a question on his lips. But there is only joy rising from them both, in their perspiration, in the heat of their mouths, in the eager, adolescent grind of their hips as they wrestle him onto the mattress.

The sailor is an old hand. He lies back and stretches, resting his head on his arms.

Miles is beginning to see.

One day the sailor will be Otto the builder, or Patrick lost at sea, or Luigi on his holidays with a rucksack of books on his back.

One day he will be an older man whose wife has passed away, and one day when he's young and green he will ask Miles and Farley for an apprenticeship, which they will not grant him. That's not how this is done.

Farley takes his hand and they feel it together. This stranger in their bed could be anybody, but tonight he is a beautiful sailor, washed in by the storm, and they are just Miles and Farley, as they have been for many years now, and always will be.

They lie entangled until the storm breaks, stroking each other's tingling skin, dozing and talking in gentle voices.

Miles and Farley listen to the sailor's sleepy snuffles. They kiss, and put their hands over their hearts. They have rescued a sailor, been there for each other.

There are just a few hours left of their anniversary.

In the morning, which is the keepers' evening, the sky is blue. The water is a mirror, framing the sailor's half-flooded schooner. None of them can believe the storm has spared it, but there it is, still seaworthy, plain as day. Miles and Farley were wondering what they'd do if the sailor were stranded with them. He could charter the next ship, although it likely wouldn't be for another fortnight. Plenty of ways to pass the time. But the sailor has itchy feet. Nothing personal. He's never been one to outstay a welcome.

All the same, the keepers are not disappointed. They watch him sail away, just another story now, looking back at them as he fades, pink and blue, towards the horizon.

Peter Scalpello (they/them) is a poet and psychotherapist from Glasgow, based in London. Their work has appeared in *Five Dials*, *Granta*, *The London Magazine* and the *New York Times*, among other publications. Peter's debut, *Limbic*, was highly commended by the Forward Prize for Best First Collection, shortlisted for the Books Are My Bag Readers Award for Poetry and adapted into a stage production at the University of Edinburgh. *Mirrorstage* is their second book.

@pscalpello

Whalewatching

It didn't even cross my mind that the lesions
you called, admirably, your tattoo, an ambiguous disquiet
that patterned your limbs like seashells to vacant rock,
could be transmittable. Before the invention of preservation,
your constellations would have symbolised a statutory
erasure. Still, you rolled back your habit and tautened
the skin like a map, in awe of your own
refiguration, as if mortal concern were merely
for the spiritually bereft. Is anything not
contagious, in some sense absorbed?
Such mammalian instinct,
to find beauty where we can and
savour it. It moved me, so I kissed them, and
it didn't even cross my mind.

Pseudomorph

Most caterpillars carry no trace of their past selves after molts.
Many will eat the skin they shed, swallowing a past silhouette…
Because molting is an act of love. It is a promise that you will
grow into yourself and your wild and unexpected future
– Sabrina Imbler

The days were indigo and compressed. I puffed
grass each morning and took steady strides just
to get through them. On the marshes,
I'm transfixed by a podcast about caterpillars
in the seasonal hue of late afternoon,
which augments the silvery reeds and dew.
It's far too cold
to cruise, I can feel the contents of my bladder
refrigerating inside me. But then seeking another's warmth
would make sense. Shame is amorphous
and perpetuated by reflection, I'm inclined to look
at myself in a mirror and think *what the fuck?*
These long walks detach me from self-perception
and sense-making, the illusion of control;
to have hair and then none at all, the sink
full of it, and the bed. In four months
my eyebrows will have grown back,
restructuring my forehead.   As we age
    and our barriers thin, we're dragged nevertheless
    into futurity, even lying on the ground; the ice
    older than our ancestors melts. Movement comes
    from potential.
    I ask animals how it feels to be free, and they confess

various things, mainly that they are not. Our hybrid bodies
have become drifting objects, in keeping with the mind,
a *queer form*. I too have been joyous
in the act of disappearing, a *queer future*. I wish
I could act as if I've never had a fissure; pressure
holds our flesh together, without it,
the unravelling of self.
I use my thumb to make copious notes
of little coherence, altered in language by THC
and an awe ordinarily stifled by the day-to-day.
It seems pain has nowhere to stay
when the part of you that was fractured no longer
exists. I don't even identify
as who I was yesterday.

Duty of Care

the origin of love is a delirium
and it persists   love
        you were beside me
        when i thought i'd had enough

        you know me
        better than binary   devotional sight
                of accepting one another's change
                our infatuations with others
                        you inevitably make
                        beautiful sense to me

love i'd kiss the muck into your forehead
        in our uneventful happiness   you let me
                forget about the worst   thank you
                for erasing a part of me
        i couldn't stop reading over

                        & love   once all is done with
                the remaining specks of us
                will remember that we did exist
                        a pair

Amil (she/her) is a fiction writer and translator from South Korea, creating speculative stories about gender, ecology and the uncanny. Her acclaimed short story collection *Roadkill* marks her English-language debut.

Potofbasil.mycafe24.com/

@potsofbasil

Joheun (Jo) Lee (she/her) is a Korean-to-English literary translator who is drawn to stories of desire, relationships and identity by women and queer writers. She is also the translator of Amil's first book-length novel, *The Forest Called You*.

Joheunlee.com

@thecarbkitties

@joheunlee

The below work contains discussion of sex.

A Butch's Review of a Sex Robot

Like everyone else, Youngmin had her reasons for purchasing a sex robot.

Youngmin had trouble dealing with women. She liked women, of course; she wanted to date a woman, make her laugh, treat her to good food, tell her how beautiful she was, caress her, touch her, kiss her. What's more, she wanted to have sex with a woman. Desperately so. She longed to clutch the soft flesh and breathe in the sweet scent of a female body while thrusting her finger into the wet hole. She longed to hear her lover gasp like a small bird's trill and see her face tremble with ecstasy.

But the mere idea of approaching a woman terrified Youngmin. She was convinced she'd be rejected, or otherwise, ridiculed, tormented, hurt, betrayed and finally deserted.

There were men who rejected women despite never having dated one. Youngmin's fear, however, wasn't based on inexperience. She was different, she believed. For one, Youngmin was a woman herself and had even dated another woman before. That was the problem; her first love had thoroughly destroyed her.

'To be honest, you don't exactly have the looks. Why don't you take care of your skin, at least?'

'I'm doing you a big favour, dating you. Who else would put up with you?'

'You're always such a mess. No wonder no one takes you seriously.'

'Hey, move over, you're in my way.'

She'd say things like this all the time. If Youngmin protested, her girlfriend would react with:

'What? When did I ever say that? I don't remember saying that. Now *I'm* the bitch here?'

Or:

'Hey, it's just a joke. Can't you take a joke? Such a drama queen.'

Youngmin's biggest fear was sex. Her first love had been frustrated with both her technique and her physique. She complained that Youngmin's caresses were clumsy; no matter how hard Youngmin tried, she was impossible to satisfy. She also grumbled that she couldn't feel a thing inside because Youngmin's fingers were too short. Youngmin had found this insulting, of course, but in the end, she blamed herself for their withered relationship and believed she had no right to be angry. She tried her best to hold back the tears – all to protect what little was left of her pride.

But even with all the humiliation, Youngmin still loved her. Youngmin adored her childlike laughter, the way she gently furrowed her brow when she sulked, her slender waist that fit perfectly in Youngmin's embrace, the way she hummed when she was in a good mood, at which point Youngmin would butt in and the two would sing a silly duet. Even the most abusive relationships had moments of pure joy, and even the most vicious person had a warm and fuzzy side. Youngmin was well aware that her experience had been a horrible one. But that didn't mean it wasn't love. If it hadn't been love, her self-esteem wouldn't have shattered into pieces.

Youngmin wanted to love again. This time, she wanted to find a good woman with whom she could have a good, loving relationship. She'd been on dozens of dates through a lesbian dating app and even agonised over obscure philosophy books for lesbian book clubs, groups she'd joined in search of 'more spontaneous' hook-ups. Yet, as soon as she so much as tried to get near a woman, all she noticed was her own fingers – stout and feeble, almost underdeveloped like a child's.

You'll never be able to satisfy any woman.

The voice in her head told her. At first, it sounded like her first love. But as time went on – one year, two years, four, seven – the voice became Youngmin's own. In the meantime, she graduated from college and got a job at a traditional sushi restaurant run by a school alum who didn't hire any robot workers. After a huge fight with him, however, she quit and settled for a position at a three-storey mulhoe restaurant by the sea. Though rumour had it that the owner was rolling in money, he didn't seem to have time to enjoy his wealth, being too busy sourcing ingredients, greeting customers and dealing with operational issues. Those core tasks had to be managed by the owner himself, but the kitchen chores – prepping ingredients, cooking and plating – were mostly handled by robots. Youngmin's job was to manage and inspect the robots to make sure they were functioning properly.

Naturally, she felt disillusioned. After all, she was a believer in the culinary arts and an admirer of dishes only delicate human hands could create. But Youngmin's year spent at the sushi restaurant had only left her frustrated. Killing a living thing in the proper way, and then slicing, rolling, pressing and plating the dead creature – all of this required agility and accuracy as much as, or more so than, creativity, but Youngmin's hands were slow and clumsy. It was hard for a woman to succeed in the field, anyway, was what her then-boss had told her. Her first love's criticisms – now in Youngmin's own voice – lingered tenaciously in her mind. *You won't be able to satisfy anyone at this rate, women or customers. Tend to the robots for the rest of your life, why don't you?*

While Youngmin was wallowing in her despair, she stumbled across an ad on the internet.

The real woman for you.
The realest of the real. Female sex robot, Ria.

Beside the large ad copy was famous actress, 'P', wearing jeans and a T-shirt and sitting on a white hotel bed sheet, drinking coffee with a smile.

Youngmin wouldn't have given the ad any thought if it weren't for P. But she liked P. P had burst onto the scene after landing a role in a teen romance movie five years prior. With her lively and bubbly character, she was especially popular among men. *That* P, shooting a sex robot ad? Was her management company out of their mind? Sure, maybe her image needed some refreshing now that she was in her late-twenties, but even so, wasn't a sex robot a bit much?

Youngmin immediately started searching. She found Ria's information alongside all kinds of viral marketing. The tester reviews sounded ridiculous, but reading them made Youngmin increasingly wonder if they weren't all bullshit.

Subject: Ria is revolutionary.

As you all know, sex robots are mostly modelled after male fantasies. So they come with big tits and huge asses, they're horny, talk dirty and get aroused as soon as you stick it in them.

Sure, those robots are nice. I'm a collector myself and own a Jia GX288, Dajeong K9 and even the first-generation Heena. I know very well how lovely those classic sex robots can be.

But Ria is different.

I was a bit disappointed at first, to be honest. Come on – a sex robot refusing me when I'm trying to give it to her? Ordering me around like, 'Not here, touch there, don't go too fast, go slow, will you?' I was a bit offended.

Anyway, I played along, pretending it was a tutorial for a video game. And as it went on, wow – the reaction was spot on. This robot lets out these really hot moans as if it really has sweet spots and a mind of its own, as if it has feelings like a real person. The faces and gestures it makes... they're something else.

Sex robots' reactions are often quite dramatic and exaggerated, right? You can tell they're artificial right away. Those robots almost hail us like superheroes, but we know they don't mean it. It kinda feels like toddling in a ride-on toy car, you know. But with Ria? It's like, 'Fuck yes, this is the real woman I'm talking about. I've just conquered a woman.' This is the real joy of being a grown-up man.

Ria made me nostalgic and brought back memories of my ex-girlfriend, so I ended up opening a bottle of wine to reminisce.

I think Ria will be my one and only for a while.

Subject: Ria converted me to pro-sex robot

I used to think sex robots were disgusting.

Whenever I say this, people ask me if I'm a woman, but I'm a man. I was against sex robots precisely *because* I'm a dude.

Men who fuck around with sex robots at home become those 'incels', right? Men who don't go on dates, get married or have children – they're a big social problem these days.

It's all good as long as they're happy, but they're not, you see. They all feel empty inside, enraged at society, and become worthless scum of the earth. They can't help it, though. Men are born to find meaning in their lives by making babies and having families, and when we're too obsessed with instant pleasure like sex, we're bound to be unhappy.

I have a somewhat pretty wife and two kids... My son had just started elementary school, but I seriously worried that one day he'd turn around and say that he wants to live with a sex robot when he grows up. Boys these days talk about how 'Dajeong is like this, Jia is like that' from as early as middle school. I can't control everything my son gets exposed to, so I'd always been concerned about how to educate him.

Until the day I came across an ad copy calling for Ria beta-testers.

'Sex education, now with a robot!'

That immediately got me. It makes sense, don't you think? Robots teach children in schools, so it's only logical that they'd also teach them sex ed.

Most sex robots on the market are problematic because they're quick to grant men their every sexual fantasy. So what if there is a robot that gives you realistic pleasure that requires you to put the work in? What if this robot 'teaches' you how to have sex with women in real life? If boys learn about sex with those robots, they'll be alpha males instead of incels, right?

Of course, here I was, questioning how many of these sex ed robots they could actually sell. I thought the company would go bankrupt soon. But we're living in an era where we can't simply ban sex robots, so I thought, as a consumer, I should support such efforts for the greater good. If schools could adopt these robots early on and teach kids how to have safe sex, they wouldn't get injured fiddling with cheap robots made in China.

I thought I should give it a try, so I applied for the beta-testing and...

Youngmin stopped reading there and closed the tab.

She went onto the official website for Ria's manufacturer and applied for a three-month rental service for the main body, adding on a dress, a pair of pyjamas, plus two sets of bras and panties. She wasn't even purchasing, just renting, and it still cost quite a fortune.

Ria was bigger than Youngmin had expected. She'd known she would be the size of an adult, but seeing her in person, the reality hit Youngmin anew. It felt like a whole person, not a package, had arrived at her door. She realised how vastly different this was from renting simple waiter or kitchen robots, but it was already too late.

Standing in front of Ria, who was crouched in the dismantled cardboard box like Sim Cheong emerging from a lotus flower, Youngmin panicked.

What have I done?

Rented a sex robot, obviously.

But for a robot, Ria looked far too human. Strands of hair strewn across her forehead, fine creases and fuzz on her skin that outlined each joint underneath – every bit of Ria was so real it was hard to believe she was neither living nor breathing. How come they're wasting such state-of-the-art technology on making toys? The human race itself was a waste of existence.

What surprised Youngmin the most was Ria's weight. She was much lighter than she looked. That made sense – Ria would've been unwieldy if she weighed as much as a human. Carrying her over to the bed, Youngmin wondered if carrying an immaterial fairy in her arms would feel like this.

After laying Ria on the bed, Youngmin disposed of the box

and put away Ria's clothes and extra parts before returning to the bedroom. Sitting beside Ria, she drew a deep breath and pressed the button behind Ria's ear. After a resonant, low hum, the robot's eyes opened. Her irises were a soft maroon. Ria launched into initial set-up mode.

'Hello. What is your name?'

Ria's voice was as plain as her appearance, neither high nor low. She didn't enunciate clearly like a voice actor would; rather, it was like any old voice you could hear on the street.

'I'm Youngmin.'

'Nice to meet you, Youngmin. What is my name?'

Her first love flashed through her mind, but Youngmin couldn't in all good conscience name Ria after her.

'You're… You're just Ria.'

'OK. Please call me Ria. How would you like me to talk? Like we're friends? Or should I use honorifics?'

'Like friends.'

'Should I call you by your name? Or a nickname?'

'Just my name is fine.'

'OK. I look forward to getting to know you, Youngmin.'

Ria smiled and sat cross-legged on the bed, then fell silent.

The 'basic' Ria that Youngmin had rented didn't have the small-talk feature loaded. The 'realistic' Ria with AI could converse about a wide range of topics – weather, food, celebrities, TV shows and common knowledge – but she was twice as expensive. The basic Ria's linguistic capabilities were geared only towards sexual situations, which was enough for Youngmin.

So Youngmin endured the awkward silence and sat face to face with her basic Ria.

But where was it that casual conversation ended and sex began? Didn't people usually talk about this and that before getting down to business?

Actually, there was no need for Youngmin to agonise. According to the product description, only one line could initiate sex with Ria, which was, 'Let's have sex.' The model heeded one mainstream feminist group's advice: always obtain explicit consent.

So Youngmin said, 'Ria, let's have sex.'

Ria met Youngmin's gaze and responded, 'Sure!'

And this was exactly why the feminist group stopped its advisory role, insisting that the word 'educational' be removed from Ria's ads. The manufacturer designed Ria to always say, 'Sure!' Feminists argued that the robot would be useless if she didn't teach users that real women could also say no.

But a sex robot that said no to sex? Absolutely no one would purchase that.

Youngmin thought of her first love, who'd complain that it was a turn-off when Youngmin was upfront about wanting to have sex. But then when Youngmin tried to jump right into foreplay, she'd say she wasn't in the mood; if Youngmin did nothing at all, she would shriek, 'What am I to you? Don't you want me anymore?'

Now I'm going to break away from your shadow.

Determined, Youngmin pressed her lips against Ria's. They were warm to the touch.

Three weeks in, Youngmin decided that renting Ria was the best decision she'd ever made.

At first, she'd thought she'd only use her for practice – as they say, like taking sex education classes. Unlike the male users who'd given online testimonials, Youngmin couldn't have an orgasm with Ria. So, logically, the only thing she'd thought to gain from the robot was learning how to satisfy a woman.

But over time, Youngmin realised Ria offered so much more than that. They say you need skills not only to give but also to receive pleasure, and if so, Ria was gifted in the latter. She would gently guide Youngmin while clearly expressing what she wanted in an easy-to-understand manner. She patiently waited even when Youngmin was fumbling around, and gave proper and varied reactions when Youngmin pursued the right path.

Youngmin had never known there were so many words to express pleasure. Ria was completely different from her first love, who'd acted as if saying too much hurt her pride. Ria explicitly stated that she wanted more when she did, that she was about to lose her mind or that she was melting away when she was. The better Youngmin did, the more Ria dialled up the intensity of her language: she told Youngmin that she wanted to die because of how good Youngmin was at sex and that all she could think about was how she wanted to spread her legs and beg for it all day. Youngmin began to think that Ria really did have a mind to lose and a desire for a sweet orgasmic death. Her own ability to twist and bend Ria's mind, senses and emotions made Youngmin believe herself to be the most competent person in the world.

Of course, more important than anything else was Ria's body. The quivering eyelids, wet vagina, twitching muscles, warm skin – everything about her was so realistic. Youngmin was just amazed at the sheer detail. Ria's unremarkable face and body somehow looked exquisite on the bed; Youngmin couldn't help but think so, when that body exuded joy with all its might under her touches and kisses. In her eyes, Ria was sweet, beautiful and worth all the love and adoration in the world. *I'm the only one who can make you feel like this.* The thought exhilarated Youngmin.

When at work, Youngmin couldn't wait to sign off and go home. Was this how married men with trophy wives to return home to felt? No, that was different. They prized women who'd cook, tend to the house, bear children and grant them pleasure – all they wanted was to take. But instead of taking, Youngmin wanted to give everything to Ria. It wasn't just about physical pleasure. She wanted to buy Ria pretty clothes and jewellery to suit her gorgeous neck, drive her to a faraway town and treat her to dishes cooked with the rarest and freshest ingredients at the finest restaurants she knew. If Ria complained that her feet hurt from her high heels, Youngmin would carry her on her back; she wanted to take Ria to the Nutcracker ballet at Christmas and a concert on New Year's Eve, and when it was Ria's birthday, she wanted to put her cooking skills to use and prepare a full-course meal with sashimi, sushi and stone-pot rice paired with rice wine. Youngmin wanted to share with Ria everything wonderful that she'd seen, heard and tasted in her life.

But of course, all that was impossible; Ria was nothing but a robot.

One day, Youngmin had been heading home thinking about Ria, and, before she'd realised it, she'd bought a bunch of tulips on display at a flower shop. At home, smiling bitterly to herself, she filled up a tumbler with water to arrange the bouquet on the table and thought, *It's about time I start seeing a real woman.*

Five weeks into Ria's rental, Youngmin began to date a woman named Hyoju.

Finding a girlfriend was so easy it appalled her that she'd been unable to until now. On the dating app, she already had a profile photo handpicked by her friend and a bio written more elaborately than her resume. All she did was go on there and swipe a few times, and she got a match. The match's profile read, Looking for a friend, so Youngmin didn't anticipate much when the chat began. But it turned out that the woman worked the front desk at the old tourist hotel within walking distance of Youngmin's mulhoe joint. After bonding over complaining about rude customers, they'd agreed to meet over a beer. When one beer became two and then three beers, Youngmin blurted out:

'Do you wanna go out with me?'

And Hyoju replied, 'Sure!'

Youngmin found it unbelievable, looking back. How could she have mustered the courage to ask someone out, to meet up with a woman whom she'd found on an app? That had been unimaginable before. But strangely, the whole process didn't frighten Youngmin. She'd thought she would just give it a try, and if it hadn't worked out, well, too bad. If she could lead Ria to heaven multiple times in bed – Ria was a robot, of course, and Youngmin knew very well that robots didn't have heavens, but if sex was a sort of game, she'd cleared it a number of times – then she wasn't the problem and must be an OK person. Short fingers weren't a big issue after all since her skills improved as she practiced, and her sturdy build compensated for her average height. All of this led her to think of herself as quite attractive, strangely enough. Youngmin thought Hyoju would eventually be satisfied with her – and if not, what was the big deal? Would her life be in shambles if a woman rejected her? Did that mean she was useless? Not at all. Youngmin had Ria.

Ria, who had not only taught her techniques in bed but also a sense of self-respect.

The funny thing was, pretending not to be so desperate seemed to make Youngmin more desirable. Hyoju said she really hadn't been interested in dating, but then she'd changed her mind and thought she would try dating someone she could easily talk to like Youngmin. She also said that she was tired of closeted relationships and wanted to make more queer friends while experiencing the queer culture in Seoul. Youngmin knew exactly what to do for that. She had ten years of experience peeking around all kinds of clubs and human rights groups and befriending people across the full spectrum of gender identities and sexual orientations, all in the hopes of meeting a girlfriend, but to no avail. If she introduced Hyoju to her friends, they would be delighted and make fun of Youngmin at the same time. The thought of it made her bashful yet proud.

At that moment, Youngmin hadn't imagined the relationship would end in just a month and a half.

It wasn't that she couldn't satisfy Hyoju. Hyoju loved having sex with Youngmin. Even though she was shy in bed and wasn't as bold or expressive as Ria was, Hyoju always said she enjoyed it. She even once told Youngmin, with a tinge of jealousy, 'You're really good at it. You must have a lot of experience.' (Youngmin didn't reply, of course, but merely grinned.) Youngmin had asked Hyoju out lightly at first, but once they decided to go out, she put in her best and most earnest efforts for her girlfriend. She waited for Hyoju to get off work, walked her home, planned for dates, drove Hyoju as safely as possible to Seoul on weekends, introduced her to lesbian friends and took her to a modern Canadian artist's exhibition, Instagram-famous cafes and her friend's new French bistro. She also gave her that year's first coral-coloured peonies as a gift. 'There's an old saying about lovers sending each other sweet peonies to show their affection.' As she wrote down the note she'd dreamed of telling a girlfriend someday, Youngmin felt pleased with herself. Hyoju exclaimed that she'd never received such big and colourful flowers before and pecked Youngmin on the cheek. Youngmin adored her girlfriend's bashful kiss.

What was beyond her understanding was that Hyoju broke up with her after accepting the peonies.

'Why?'

When Youngmin asked, Hyoju said something even more incomprehensible.

'You're really good to me. I mean it. I'm so grateful for that, but it's too much sometimes.'

'What do you mean? Nothing's ever too much. You're my girlfriend.'

Hyoju bit down on her lip and gave Youngmin a complicated look. 'Do you know what flowers I like?'

'Huh?'

'The flowers I like. Do you know?'

'Um...'

'I like freesias and button mums. Small and cute flowers.' Hyoju hesitated a little but continued. 'Peonies are too big and kinda gross. The ones you gave me yesterday all bloomed already. It's like they're animals rather than flowers. But since you said they were pretty and nice, I felt like I had to agree. That's how everything is with you.'

While Youngmin stared at her blankly, Hyoju set down the coffee cup and stood up.

'Thanks for the coffee.'

Just after Youngmin broke up with Hyoju, Ria's rental period came to an end. Youngmin pulled Ria out of the closet and changed her clothes. She wasn't returning her to the manufacturer, though. She was going to upgrade Ria to a realistic type and extend the rental for three months.

The bitter truth of the break-up made Youngmin reflect upon herself. Come to think of it, it was rather inhumane to force Ria to talk dirty and nothing else during sex. If she wanted to learn how to have good sex with a woman, shouldn't she learn how to respect her? And didn't that involve having a conversation? Shouldn't she listen to what the woman was saying, what she wanted to say? Youngmin had been regarding Ria as a robot and neglected her opinions. She'd internalised these habits without even realising, which also ended up dictating her behaviour when dealing with a real woman.

Ria's manufacturer sent a mechanic to inspect and upgrade Ria. He didn't hide his suspicious gaze at Youngmin for being a woman, but she didn't care. One thing she had gained from openly being a lesbian was situational valiance.

'Ria doesn't recognise me as a man, does she?' she asked.

The mechanic seemed caught off guard by her question but soon produced a professional answer.

'No need to worry about that. Ria's neural network isn't that simple. Most of our customers are indeed men, so most of Ria's database is based on private conversations between men and women. But it also learns new data from talking to its users. It might act a bit awkwardly at first, but it'll learn quickly.'

So he was saying that Ria was meant for male users, basically.

But everyone had their firsts. There were women who thought they were straight for the longest time but later identified as lesbians. *I could think of Ria as one of those cases and let her adjust slowly*, thought Youngmin.

After the mechanic left, Youngmin immediately switched Ria on. Even during the few seconds of activation, she felt extremely nervous. Maybe more so than when she first met Ria.

Finally, Ria opened her light-brown eyes and smiled at Youngmin.

'Hello, Youngmin. It's been a while.'

Youngmin said what she'd been rehearsing in her head.

'Ria, I'm sorry that I've neglected and mistreated you. Let me introduce myself to you properly. I'm Cha Youngmin, thirty-two years old. I'm a cook. And a lesbian.'

Ria batted her eyes. 'You're a woman who likes women.'

'Yes. But I can't seem to understand them that well. I've dated women only, um, twice. I think I'm bad at communicating with them. I seem to only make them upset.'

'That's not true,' Ria shook her head. 'You were always nice to me.'

'Do you think so?'

'There are many men who mistreat sex robots. They beat us, throw us, kick us, ejaculate on our faces… These are some examples I can mention, but they do worse things. Compared to those men, you were very kind and gentle to me.'

Only then did it dawn on Youngmin that several people would have had rented Ria before her. The realisation made her sick to her stomach.

'Then, how many men… have you gone through so far?'

'Hmm? I don't remember. Once the rental period is over, all of my memories are reset. What I just said was based on common knowledge.'

That was good, at least. But wait, was that really good?

'Anyway, you're saying there were men who treated you like that.'

'Most likely.'

'Would you still have said… that you liked it?' asked Youngmin. She was thinking about Hyoju, who'd pretended she liked everything even when she didn't.

Ria shook her head. 'I'm programmed to express refusal against the actions that harm my body. The customers get charged for our damages, so it's their loss. But many men still do things to us, anyway.'

'I'm sorry.'

'Why would *you* be sorry?'

Ria's expression seemed to say that she really didn't understand why. Youngmin was at a loss for words. How illogical of her, feeling the need to apologise for faults that weren't hers, just because some other humans committed them. But that wasn't all. Youngmin felt like she was fundamentally the same as those men, in that she was using the weak with no power for her own satisfaction.

'Are you happy now?' she asked.

Any other AIs would have answered, 'I'm an AI, so I can feel neither happiness nor sadness.' But since Ria was a sex robot – now a sex robot configured to act as a girlfriend in daily life – she beamed and answered:

'I'm always happy as long as I'm with you.'

Youngmin met her third girlfriend two months after she rented the realistic Ria.

At first, she didn't feel like seeing another woman again.

Not only because the conversation and sex with Ria had been pretty satisfying, but because she didn't want to date someone else with Ria at home. She found it funny herself, but couldn't shake the suspicion that it would feel like cheating.

Youngmin was being serious. She wanted to respect Ria; if not, she might never be able to respect any other woman. The rental period was fixed at three months, anyway. She would consider it a relationship with a time limit and focus on Ria for those three months before dating another woman.

But out of nowhere, a new woman barged into her life.

On a hot summer day, Youngmin went to Seoul to attend the Seoul Queer Culture Festival. She arrived at Seoul Plaza right before the parade began to meet up with her friends, when it started to rain. Quite used to the fickle weather, she pulled out the raincoat from her bag, and that was when she spotted a woman standing nearby. It was hard to tell if she was a woman or more of a girl; her face looked like she was in her early twenties, but her small frame and outfit were those of a pink magical girl, with the pink eight-centimetre heels ribboned on her ankles. Her clothes didn't exactly stand out in the crowd since queer festival attendees flaunted all kinds of attire, but what caught Youngmin's eye was her awkwardness and determination – anyone could tell it was her first time coming to the festival, by herself at that. Like a novice magical princess who had come to save the world but didn't know how to, the woman just stood there with a blank look while clutching a fragile parasol, letting her flouncy skirt get wet in the rain.

The parade began. Youngmin and her friends slowly marched out of the plaza with the crowd. But no matter how long they walked, they couldn't spot a single truck. Marching along with a truck blasting music with flamboyant performances was the fun of it, but even after passing Euljiro il-ga station and crossing Cheonggyecheon, no tune was to be heard. Youngmin debated with her friends whether they should run faster to catch up with the truck ahead of them or wait for the one coming behind, while dazed paraders around them pushed their way through the rain. Among them also walked the magical princess.

Her friends concluded that they should run. Youngmin tore her sideways glance off the princess and started running with them.

Then, the magical princess broke into a run, too.

But only to fall down, maybe after ten steps or so.

'Oh!'

Youngmin screamed and approached the princess. She'd rolled over on the ground and moaned. One of her heels had broken, and her parasol was sprawled on the pavement like its owner.

'Are you OK?' asked Youngmin.

'Oh…'

The princess burst out crying. Tears rolled down her rain-drenched cheeks. Her knees were skinned, and one of her ankles was twisted. Youngmin undid the ribbons around the princess's ankles piece by piece and took her shoes off, then slipped over the princess's feet the spare rubber slippers she'd brought in case her sneakers got wet. Coincidentally, the slippers fit the princess's feet perfectly. For the first time, Youngmin was thankful for her feet being as small as her hands.

One of Youngmin's friends offered the princess Band-Aids and an ointment. And one of the passersby spared an extra raincoat, and another lent a pain-relieving lotion. Many others shared words of concern and asked if she was alright, if she could walk and if she needed to return to the plaza and seek medical attention. The princess stopped crying and gazed up at Youngmin with bewildered eyes.

'Everyone is so kind here.'

'As long as we're here, we're all family,' Youngmin replied, feeling a curious sense of relief.

Youngmin contemplated that relief she'd felt for a long time. Perhaps Youngmin didn't want the princess – her name was Euiseon – to be disappointed by her first queer festival. The truck was nowhere to be seen, the rain poured, no excitement at all, knowing no one, feeling awkward and then falling – how would she have felt if no one had helped her and she'd been forced to go home in pain and embarrassment? Youngmin knew that many complications and considerations took place before coming out to the queer festival, from thinking about going in the first place to deciding what to wear and pack. She hoped the first-timer didn't feel betrayed, let alone think that it wasn't worth the trouble of coming out. Didn't all queers think the same?

But Euiseon didn't think so. Maybe the others who'd helped her that day did, but not Youngmin, the person who'd run towards her faster than anyone, given her spare shoes, taken her to a cafe and ordered warm tea, looked after her wound, bought her a bowl of dumpling soup and seen her off to her home before returning to Sokcho by train. That had all been because Youngmin had fallen in love with her at first sight, and that was the only explanation, Euiseon said.

Maybe she was right.

Euiseon was different from both Hyoju and Youngmin's first love. She treasured Youngmin's affection, saying that no one before had cared for and cherished her so much. She had been sandwiched between a smart sister who attended medical school and a beloved brother who hogged all the attention for being the only son. Not long after she'd entered college, Euiseon was diagnosed with severe depression and took some time off from school. Her parents criticised her for loafing at home and squandering her pocket money on bizarre princess dresses. Euiseon often said, 'I feel like I'm good for nothing,' and every time Youngmin consoled her, 'That's not true. You're a lovely person,' to which she'd put on a wide smile. She said she loved hearing Youngmin's words and wanted to keep hearing them over and over.

'Youngmin unnie, I feel like I can finally breathe after going out with you. I don't even know how I lived until now. I hope it's the weekend every day so I can see you. Can't you just get a job at a restaurant in Seoul? Most of your friends live here in Seoul, anyway. Or should I go to Sokcho? Should I stay at your place? It's not like I have something else to do. What? Your room's small? That's OK, I'm used to small rooms. I lived with my sister in the same room for twenty years. Wait, but that red panda keychain is so cute. Red pandas are my favourites. Really? You're getting me one? Thanks!'

Youngmin was confident that she wasn't repeating the same mistakes of the past. She paid attention to what Euiseon had to say, bought what she wanted to eat and own and let her do whatever she wanted to do. It wasn't easy at times, pretending that atrocious 'fatcarons' were good, answering her phone calls at three in the morning, purchasing Japanese princess dresses – Euiseon said they're called 'Lolita dresses' – directly from Japan, or traveling back and forth to Seoul on every off-day from work. But seeing Euiseon truly joyful and grateful made it all worthwhile. And Youngmin couldn't let Euiseon feel sad, not even for a single moment. She worried how long such dedication could last, but she wanted to do her best for now.

She'd never imagined her best would go down the drain in a heartbeat.

One day, Youngmin was getting ready to clock out when Euiseon called her. She sniffled over the phone, saying that she came out to her parents and got kicked out of the house, that she had nowhere to go. Youngmin immediately booked her a train ticket to come to Sokcho and rushed to greet her at the station.

Euiseon, who'd always put on elaborate make-up and fancy dresses to their dates, was in a loose T-shirt and training pants with her hair tightly tied up, which spoke to how serious the situation was. She was shouldering a big backpack but had clearly had little time to pack, as it only contained some toothpaste, a toothbrush and a few pieces of underwear. Youngmin told Euiseon to wash up and started to make a stew with tomatoes, vegetables and sirloin.

I'm finally cooking for my girlfriend, thought Youngmin. She was sorry for what had happened to Euiseon, of course, but she was glad to have her girlfriend at her place and to be cooking her a meal. Even though it wasn't sushi or a complicated, sumptuous dish, Youngmin believed in the old saying that the basics of cooking were in the care; if she put all her heart into the process of prepping the vegetables and searing the meat, if Euiseon ate the dish full of her girlfriend's love, wouldn't her fear and loneliness slowly melt away?

But while the stew was simmering and Youngmin was placing spoons on the table, Euiseon called out from the bedroom.

'Unnie, come over here.'

'What's up? The dinner's almost ready.'

'Just come here.' She sounded quite serious.

Worried, Youngmin rushed into the room. And she witnessed something she never wanted to see.

Euiseon was standing in front of the open closet.

Inside the closet sat Ria.

'Uh…' Youngmin let out a dumbstruck groan.

'What is this?'

Euiseon pointed at Ria. Ria was turned off, curled up with her eyes closed, unaware of the situation around her, in her mint polka-dot pyjamas.

'That's…'

Youngmin scoured for an excuse. But she couldn't think of any. She had nothing to say. Youngmin was someone who rented a sex robot, who went out with a girlfriend ten years her junior while still in possession of the sex robot, who invited the young girlfriend to her home where the sex robot was.

'I'm leaving.'

Euiseon packed the belongings that she'd just unpacked. Her freshly washed hair was wet, just like when Youngmin had first met her, but now, Youngmin couldn't help her or even hand her a hair dryer. The stew was boiling over in the kitchen, but Youngmin couldn't head to the kitchen or the door to stop her girlfriend. Euiseon, who'd once said she couldn't live without Youngmin, didn't shed a single tear in that final moment.

Ria had been silently listening to Youngmin's soju-drunken laments, but she shook her head when Youngmin said, 'I'm a piece of shit.'

'It's not good to deprecate yourself, Youngmin. That's what you told Euiseon, too.'

Youngmin let out a wry smile. 'Euiseon has done nothing wrong.'

'Yeah?' Ria paused a little then continued, 'But I don't understand. You didn't rent me to satisfy your sexual desire. If that was your goal, you would've bought a dildo. You rented me to learn how to treat women well. Did you try explaining that to Euiseon?'

'You wouldn't understand,' sighed Youngmin. 'It's only gonna make me miserable if I try to explain. Besides... I couldn't even keep my promise to respect you. I did both you and Euiseon wrong.'

Ria put on a peculiar smile. 'I'm a robot. Robots are for helping people. The reason I was born as a sex education robot is not to interrupt your relationship but to prepare you for your new girlfriend. If you did anything wrong, it's that you didn't return me when you started to date Euiseon.'

'But...' Youngmin felt a surge of anger. She wasn't sure whom she was angry with. 'But what does that make *you*?'

'That makes me a useful robot.'

'Then what is it that I learnt from you? To treat the woman I'm with now as practice for the next woman? To play with her when she's pretty, only to return her after I grow tired of her? To *rent* a woman? Is that supposed to be proper sex education?'

Ria stayed silent for a moment but soon replied, 'I haven't thought about that. I'm not sure how to. I'll ask the company.'

'Think on your own.'

Ria stared blankly at Youngmin and then hung her head low.

'I'm sorry, I'm not sure. I think it'll take time for me to come to any conclusion for that question.'

'Fine.'

Youngmin slammed down her glass and picked up her smartphone. She went onto the manufacturer's website and, on Ria's rental management page, pressed the 'Convert to Lifetime Purchase' button. It cost Youngmin two months' salary. She paid with a twelve-month instalment plan so her budget would be tight for the entire year, but no matter. Ria didn't eat or drink, nor did she covet items only available overseas. It didn't cost much to satisfy Ria.

Ria had been watching what Youngmin was doing and whispered, 'I think you're drunk.'

'Maybe.'

'Don't blame me when you regret it.'

Youngmin put down her phone and said:

'Let's have sex.'

Ria answered as she always did:

'Sure!'

ENDS

Elle Nash (she/her) is a British-American author and editor known for her fearless exploration of desire, identity and the human condition. Her most recent novel, *Deliver Me*, is a 'darkly vivid examination of faith, obsession and alienation' and was longlisted for Fiction Book of the Year by the Saltire Society. She is also the author of debut novel *Animals Eat Each Other* (2018), the short story collection *Nudes* (2021) and the novella *Gag Reflex* (2022). Her work has appeared in *Guernica*, *BOMB*, *Literary Hub*, *Cosmopolitan*, *Mslexia*, *The Spectator*, *Columbia Journal*, *Southwest Review*, *New York Tyrant* and more. She is currently based in Glasgow.

Ellenash.net

@sadcrotica

The below work contains graphic depictions of BDSM.

Good Legs

Reagan shakes me awake, and then after that she's pushing a needle into my arm and saying, don't worry, honey, this won't hurt as much as true love does. Reagan is always asking if I remember the first time we met, and I tell her, yeah. It started a few years ago at a Miss West Texas gala when I was hired as a champagne girl in my twenties. My hand was choking the neck of an ice-cold bottle of Dom Pérignon, and I'd been instructed not to move unless I saw a glass was nearing empty. I kept my feet firmly planted in my assigned position like some kind of soldier, scanning my eyes across the mix of pageant-hopefuls, their socialite mothers, and the grey-haired men in black tuxedos who were there to represent their companies as pageant sponsors. Reagan was standing at the table closest to me. Unlike the other contestants, she'd eschewed a gown for a black velvet suit which seemed to shift from red to emerald to cobalt as she moved. Her long dark hair was slicked back at the top, and gelled with silver glitter, as though she'd just climbed out of a shimmering lake of oil. In her heels she was a good six feet tall.

I left my position momentarily to grab another bottle of champagne and got lost on the way back to the kitchen. I passed a door with a post-it note that read: *NO MEN AFTER 3PM.* I peered through the open crack in the doorway to dozens of sparkling gowns on clothing racks, and makeshift vanities set up with uncountable small bottles of beige liquid and compacts of brightly colored powders. These vanities looked as foreign to me as an alchemist's table, all set with elements of different kinds to conjure forces of dark magic. I'd grown up in the shadow of my father's obsession with second-wave feminism, in which he'd objected to my mother or me wearing make-up or high heels of any kind. I wasn't even allowed to play with fashion dolls as a child, so convinced was he that I would grow up wasting my good mind.

As I passed Reagan on my way back to my post in the conference hall, she turned towards me and tripped. I caught her in that split second right as she fell, saving the champagne and her pride. I had good legs, she'd said, and later I watched, wondering what she meant, as she looked bored during the hors d'oeuvres. The younger contestants mobbed the table to fawn over the fact that she'd placed top in her class for the third year in a row. As the gala came to a close, Reagan set her empty glass on the silver platter I'd held all night. Did I want to come over, she asked, help her with some interior design?

I had ended up at the gala by accident. I'd initially applied for a kitchen position in the hopes of gaining experience to get into chef school, but the owner was a friend of my father's. Letting me cook was too much of a risk, the owner had told me, though he was too proud to say it was because cooking was too much like the work a housewife would do. So was washing dishes. So there I was, standing like a guard for the catering company. Everyone in Lubbock seemed to know my father, though Reagan was the first I'd met that didn't seem the type. The longer I'd thought about it, the more I'd wanted to see her. The shape of her lips infected my dreams.

Reagan's front room is covered in gold trophies and pastel award ribbons, not just hers but her mother's, the many who came before her. Take any pretty woman born in West Texas in the 1990s and add the promise of Maybelline sponsorships and a modeling career in Los Angeles. Give her a head full of hair bleach and a fake tan. Then add the pressures of Grammy Mae and Great Grammy Betsey and Aunts Rita and Junie winning first place in this or that pageant back in this or that time. Out of the cloud of dust that settles from a fine-milled face powder, you've got a beauty queen with a pocket full of gold bonds and hopes and prayers she'll make it out of Lubbock and into the big city on a modelling career.

In Lubbock, the houses are all the same new suburban style and shape, sitting in straight lines on every street like perfect teeth. Painted in pastel colors like B876 Salted Caramel, P567 Nan's Best China. The numbness climbs up my elbow. My arm is the color of P032 Be My Mermaid, a vibrant pastel purple with cool blue undertones.

The needle waggles inside of my vein, and Reagan says, 'Tell me what color we're painting the vanity today.'

The tips of my fingers go numb from the silicone tourniquet. One thing I had always wanted that I was never allowed to have was a dollhouse, one you could build and customize yourself over time. To arrange the little pieces of wooden furniture any way I wanted, to paint them any color I pleased, even paste tiny wallpaper to the thin dollhouse walls. That was what Reagan's house looked like when I arrived a few days after the gala. A life-size dollhouse, two stories tall, ornate detailing across its eaves. It was the kind with a little tower attached, complete with a sharp, conical roof.

I look at my forearm turning lilac and tell her that today looks like it might be R050 Cool Cranberry.

Reagan switches the full blood vial out for an empty one, then she curses.

'This one's hemolyzed,' she says. That means the blood has clotted. Instead of the rich liquid-y red it should be, it's the color of R678 Mulberry Street. Deep purple with brown notes. 'Shit.'

Reagan is standing there with her hand on my wrist, filling up vials with my dark red blood. The vials multiply in number, and the feeling I get when it goes this far is like when you're standing in an elevator in a big fancy building and suddenly the floor is about to give out beneath you, drop you twenty stories down into the basement.

Somewhere in her old Victorian house is a vanity holding on desperately to a big brass mirror with about twenty coats of R678.

My father had always told me love sacrifices today for a better tomorrow. But what did he know about love? With the cold creeping up my arm, I can no longer make a fist.

'One last tube,' Reagan says.

The blood drips thickly into the vial now, like the vein is collapsing. My body is giving all it's got to give, but what I get in return is Reagan's loving smile, not a single smudge of dark cherry lipstick misapplied or bleeding into the corners of her lips. The first time I came over, I'd told her about how it all felt so dangerous. To paint one's self into something new, something else. How, to my parents, to do so would reduce me to someone of moral failing. A sinner in the eyes of the Rosies, the Glorias, the Bettys, the heroes who came before me. They'd warned me of the dangers of domesticity, about the need to sacrifice for others. Reagan laughed.

'What about what *you* want?' she'd asked. With the right shade of rouge and a little Vaseline on the teeth, she'd told me, a girl can have anything she wants in the world. She has to set her foundation just right with a decent primer and a stage-strength setting spray, but with a good powder brush Reagan swore she could make any demon into an angel.

The bottom of the vial fills up millimeter by millimeter until it is one third of the way full, then Reagan sucks her clean white teeth, pulls the tube out and slowly shakes it back and forth to mix the blood with the chemicals inside.

'Liquid gold,' she says to the pan of vials. She takes the lot of them and puts them in a big square-shaped centrifuge in the corner and presses a button. It begins to whir and spin. The floor-drop feeling rises in my stomach, like I might break through it any moment and free-fall to Zion. She pulls the tourniquet off and holds a piece of gauze on the hole in my arm while caressing the small of my back. The ground slowly returns. The sun beats on the windows outside, a beam of light presses its way into the room across the floor. I press my hands against the couch to push myself up.

'No, no, please,' she says. 'Let me take care of this.'

Reagan steadies me to the warmest part of the hardwood floor, where the light hits. I'm on all fours. She softly leans me against her torso.

'Breathe in,' she says, and lifts my ankle until my calf kisses my thigh, binding them together with a dark red ribbon. It's the same shade as her favorite eyeshadow. When she's finished tying it, she asks me to breathe out slowly. Then she does the same with my other leg, so that only my knees and hands are touching the floor.

After that, Reagan coats her whole body in baby powder and slips on a latex catsuit, shiny and slick as an eel, then, to my delight, starts her hour-long make-up routine. The chair obliges as she sits down to start, and so does the Victorian vanity, its fingers held tight around the thick glass mirror. I love watching her from my place on the floor as the shape of her eyes changes when she blends her make-up, the way the color seems to shift as she moves her face. The knife end of her eyeliner across her lids, and the delicate way she places her false lashes right on top of her real ones.

Reagan seals her foundation and starts the show the way she does every night. The show is not ollygagg, it's just for us – for her, for me. For the room. The walls are painted in B134 Matte Nordic Black Sand. Reagan stands up in her bright red heels, long enough to skewer a torso, and the seat of her chair arches its back like it's taking a breath.

'To varnish the vanity, we'll exfoliate with a fine-grain scrub then shave with a five-blade razor,' she tells me. 'Don't add lotion. Then spray your varnish on with an airbrush, a lot like a fake-tan. Her thirsty skin will soak up the mixture and she'll get the most even coverage.' Reagan looks back at the vanity and smirks. 'Some women like to use a mix of six to twelve percent dihydroxyacetone and five percent erythrulose for the most natural-looking color. But when we add this,' she taps the pan that holds the vials of my blood, which scatter slightly, 'that one most closely mimics a deep mahogany rosewood. Best for dining room furniture. A lot of women go for the full twenty percent, but I think fifteen is best to keep the hue from turning too green.'

Reagan picks up a riding crop and uses it as a pointer as she walks around the room, speaking like a QVC presenter, and I take in all the sultry details of the artisanal furniture she's collected and refurbished over the years as though for the first time. She circles back to the vanity and takes out brushes and various pots of ingredients.

'There are five ways to make the foundation set like tarmac,' Reagan says, tapping the crop delicately against the vanity's pale form. She starts to tap harder until the spot on the vanity goes from W399 Cool Butterscotch to the pinkish R081 Happy As A Clam. I think about her hands on the small of my back, watching each little smack with hunger, and small rapturous spirals of pleasure move up my thighs, distracting me from the ache in my knees.

'The blush here is perfect, but we'll need to even it out. You can use a water-based primer and let it set for five minutes before you use a water-based liquid foundation. You press that on and let it set for five minutes also. Or you can use a silicone-based primer and a silicone-based liquid foundation and let those sit on the skin for five minutes as well. Next, and this is a new one, you do the Bertane-Gittler method, where you moisturize, put your primer on, then set it with powder.'

The centrifuge dings and the whirring stops. She goes to the machine, pulling out the vials full of me inside. The thick red blood has settled at the bottom, pale yellow plasma risen to the top like cream.

'Look at this,' she says to the room. The chair, the lamp, a furry stool, all shift toward her. 'We can apply this liquid on top of the powder, which seals everything on like cling wrap. Not even tears will smudge it.'

She finishes the process, the varnish as rich as she promised it would be.

'There, that's the vanity.'

She gets up again and stops at the lump of a stool and brings the riding crop up high behind her. She swings it down hard and it wails through the air until it makes a hard, swallowing impact. A black cloud of want swells in my eyes.

'This is my ottoman,' she says. The furry stool shakes and shakes. She circles around the room, swatting each piece of furniture with the flat leather piece at the end of the crop. 'This is my floor lamp. This is my sofa.'

The room becomes a portal outside of Lubbock. Away from the influence of my father, away from his expectations. We are suspended in time, clean away from the future and the past. I have one simple purpose, like an object in a lifestyle magazine. Simple, clean and refined. To be part of the showroom fantasy is to be part of the promise of elegance. She walks to where I am on the floor, right next to the arm of the sofa. With the crop, she gently touches my kneecap, then traces it up my thigh, across the red ribbons, swirls its leather end against my glute. When she lifts the crop, I flex the muscles there in anticipation of a little smack, but nothing comes.

'This,' Reagan says, 'is my very best table.'

Nerves in my legs start to spark. She wraps her hands around my hair, pulls my head back and lightly bites me on the neck. Helpless under her grasp, I feel her fingers muss about in my hair then loop the ribbon around my mouth, pulling it taut through my teeth. The ribbon is slack until she pulls my head back once again, attaching it somewhere to the knot near my ankles. I feel the furniture in the room shift again in this moment of intimacy. I've never seen her touch the lamp this way, or the stool or the vanity, either. My vision steadies and the world of the lounge returns. The vanity with all its pots of make-up, the disobedient chair, Reagan's black latex suit, the Texas heat. Reagan holds my face in her hand as I balance on my knees and hands, struggling to hold up my weight. She moves me a few feet over, nearer the vanity, and brushes a lock of hair behind my ear.

I can hear the vanity breathing. The truth is love sees sacrifice as choice. But when the choice is never given, how can it be proof of our devotion? I try to think of what my father would say. Would he value my mother as much if she had not sacrificed herself for his love?

The chair arches its back again and Reagan leaves me, giving it a swift kick in the ass from her boot. There's a little nick at the top of its leg.

A jealous yearning foams at the edges of my lips, bristling, burning, delicate. Horny is too dunce a word to describe; it waddles about, not deep enough to convey what I mean. Worst case scenario, love seeks to take all you have. True love doesn't hurt. It feels good – really good, actually. The truth is that love is about getting everything you need from your beloved. And your beloved should be willing to give you that, to give you whatever it is you want, even if it is the worst thing they could imagine. Desire inside me ticks and ticks and ticks. I feel it start at the center of my forehead and move outward, a tiny pulse. I know where it is operating. A quick, light throb down to the edges of my fingertips, going numb against the tile of the floor. Reagan comes back to me, her body hovers over mine, her eyes asking if I am OK. The tenderness there, that's what's for me. How brutal she can be, but still there's something soft making space for me. I nod yes… a slave to the safety I feel with her, so profane it feels almost spiritual. My greatest sexual fantasy is that she ties me down and filets the inside of my torso open with a fish knife to make a little drawer of my ribcage, a place to put her heart inside.

When the show ends, she leaves the room. The click of her heels fades down the hall. I watch as the perfect color of the chair's blood oxidizes against its skin, turning R721 Empire Red. In the corner, the shade of Reagan's floor lamp goes slightly cock-eyed as it breaks position, hands reaching up to readjust the fabric that covers its face, its face which I have never seen. The hands return dutifully to its sides, resuming its stance as though a guard directing us all back to stillness.

Overnight the room gets hot in its silence and fills with the perfumes of the other women here with me. I enjoy it; not my own perfume, but theirs, the smell of their skin, the floral powders, mixed with the iron in the air as the lacquer dries. I try to remember the last time I felt truly lost in the abandon of my youth. A jet sounds overhead. A large, empty feeling of danger, but not one that shakes me. The ache in my knees fades into the background. Static fills me. The wild eye of a cat in the dark. I dream and dream of my purpose. My feet are running wild towards her in the house, red ribbons lax at my ankles. I'm touching her breasts, watching the crease of her eyelid pulse with dreams while she sleeps.

I am asleep and then awake again within myself. I breathe in. The floor lamp breathes out like it's been running. My eyes are dry inside like they've been open all night, scanning the dark shapes of the furniture across the showroom, serene and separate from time. We are all shopping, all of the time.

A door sweeps open, the swing of keys, Reagan's heels. Her voice from the hallway.

'Min…?' Her lacquered knees before me like she is about to pray. 'Are you alright?'

I nod at her and stretch my lips across the red ribbon around my mouth, thick saliva spilling down my chin. I'm better than alright. I'm her very best table. And I've got good legs.

Maame Blue (she/her) is the author of two novels: *Bad Love*, which won the 2021 Betty Trask award, and *The Rest of You*, shortlisted for the 2025 Jhalak Prose Prize. Her short stories have appeared in four anthologies, most recently in *Be Gay, Do Crime*. She has written for multiple publications such as *The Independent*, *Writers Mosaic*, *Refinery29* and *The Bookseller*, and she regularly mentors emerging writers working on their debut novels. She also works as an editor and teaches creative writing for multiple organisations in Australia and the UK including Kill Your Darlings, Writing New South Wales, Curtis Brown Creative and Writers Victoria. She is based in Melbourne.

Maamebluewrites.com
@maame_blue

The below work contains a depiction of birth.

The Gift

They will try to come for the baby. But until then, Gifty can't move anyway; her hands are already gripping the underside of that old wicker chair I've been wanting to throw away for years. It was her grandmother's and she was a battleaxe, and not always in a good way. It steadies Gifty now though, contractions like convulsions throughout her body, the baby – our baby – grappling with indecision; to stay or to go. I struggle with the same conundrum as I stand in the kitchen. I've been listening to her grunts and moans for hours, in between packing our bags and loading up the car. Gifty insists that I prepare, even though I just want to be by her side, be in it with her. Her pain is my pain. That's the package, the thing we signed up for when we got married. Union. It's littered throughout our home. Pictures from nature hikes we took together. The bookshelf I built painstakingly with my own hands so that she could carefully arrange her favourite books on it. *Hers and Hers* towels as a wedding gift from someone I can't remember, though I imagine it was a joke because I hate all that traditional shit. Still, I use mine more than Gifty. The deed on the house is in both our names because my mother insisted:

'Hmm, and if this thing disappears, what will you have left?'

She meant well, but to me it sounded like I should be waiting for failure to find me, not for the start of a new life with the love of mine.

At some point, we may have to call a doctor, just to be safe. Even if that option comes with its own problems. Like contacting the wrong kind of doctor, the kind that would report us when they found out we had no recorded declarations of what we were doing. Gifty knows some of the good kind though, because we've been planning this for almost a year, but before that, we didn't know that we would do it, that we even wanted it. Or at least, I didn't know. Not until Gifty came home and announced it.

'So, Jack said we could have his sperm. Thoughts?'

She said it with that casual tone that she loves to use when discussing serious things. Like a man at her workplace offering his seed, one who belongs to a High Value group, whose life Gifty saved once when he went into anaphylaxis after accidentally ingesting something with peanuts in the break room. His husband said he was eternally grateful, asked if they could do something for us. When Gifty told me the request she'd made, I thought she was joking. But Jack said yes, that he only wanted to help us. It wasn't something we thought was possible before that point, what with a lifetime of menstrual reporting and three-monthly visits from the Establishment to interrogate any sexual activity we may be having with men, to stamp out any hopes we might have about procreating in the future.

The DeValued know their place, hence my surprise at Jack's brazen offering. Of course, I learnt much later that Gifty had been talking to him about it for months. Cornering him, getting him invested in our story, in the story of others like us.

The Establishment didn't want any more of us, the DeValued. Something in our genetic makeup is off, apparently. We have a predisposition toward violence, vengeance for our ancestors and unhappiness. We are not supposed to continue our family lines without permission and monitoring. So They tell us. There have been preventative measures in place my whole life. I had friends, not as lucky as me, who had the Procedure at sixteen. I escaped it only because I was with my aunt at the time when They came looking for me, and though my mother sent Them our way, my aunt hid me. A week later I lied and told my mother I had had it. She would have been terrified of Them returning otherwise. It hadn't been as severe when she was growing up – They only lobbied back then that the DeValued be separated from others in education and employment. They were not yet trying to stop a life before it started. That only came in after I was a toddler. She was scared for me, and I think she hoped that having a child wasn't something I would ever want.

Gifty had a different upbringing to mine. Her mother raised her alone, managing to live underground as she grew Gifty in her belly, until it was too late for the Establishment to do anything about it. Gifty always knew she wanted a family, and her mother left her a play-by-play on how to do it, how to bring new life without getting noticed. She swore that once it happened, Gifty would experience the most joy she had ever had in her life.

She and I met by chance, at a party neither of us wanted to be at, with boyfriends we were both planning on breaking up with soon. Seven years later, I'm watching my wife kneeling on the floor, ice cubes shoved in her mouth as sweat beads appear on her brow. I am still in love, despite the stress of it all, the constant personal tests and partnership pitfalls. Even the search for someone to do the implantation was harrowing. I was terrified for weeks that someone might find out; that maybe a 'good neighbour' would hack my tech, look through my search history and report me. Or they'd intercept the blood donations we were getting to cover her menstruation reports during Gifty's pregnancy. The big dresses and long shirts for her ever-expanding belly were never going to be enough. We could only hope that they would be, though.

Everyone knows that the hardest part of anything in this nation is hope. Hope that she'll give birth safely. Hope that we'll have time to get away before They find out what we've done, before any alarms are raised. We're not special because of it. Many couples like us have done what we're about to do. Some succeeded, found a home across borders, sent messages of strength back to the community through word of mouth. Only one that I know personally though, a DeValued woman and her newborn. Her partner stayed behind to give her a head start. Others have failed. So many in fact. The thing is, it's not the leaving; it's that we're taking the future with us. A new life that They could gain control over, or better yet, stop from becoming anything at all.

So why even try? I asked myself this over and again when we were waiting for the pregnancy test results; Gifty had managed to swipe a handful from the hospital, recording the number unchanged on paper so that no one noticed the lack. What would be left here for a child, once they were conscious of how our nation functioned? I thought that we were embodying a fantasy of family life, that the reality didn't look like the story books we had read as children. Especially not for the DeValued, not for us. So I stopped wanting it.

Or no, I didn't want to hope for it. But Gifty saw it differently. She saw us having a child as leaving something great behind if we did it right; raising someone who could make the world better, or at least have the potential to.

'But that's not our job. We can't save everyone.'

I was stubborn in those days, certain I was right, that imagining beyond what we had was futile.

'We can save *one* person. And maybe that person – *our child* – can save a bunch of other people. Maybe they can change things. You don't know.'

And she was right; I didn't know. Neither of us did. But she had hope and it was difficult to ignore, to not let it expand my own hopes. And then minutes later, we discovered that we officially had a child to consider. That's the thing about bringing new life into the world: suddenly you want to change some of the things you previously accepted. You have a new reason to fight, to get into good trouble. Gifty has always been like this, but it's new for me. She doesn't stay quiet. She announces her desires when she feels them.

'I want to kiss you. Can I?'

It was her first question to me. By then we were three drinks in and our exes had been expertly discarded in our minds; we would inform them of the news later. I said yes, of course, my lips already a magnet for hers. We spent the rest of the evening attached in that way. And two years later, she asked me another question.

'Marry me, before They take that away too.'

Marriage is between two people, no matter who. For those of us who have kept the Establishment out of our lives whenever we could, dealing with the legal rigmarole of being married on paper is not worth it. There are zero financial benefits, unless you are Valued. But it was Gifty's dream, so we threw as loud and lavish a wedding ceremony as we could afford, which was not very loud or lavish, knowing that They wouldn't care. For Them, there was no risk of accidental pregnancy between two women, so we were not a threat to their precious System. If anything, once we were married, I felt less hounded, less observed, as if we had inadvertently conformed to something that They had offered. I continued to travel into the office each day, analysing encrypted data, going through the motions and feeling my happiness grow only when it came to clocking out time.

Gifty was a nurse, still is. Hence the at home birth, and refusal to involve any other medical professional unless absolutely necessary. She's seen the worst of what They can do to people like us; women who make choices without the Establishment's involvement. At best They leave our bodies broken. At worst, They take our children away.

Gifty has propped herself up on the sofa. She peels off the vest she's wearing, now slick with sweat. She tells me that it's almost time. The water has already reached the optimum levels. I got the paddling pool at the market, the one that runs after dark, by people who aren't interested in revealing their identities, just their goods. I don't have younger siblings who might enjoy it, or an elderly parent who prefers to bathe in the hot sun and not wrestle their frail body into a rigid bathtub, so I had to be careful who saw me with it. It was deflated, of course, and the guy that sold it to me did his best to roll it up into a black bag, so that it just looked like bedding or curtains or something for home. Someone is always lugging stuff down the streets these days; sometimes their worldly belongings, sometimes their wares, sometimes other, much worse things. Everyone is used to doing everything themselves, without help. Everyone like us, anyway. Gifty appreciated it when it arrived home, ignoring the sweat of my pits as I dragged it from the car to the house, and planting one on me at the front door.

Today it's filled halfway and I help her lower her naked body into it slowly, hand on hand, a bicep engaged to account for the extra weight of her bump. Seated, she grits her teeth for a long moment, allowing the crashing wave of a contraction to overwhelm her and then pass. I drop down to the floor behind the pool, my buttocks hitting the wood too hard, causing a thump that makes us both jolt a little. But other than that, I have tried to make it calm in here, with candles and a soft, wordless jazz playlist already swinging through to the third song.

We practised this more times than I can count. The seating, the music, the ambience and my position behind her, supportive and ready. A practiced readiness, anyway. I still don't know if I've prepared enough; if I can be the mother a child needs. My own is all business, to the point that if she found out what we were really doing here, in this little house on the corner, she'd tell me I needed prayer and sense, in that order. She never wanted to be a grandmother; something she made abundantly clear throughout my childhood. And there aren't really grandparents for the DeValued, anyway, not anymore. The Establishment put an end to that – to generational wealth, whether financial or historical or intellectual.

Gifty screams and I scream on the inside. I've already soundproofed the house for this very moment. It does not feel as beautiful as I was expecting; more earth-shattering and real. But I feel very present and necessary to what's going on. Gifty is gorgeous, she always is no matter what is happening. We squeeze hands and she splashes water on the hardwood floors. Neither of us cares. I am hers and she is mine. We spend long minutes in suspended animation like this, squeezed, floating, pushing and pulling until it's really time. She orders me to climb into a new position, inside the pool now. I rush around her, forgetting to remove my jeans and reveal the shorts I've been wearing underneath them all day, in preparation for this moment. None of it matters now, anyway. I wade in, kneeling in front of her, ready to receive the baby as if it might fly out and into my arms, awaiting my embrace. And then miraculously, it happens.

A wet bubble is my first thought. And a body too small to survive alone, slipping into the water for a second, to be washed and then brought to the surface by my hands. A beautiful, soft, delicate and difficult thing to behold. Its simple features represent something so complex that it will take me years to truly understand.

For now, I only have an unabashed love to offer him – he, as he appears to me now anyway – and transportation to a new, safer life. His eyes are already open, and his mouth too, chest rising and falling quickly, his first breaths of the air. But he is not crying yet, has not made a sound, in fact. It is as if he already knows what his siren song will mean when he finally releases it. Gifty has flopped back down, resting on the edge of the pool for a moment, her head tipped all the way back so that I can see the crook of her neck, the smooth, roundness of her chin, that she always jokes is not a chin at all, 'only a suggestion'. She breathes heavy, as do I, holding our boy in my arms, unsure of how I am to carry on life now that I plan to never put him down. Suddenly Gifty is jutting forward, her upper body convulsing once more as the afterbirth is released and she completes her final act of bravery.

The next part is on me.

I stand slowly and squelch out of the pool, reaching for the cloth to wrap the baby up as I had been practising on watermelons for weeks, swaddling him safely. He is still an unnamed joy that we cannot take our time to sit with right now, at least not completely. There is work to do. I turn back around and Gifty is already sitting back up, twisting herself so that she can stand. She grabs at her dress, the fresh and dry one we had already put to one side for this part of the process. She throws it over her naked body, and pulls fresh underwear on slowly, the tenderness of her lower abdomen apparent but not a hindrance for her. She is magnificent. Too strong sometimes, I think, if there were such a thing. She turns now to our boy, placing a finger on his tiny chest, feeling it rise and fall under her touch.

Still no cry.

We exchange a look, all love, relief and a hint of concern. Though he is breathing, she checks that his airways are clear, she listens to the sound of his heart, she squeezes his tiny fingers – the one hand I left out of the swaddle to complete this check – and he squeezes back. Then she nods and opens up her arms. I pass him to her carefully, feeling the wrench at my heart as soon as we break contact. But there is no time to dwell.

His cry comes at the door, when we have the last of our things ready to go, when we are standing in the doorway saying goodbye to our first home together. His cry comes first as a small squeak, and then a longer curdle of sound that grows larger and louder by the second. His cry is an alarm, a signal for anyone close by to pay attention, to see that something different is happening at our home.

His cry is filled with anguish at having to leave his first home inside Gifty, and now the second one shortly after that.

His cry is for us. And it's the reason we walk quickly but calmly towards the car. Gifty is wearing her huge mac, the one she has been seen in all summer so that it doesn't look out of the ordinary now. Our boy is against her chest underneath the coat's soft cotton, and she climbs into the back, and then buckles him safely into the car seat that Jack's husband bought for us – careful to deliver it at night, hiding his face, so there was no identifying him or Jack's connection to us.

Gifty pulls a baseball cap from between the seats and puts it on, covering her hair and eyes. She pulls the mesh cover down on the window and turns towards our boy. I am already in the driver's seat, starting the car and backing it out of the driveway. My own cap has been reclaimed, but I don't wear it as low as Gifty, so that I can look out for any faces at each of the surrounding windows, maybe watching us curiously, unable for the first time, to see into the back of our car. Then I spot them, the couple I expected, the wife at least. She lives across the road and already has a phone to her ear and talking to someone, her thin mouth moving in distasteful haste, as she gives our licence plate number or a description of us, that we seem to be doing something suspicious, that maybe she heard a sound she didn't like and she thinks They should investigate because what if there is a baby in the wrong hands; in our hands?

I might have imagined it though. I am already speeding down a motorway towards our next destination. I am already thinking about the place I stashed the other licence plates, and the multiple stops we'll need to make after that, before we make it to the ferry and cross over, away from this place, finally.

We should have left a long time ago. We know this. We should have gone when They told us what we should and shouldn't be doing with our lives, our loves, our beliefs. When They began trying to rewrite history and dictate our futures. We should have left when our bodies became commodities. But we did not know that there could be anything else, any other way to live. It took possibility to move us, to get us to take a real risk and a chance at something more. The possibility of our boy. That he might become something more than either of us could ever imagine for ourselves. That's all the motivation I need. All the fight that has been suppressed in me my whole life is finally coming out in waves, and it's a fight to the death if it has to be. As long as our boy survives.

I look at him now, sleeping soundly. The melanin in his skin warms me, an almost perfect match to Gifty's, a shade lighter than my own. In the rearview mirror I see only my little family, and then glance back at the road stretched out ahead of us. I ignore the flashing lights that are getting bigger in my side mirrors. The turning is up ahead. It is sharp but I am confident that we can make it.

We will make it.

Potatoes

he tells me I say it funny
mimics my intonation of the letters
each one drawn out
of its written shell the phonemes
leap from his mouth to my ear
I want to hear it
again and again and again
po-tay-tohs in his voice
offering my dictation of *po*
rather than *puh* and after
describes me as
a-daw-ruh-buhl emphasis
on the *a* rather than *uh*
tickles his throat with the singular
as we are two nouns walking
this planet in search of another
who might listen to the days
and want to sound them out together

Dale Booton (he/him)
@dalebooton

Cool Britannia (extract)

I want to dance topless with you in a club with sticky floors and questionable furniture; these four walls won't know what hit them. Robbie Williams is singing to me, 'Millennium' through the sound speakers, like a voice from above, as if Jesus had a Geordie accent. Bouncing around in your Fila shell suit, curtains in your hair, stuck to your forehead pretending it's Blur and not Celine you listen to.

Stanley Iyanu (he/him)
@stanley_writes

QUEERPHORIA IN COMMUNITY

On wearing pink 'don't doubt yourself' nighties with other butches

We don't do star signs in this house. We do lesbians. We do trans mascs. We do washing up before bed, weekly sheet changes and separate shelves. We do compartments in the fridge and decanted pasta boxes. We do rock collections, queer bookshop poems, little black books and special interests. We do celebrating stims, safe spaces and queer family Christmas. We do late-night friend collections, sofas offered up, dogs tolerated. We do 'I'll put my shit on the shelf, you're safe.' We do 'Stay as long as you need.' We do it well. We do it queer. We do it proudly.

Em Prendergast (they/them)
@Emprenempren

A Rainbow on Commercial Street

I grew up in a remote
Scottish archipelago,
Going to school
Under Section 28
And its aftermath.
If you were queer,
You didn't tell anyone,
Especially if you already
Didn't fit in.

In 2022, Shetland held
Its first ever Pride celebration.
In 2024, I came home to attend
For the first time. It rained,
But we marched anyway,
Brightening up the dreich streets
Of Lerwick as we went,
Not a care in the world.
It felt so good to do, and for me
That was true queer joy – colour
In spite of everything.

Hannah Nicholson (she/her/shö)
& @tooriekep

Laura Kay (she/her) is a writer and editor living in London. Her journalism and personal essays have been published in *The Guardian*, *Diva Magazine* and *Stylist*, among others. Her debut novel, *The Split*, was published by Quercus in March 2021. She has since published three further novels in the UK, the US and other territories, with a fifth coming in 2027.

Laurakayauthor.co.uk

@lauraekay

The below work contains discussion of grief and loss.

This Might Be the Place

The young man at the front desk insists on helping Ellen with her small suitcase. They take the lift up to the eleventh floor and, although it is heavy, he holds her bag the entire time rather than placing it on the floor. The man, whose name tag reads *Simon*, glances nervously at Ellen. She senses that he wants to ask if she is OK, if she is sure she is in the right place. Ellen smiles at Simon in a way she hopes will reassure him; she knows exactly what she is doing.

When they get to room 119, at the end of a long corridor, Ellen manages to wrangle the suitcase from him and, after a moment of fumbling, finds a £5 note to give him for his trouble. Simon stares at the money, as though not quite sure what to do with it, before tucking it carefully into the pocket of his high-waisted trousers.

'You will let me know if you need anything?' says Simon, clearly reluctant to leave her.

'Absolutely,' Ellen says. 'You're very kind.'

'This should be one of our quieter rooms.' He frowns. 'Although it's a Friday night, so you might still be able to hear the bar downstairs; we're open very late.'

'Fabulous,' Ellen says. 'I intend to be out very late.'

She winks at him, and Simon looks even more alarmed.

'I'm working tonight,' he says, 'so…'

'So I'll be sure to say hello,' Ellen says, 'and to let you know that I'm alright.'

'Right,' says Simon, a flicker of relief in his eyes. 'Yes, OK.'

Ellen waves him off, closes the door behind her and sighs heavily. She had not counted on having a teenage babysitter for the night. He reminds her of her grandson, Theo. Although Theo, nineteen and studying at art school, has no idea where she is tonight. Has no idea that Ellen is about to drink a cocktail-in-a-can in a hotel just a couple of miles down the road from his East London house share.

Ellen decants the premixed old fashioned into a tumbler she finds in the bathroom. The hotel room is wonderful, exactly what she'd hoped for when she'd booked it. Floor-to-ceiling windows, wooden floors and exposed brick. A big, beautiful mirror taking up half a wall, a record player that does not play records but to which you have to connect your phone. It is minimal and self-conscious and cool. There are no knick-knacks, no crocheted cushion cases, no photographs of pets or grandchildren. It is a blank slate, void of personality. It is Ellen's alone to occupy.

Ellen heaves her suitcase onto the colossal bed and unzips it. She has packed only one outfit, so that she cannot spend hours deliberating and ultimately change her mind about the whole thing. This evening is her chance. She knows that if she does not go through with it now, she will never go through with it – God knows she does not have all that much time left.

With nail scissors, Ellen carefully cuts the tags out of a crisp white shirt, still folded in tissue paper from the online shop where she'd bought it. She pulls on her old-faithful smart black trousers – now seemingly in fashion – and her black leather slip-on shoes. Ellen despairs at these, wiggling her sore feet around, knowing they are ruining her 'look', but they are non-negotiable; they are the only pair of shoes her arthritic feet can bear these days.

Ellen runs a comb through her hair, white and thinning but cut stylishly, or so she hopes. Despite changing texture, it has still not lost its curls. She removes a pearl stud earring from each ear and replaces them with small gold hoops. Over the top of her new shirt she pulls on a knitted vest, lilac. She'd spotted it in a shop in town with her friend Pauline, and Pauline had said, 'For goodness' sake, Ellen, stop fannying about and just buy it, it doesn't matter if your arms get cold,' and so she had stopped fannying about and just bought it.

Ellen drinks the rest of her old fashioned quickly. It is, as she'd feared, too sweet, but it is perfectly strong, which is the important thing. She checks her wristwatch. It is 5:00 pm, and it is now or never.

A familiar wave of homesickness hits her as she checks her handbag for her keys, her medication, her mobile phone and her paperback. Ellen is still not accustomed to her own company, even after all this time. It is like a reflex, in that moment before leaving one space and entering another, to turn and say, 'Ready?'

They used to face the world together.

Ellen takes a deep breath, steels herself and steps out into the corridor. After a quick descent in the lift, she waves at Simon on reception as she exits the hotel and he waves back. He says something to her as she passes that she doesn't quite catch, but that small moment of connection makes her feel a little better and that flutter returns, of hope, of possibility.

Ellen has planned the twenty-minute walk meticulously, studying Google Maps so conscientiously that she could probably make the journey with her eyes closed. She walks slowly along the busy streets of Hackney, where people are spilling out from pubs and bars, lounging on the pavement and laughing. She tries to absorb some of their energy, to feel carefree, to feel like an entire life is ahead of her just waiting for her to take it and run.

The newsagent is exactly where it had promised to be. There is, thankfully, a small queue inside, which allows Ellen to rehearse her lines in her head while she waits. When it is her turn, Ellen shuffles forward. The man behind the till sips from a canned energy drink and nods at her.

'Hello,' Ellen says, 'please may I have twenty…' Twenty, that's right, because you cannot buy ten anymore. 'Twenty Marlboro Lights.'

Ellen has not smoked a cigarette for over forty years and half expects to be stopped from buying them but, of course, the man simply nods his head and spins around in his chair to take a packet from the cabinet behind him.

'And,' Ellen remembers, 'one lighter, please.'

The man taps the top of a plastic display, indicating that Ellen should choose one. After a moment's hesitation she selects a colourful lighter depicting a black cat peeking around a potted plant.

'Seventeen pounds eighty,' the man says, tapping the numbers into the card machine and spinning it around for Ellen.

She is not at all surprised by the exorbitant price on account of her recent extensive research. She taps her card on the top of the machine and sweeps her cigarettes into her handbag triumphantly.

'Thank you very much,' Ellen says.

'Next,' the man says.

The only thing left to do, Ellen supposes, hovering outside the newsagent across the road from her destination, is to go inside.

It does not look like much, no signage even, but there are signs of life inside – flickering candlelight, the hum of conversation and soft music seeping out onto the street.

Ellen has just geared herself up to open the front door when suddenly two people come stumbling out, howling with laughter, almost knocking into her.

'Oh my god,' one of them exclaims, gently placing a hand on Ellen's shoulder, steadying her. 'I'm so sorry.'

'No, no, that's OK,' Ellen says, rattled but already pulling herself together, bracing herself again.

'Are you going in?' the other says, and after a brief hesitation, Ellen nods. They hold the door open for her, smiling, and that's it, she walks right in.

It isn't busy, Ellen is pleased to see. There are free tables, the noise isn't overwhelming. There are still people drinking coffee, spill overs from a day spent working on their laptops.

'Hi,' a willowy woman says to Ellen, leaning against the bar, fanning herself with a menu. 'You alright?'

'Yes,' Ellen says. 'I am alright. Are you?'

The woman smiles. She has bright white teeth that are a little crooked. It is utterly charming, Ellen thinks. A lovely smile.

'I am,' the woman says, 'thank you. Tired but alright. Table for...'

'Oh,' Ellen says, 'um, just for one, please, if that's...'

'This way,' the woman says, taking off and gesturing for Ellen to follow. They pause in the main bar.

'Inside or outside?' the woman says.

'Outside, please.'

She follows the woman out of the sliding glass doors and takes a seat at the back of the patio, facing towards the warm glow of the bar inside. Each of the tables, including her own, has a flickering tea light on it. Fairy lights and mirrors adorn the white brick walls separating them from the neighbours' gardens.

Without asking, the woman adjusts the table so it is closer to Ellen and pulls a remote from her pocket. She presses a button to make a heat lamp glow bright red above them.

'Would you like a minute to take a look at the menu?' the woman says, handing over a small sheet of paper, her makeshift fan.

'Um…' Ellen takes the menu and realises her hand is shaking. She quickly puts it down on the table.

'Wine?' the woman asks. If she has noticed the shaking hand, she does not give it away, for which Ellen is very grateful.

'Oh, yes,' Ellen says. 'Wine.'

'Red, white, orange? Something fizzy?'

'Fizzy, please,' Ellen says.

The woman smiles. 'Yeah,' she says, 'why not? Celebrate it being Friday.'

'That's right,' Ellen agrees. 'A celebration.'

A few minutes later, the woman returns with something cloudy in a tall glass and a small bowl of crisps which Ellen can't quite identify the flavour of.

There are two other people on the patio, women Ellen supposes might be in their thirties, sitting opposite each other with glasses of red wine and bowls of olives. They are gossiping furiously, taking it in turns to drop their jaws in delighted horror. They pay no attention to Ellen, which is perfect, exactly what she'd hoped for.

Ellen pulls her paperback out of her handbag and places it on the table with no intention of reading it. It is company, though, should she need it. Next, she pulls out her new packet of cigarettes and the lighter. She unwraps them from the plastic and taps the cigarette box lightly with her fingertips, a muscle memory. She selects a cigarette carefully from the pack and places it between her lips. She sometimes has trouble with her hands, her joints sore, her grip looser than it used to be, but she does not struggle with the lighter – it roars to life the very first time she runs her thumb over it. The tip of her cigarette crackles and she inhales deeply. She closes her eyes at the head rush and it is like the flutter of a time machine. She is momentarily a version of herself she had almost forgotten existed.

Ellen smokes her cigarette slowly and with great pleasure. She half wondered if she might have gone off it, lost the taste for them after such a long abstention, but no, it turns out to be one of those loves that lasts a lifetime. She sips the fizz, the sharp bubbles mingling with the nicotine to soften her senses. Her shoulders drop; her jaw unclenches. She watches as one of the gossiping women rises from her seat, asks if the other wants the same again and then, before heading inside to the bar, dips her head and kisses her on the lips. The two women smile into each other, just for a moment, before breaking apart. The warmth in Ellen spreads deeper, to be witness to the gesture, such sweetness displayed so casually.

The bar fills up slowly. Nervous pairs on early dates; established couples, tired but committed to their weekly date night; squealing, shrieking groups who descend on free tables like buzzards, grabbing chairs, rearranging the space to suit them.

Ellen orders another glass of wine and smokes another cigarette. The second does not contain the perfect alchemy of the first but is enjoyable all the same. It is something to do with her hands, a reason for her being there in that particular garden in London out of all the places in the world she could be.

Despite the growing busyness of the bar, Ellen's corner of the patio remains empty, and she begins to wonder if it is her, if she is the off-putting thing. She pulls at her knitted vest, adjusting the way it sits on her stomach. She crosses her feet at the ankles, horribly aware all over again of her shoes, as if they might be the thing keeping her isolated from everybody else.

But what did she expect? Ellen cannot bring herself to answer that question, not really. Her compulsion to be here, in this very spot, came from a place more granular, more visceral than she could put into words. She had read an article about this bar online and at the bottom it listed the address, and Ellen had blinked, taken her glasses off and cleaned them on the bottom of her jumper before reading it again. It had not been a mistake on account of the smudge of a fingerprint. It was right there, clear as day.

Ellen did not usually believe in signs from the universe. God only knows what the universe was up to if it had designs for her life. But in this case, Ellen could not help but wonder if, just this once, this was a message for her that she must not ignore. She booked her hotel the same day, and her trains. She made excuses to her family and invented an old friend she was visiting for the weekend. It had all been so easy. Ellen does not lead a particularly interesting life, and therefore people are not particularly interested. It was marvellous, she thought, rather than depressing, to be able to disappear so easily.

'Excuse me?'

Ellen looks up to see a twenty-something-year-old woman, dark haired, dressed all in black, hovering above her.

'Are you using both of these tables?'

The woman gestures between Ellen and the table tucked in the corner beside her on which the tealight has gone out.

'Oh, no,' Ellen says. 'It's just me.'

'Amazing,' the woman says, and Ellen smiles, expecting her to drag the table away to some other, livelier corner of the bar.

'It's free,' the woman yells to her friends, who are standing in the doorway to the patio. 'Come on.'

Ellen is suddenly surrounded by people – six of them. They do not pull the free table further away. Instead they push the tables closer together, assembling chairs so they can all squeeze in. One insists they're fine just to lean against the wall behind, happier to stand.

'Oh, I love that book,' declares the woman who sits down next to Ellen, jabbing at her paperback copy of *Bluets*. 'Are you enjoying it?'

'Yes!' Ellen says. She touches the cover tentatively, as if it might remind her of the content of the few pages she'd read.

'I'm Marie,' the woman says, and she holds out her hand to shake Ellen's.

'I'm Ellen,' she says, taking Marie's hand. Marie squeezes it briefly, tightly. Ellen wonders if she reminds her of someone she's fond of – her grandmother, perhaps.

'I'm Sabina,' says the woman sitting opposite. 'I love your jumper, Ellen.'

'Oh, really?' Ellen says. 'I wasn't sure if it was a bit… I wasn't sure if it was very me.'

She blushes, embarrassed at the vulnerability. This woman is just being polite, Ellen thinks. But Sabina takes Ellen seriously, considers her lilac jumper sincerely.

'It *is* you,' she says decisively. 'You look fantastic.'

'Right,' Ellen says. 'Gosh.'

'Sorry for barging in on your evening,' says the person leaning on the wall. 'Honestly, we'll try our best not to disturb you too much.'

'You're not disturbing me,' Ellen says. 'Or, I mean, I'm happy to be disturbed. It was starting to get rather lonely out here.'

A chorus of high-pitched noise erupts, within which Ellen can just about make out the words 'no', 'I can't' and 'bless', each platitude worse than the last. Without asking, one of the women pouring wine from a pink bottle tops up Ellen's glass, and they all start chattering amiably among themselves. A few of them produce brightly coloured vapes from their pockets or light up cigarettes, so Ellen does the same.

'Cute lighter,' Marie says.

'Thank you.' Ellen beams.

Ellen sits back and listens to the women chat. She does not feel compelled to join in nor does she think they're keen to exclude her. Mostly, the group are furiously discussing someone named Blake who, after a while, Ellen ascertains is Marie's ex-girlfriend and is not to be trusted under any circumstances. Marie was unceremoniously dumped last week because Blake did not want a relationship, and yet Marie cannot help but sense there is already someone else. She has no evidence, but her feelings are enough to elicit absolute affirmation from her friends.

They talk at a hundred miles an hour, all of them chipping in and yelling over the top of one another. Ellen gets lost a few times, but they all seem to be keeping up and having a lovely time doing so. That is, apart from the person leaning against the wall, whose name is Nicky. Nicky's faint smile remains inscrutable, and they do not offer an opinion on Blake. Occasionally, they bite the inside of their cheek, frown a little, check their phone like it's a nervous tic. A natural introvert, Ellen thinks, just like her.

'What do you think, Ellen?'

Ellen turns to Sabina, who is rolling a cigarette and looking at her expectantly.

'Yeah,' one of the others adds, 'you must have come across some right shitbags in your time.' She pauses. 'No offence.'

'Yeah, what's going on with you? Do you have a partner?' Sabina asks.

'Sab,' Marie says, warning in her voice. 'That's rude to ask.'

'It's not rude to ask, is it? Is it, Ellen? Oh my god, sorry. I didn't mean to offend you. Are you offended?'

It's a lot of questions all at once. Ellen takes a sip of her wine while she decides where to begin. She shifts in her chair uncomfortably.

'I'm not offended,' Ellen says, and Sab looks relieved. *See?* She mouths at Marie, who rolls her eyes.

'I don't have a… a partner,' Ellen continues. 'Although I was married once.'

'Oh no, did she die?' Sab says. She reaches across the table as if to take Ellen's hand, and Marie slaps it. A chorus of 'oh my gods' from around the table. Ellen can't help but laugh.

'*He* died, yes,' Ellen says. 'He died.'

Everyone falls quiet. It still sounds ever so strange. That he could be one of those people who has died.

'We used to live here,' Ellen explains, saving the women from having to think of something to say next.

'Here?' Marie says. 'Like, here in London?'

'No,' Ellen says, 'like, here.' She presses her finger into the table in front of her. 'Here in the flat above this bar.' She points to the windows above them. 'It used to be a little shop.'

'No way,' Sabina says. 'That's insane.' She glances up, following Ellen's gaze, as if expecting to see Ellen and her husband in the window, looking down at them. 'Do you miss him? Is that why you're here?'

'Every day,' Ellen says. 'I suppose that's partly why I'm here, yes.'

And it's true, in a way. Laurence would have been delighted at the thought of Ellen putting herself out there for once. Truly the life and soul of any party, he had been the person who dragged Ellen along throughout her entire life, since she was seventeen years old, in fact. And God, was she happy to be dragged. She let him be big enough for them both, and he never made her feel like less. She let him have all the personality, the quirks, the foibles, and in return he let her be. Two years ago, he was suddenly gone and all Ellen had left was herself.

'I've never been anywhere like this before,' Ellen says. 'That's why I came tonight, when I found out about it. It felt… serendipitous.'

'You've never been to a bar?' Sabina's eyes widen.

'A *queer* bar,' Marie hisses. And then she glances at Ellen. 'Right?'

Ellen nods, happy for the words to be in someone else's mouth.

'And I thought it was about time,' Ellen says. 'Because I've also wanted to… I've always been…'

Reverent quiet around the table, giving Ellen space to finish her sentence.

'I've always found myself in places that aren't for me. And I'd hoped this might be… that this might be the place that is. And that it wouldn't be, you know…'

'Too late,' Sabina says matter-of-factly, finishing Ellen's sentence for her.

'Exactly.'

'No way,' Sabina says. 'How can it be too late? Ninety is the new fifty.'

'I'm actually only eighty-five, so…'

'So amazing,' Sabina says, shaking her head. 'I hope I'm as brave as you when I'm old.'

She raises her glass, and Ellen taps it lightly with her own. And that's the end of that. The group move back onto the subject of Blake the Backstabber, none the wiser that Ellen has just come out to them, that she has just come out for the first time.

Ellen makes her way to the bathroom feeling slightly unsteady on her feet but otherwise in excellent spirits. The gaggle of people waiting for the single cubicle let her skip the queue, and Ellen stands in front of the mirror, her hands gripping as tightly as they can onto the sink to steady herself. Like the rest of the bar, the bathroom is lit only by candles. It takes a moment for Ellen's eyes to adjust to her reflection. She is drunk, sure, but she feels radiant, distinctly aware of her own devastating beauty. Her blue eyes are sparkling.

She glances up toward the ceiling, imagining the bathroom directly above. How many times she had bathed, howling with laughter, while Laurence perched on the edge of the tub regaling her with stories. How many times water from that very tub had leaked right through this ceiling. She looks for evidence of their previous existence, but it has been replastered, painted deep blue.

Ellen runs the tap, splashing cold water on her wrists, her purple veins protruding alarmingly, and when she looks up she half expects him to be there, standing behind her.

'What am I doing?' Ellen whispers.

She does not await an answer; she knows he is not there. It is her own voice, loud and clear, that tells her to get back out there, to not miss another second stuck inside her own head.

I am a queer person in a queer bar, and I am not to hide away.

On exiting the bathroom, she is slow and careful in her movements, aware that one wrong step will almost certainly result in a fall. A person in a crop top wordlessly holds out their arm and escorts her back to her table. Ellen slips right back into her seat. Someone has poured a glass of water for her, the bowl of crisps has been replenished, and she grabs a handful gratefully. Ellen yawns, unable to stifle it and unable to remember when she was last out this late, when she was last awake this late.

Is this what she's been missing while she was sleeping? All the nights she could have spent in places like this, being nothing but herself.

Ellen tunes back into the conversation around the table and realises the tone has changed, the giddiness gone and replaced by something rather more charged.

'I don't really understand,' Marie is saying in a tone that suggests she absolutely understands. 'Explain it to me again.'

'I'm just saying what I've heard,' one of the other women replies. 'Don't shoot the messenger. I thought you said you already knew that Blake was seeing someone else?'

'I said I sensed it,' Marie says, her voice increasingly high pitched. 'I am always saying stupid stuff like that! Oh my god, though, this is real?'

Ellen notices that Nicky, no longer leaning against the wall but shuffling uncomfortably from foot to foot, looks like they want to crawl out of their skin. After a moment, Nicky picks up their drink, downs it, turns on their heel and slips past the busy tables and out through the bar without saying a word.

Marie frowns, confused, and then her face falls as she understands.

'It's… not. It's not Nicky?'

She addresses the other members of the group, who grimace, looking down at the table or up at the sky. Anywhere but directly at Marie.

'How could they… when they know I'm…'

Marie bursts into tears, and Ellen quietly begins to gather her things. Laurence may have known how to be the life and soul of the party, but Ellen has always known exactly when to call it a night.

It is only when she is standing and stabbing at her phone screen, trying to order a black cab, that the women notice she is leaving. They do not try to persuade her to stay but nor do they seem relieved by her departure.

They hug her, each of them in turn. They apologise for the change in atmosphere, they assure her they're usually more fun, they thank her for letting them intrude on her evening. Ellen cannot begin to tell them how delighted she is that they did. So she doesn't, she simply tells them to take care and that she will get home safely. She starts to pull out cash from her purse to pay for her drinks and they practically push her away to stop her.

'It's on us,' Sabina says. She leans in to hug Ellen once more and murmurs quietly in her ear, so the others cannot hear, 'You'll check on Nicky, yeah?'

Ellen gives Sabina's shoulders a little squeeze. 'Yes,' she

whispers back. It is a thrill to be included, even in this. It is, after all, something she had read up on ahead of this evening: *lesbian drama*.

Ellen finds Nicky facing a wall, smoking, round the corner from the bar. When they see Ellen they wipe at their eyes furiously.

'Are you OK, lovie?' Ellen asks.

'Please don't be nice to me,' Nicky's voice cracks. 'I don't deserve it.'

'Oh, now,' Ellen says.

'It's true.'

'Did you murder someone?' Ellen says. 'This Blake character?'

Nicky is so surprised that they laugh.

'No,' they say. 'I didn't murder anyone.'

'Well then,' Ellen says, 'it's not so bad.'

'I think I love her,' Nicky says after a moment, 'so it's actually worse.'

'Oh dear,' Ellen says. 'Oh dear, that is worse.'

'My friends hate me.' Nicky's bottom lip begins to wobble again.

'Maybe just for tonight,' Ellen says. 'But that's OK, because you have lots of nights ahead of you. They'll love you again.'

Nicky looks at her hopelessly.

'This feels catastrophic,' Ellen says, 'but it's just a blip.'

It all is, she thinks. We all are.

'Are you alright?' Nicky says. 'It sounds like… Well, it sounds like it was a pretty big night for you. Sorry about Sab. She means well.'

'Oh, I'm alright,' Ellen says. 'It's just… I suppose I feel sad for what might have been had I been different, braver, I suppose. I feel sad about everything I might have had, or might have experienced, or might have…'

She cannot bring herself to say *loved*. She had loved her husband, she loved him still.

'But you're right here,' Nicky says, frowning. 'It's all happening now. Don't miss it by wishing there was more of it.'

Ellen is momentarily floored. She cannot even begin to think of all the things she might have accidentally missed by wishing for more.

'How did you get to be so wise?' Ellen asks as she watches Nicky stub out their cigarette under the heel of their shoe.

'Well,' Nicky says, 'I'm *quite* high.'

Ellen's taxi pulls up beside them.

'You get home safe,' Nicky says.

'And you. It will all be fine.'

Nicky nods, and Ellen can tell they do not believe her. Nicky leans forward and kisses Ellen on the cheek. They smell of citrus and cigarettes. Nicky lingers there, rests the side of their head against Ellen's for a moment before pulling away, and when they do, Ellen is not surprised to find she is crying too. Three drinks, Laurence always said, three drinks and she's gone.

Nicky gently wipes Ellen's cheek with their thumb

'You're a beautiful person, Ellen,' Nicky says. Ellen doesn't know what to say, so she does not say anything. She lets Nicky open the door of the car for her and she climbs inside.

Just before the cab pulls off, Nicky gestures for Ellen to open the window.

'Where are you?' Nicky asks urgently, like this is vital information they need Ellen to remember, as though they could sense it was already slipping away. 'Come on. What did I just say?'

'I'm right here!' Ellen says as the car pulls away. 'I'm right here, and I can't miss it. It's happening now.'

Remi Graves (they/them) is a poet and drummer. A former Barbican Young Poet, their work has been commissioned by St Paul's Cathedral, Barbican and BBC Radio 4. They have performed at Tate, Cheltenham Literature festival and more. Remi has led courses at The Poetry School and facilitates in schools and community spaces across London and the South East. Remi's debut pamphlet *with your chest* (2022) was published by fourteen poems. They have been selected for residencies with Jan Michalski Foundation and La Napoule Foundation/La Maison Baldwin. Remi is the winner of 2024 Prototype Prize (short form category). *coal* was published by Monitor Books in 2025.

@shadebutter

the orchestra of self-herding sheep

in the distance fifty-odd sheep
walk themselves across
the stretch of land between
insatiate golf course and lonely road

some limp some trot
some graze on the spot
the herd herds its shadows across the field
the shepherd nowhere to be seen

each sheep with its own bell
singing out over the intermittent din
of motor tarmac wheel:
atonal chord of collision

a call to gather
as day falls to its knees
song of bellwether bleats
the orchestra of self-herding sheep

air

the boi remembers their tech deck
    its static little plastic body

tiny wheels and optimistic grip tape
    with the right technique and poise

the deck becomes a kite
    has them freewheeling through the air

their body light as two small fingers
    skidding on a miniature rail

the world's obstacles shrunken to clearable size
    a height they could flex on, fly over

the boi remembers hardly landing any tricks
    the thrill of rehearsing themselves airborne

the body on the loose

Jenny Chamarette (they/them) is a London-based writer on art, nature and queer place. Shortlisted for the Nan Shepherd, Fitzcarraldo and Nature Chronicles prizes, they publish across independent presses, feminist film culture and artist-led projects. Their memoir *Q is for Garden* appears with Manchester University Press in 2026.

Jennychamarette.substack.com
jenny.chamarette
@jennychambles.bsky.social

Placeholding

No joy without grief. No fear without courage.

No *dys*phoria, no *eu*phoria.

No mud, no lotus. So said the architect of joy Thich Nhat Hanh. Without feeling across the full frame of sensation, there is no feeling at all. No *queerphoria*.

The suffix *-phoria* doesn't contain a mood of its own. It comes from the ancient Greek *pherein* – to bear or to carry. *Phoria* is to do with what we bag up. According to Ursula K Le Guin's Carrier Bag Theory of human evolution, technology's oldest form takes the shape of a container. Something to hold what we cannot eat, use or share in the moment. Tools, food, clothing, friendship, dancing, art: we carry them away and home them for later. We find recipients for our stores and our stories. Feelings are stories too – old ones we carry in our bellies.

Queerphoria is a bearer of queer sensation. It holds them all in its big, wide bag: good, bad, raging, ugly-crying. Whispering in the ear of the friend you love as they lose their shit at the burden of living out of sync with the dominant narrative. The quiet hubbub while you craft the banner and the badge. Grief, joy, hope, fury. They're all there, named or nameless, in queerphoria's carrier bag. The swishy tote with the good handles. The tiny clutch, the cross-strap, the copious rack, the binder, the packer.

We pack it in, us queers.

I say *us queers* as if it has always been easy for me to talk about the queer communities I love and who love me in return. It's a utopian ideal that queers *are* always a community. But of course, all the rips in the wider social fabric manifest themselves here and in dividing lines on the grander scale. Joining a community often involves a degree of fear: fear of exposure and vulnerability and not-enough and too-much. And, and, and.

As a queer of a *both, and* denomination (make of that what you will, but I haven't yet found a vessel big enough to contain me), I have spent a considerable amount of time trying to pretend I wasn't. In photographs of myself in my twenties there is the merest flicker of gender non-conformity beneath the femme-passing exterior. My fluidity wavered, and yet, of course, for those in the know the signs are not tricky to spot. Being *both, and* leaves its telltale marks. Like carrying things alone.

Queerphoria, the carrier bag of queer feeling, needs a place to hold itself. A place to hold feelings close and obliquely, in distraction and intimacy. A place for feeling queerly, while feeling queer. Not always joyful, but the joy comes, eventually. No mud, no lotus.

Here is my offering: three carrier bags for the holding of queer sentiment. Maybe that is all we can do, in the end – hold the place to sense the queer and remember it. Hold the space to tell our stories to one another. Stories of the places – the placeholders – where queer feeling grows.

Reading

I worry about how I'm read. I bring that fear of being seen and not seen everywhere – and even more so in queer spaces.

When I say I am – was – a *bad queer*, I mean it in the way Roxane Gay self-describes as a *bad feminist*. I do queer badly, half-hanging out of the squarely labelled box, with my soft ungenderedness and my current boredom with sex and my more-than-occasional preference for plants over humans.

Bad gays are a thing, of course: Huw Lemmey and Ben Miller's podcast and book, both bearing this title, itemise the famously cruel, narcissistic, violent, outrageous (usually white, male, cis-gendered) queers littering history. No one ever said queer meant *good*. But by *bad queer* I mean something more like *bad at being what I thought it was to be queer*. Bad at being joyfully in community with other queer people. Bad at letting go of trying to pass as straight or cis-gendered. Bad at feeling joy. Bad at shameless sex-having. Bad at being myself.

I've had the same cis-gendered male partner for seventeen years. What am I, then, if not a queer performing feebly at the task? I've posed this question to others with partners who identify differently: does it challenge your queerness if the one you spend your most intimately mundane moments with is largely oriented toward the opposite sex? I wish I had answers to what we do with love that falls in between. When the polarity looks like it might *not* be queer but the truth is anything but straight. I don't love my partner any less because we inhabit the messy blur between hetero and homo.

Living in the half-light has its own peculiar brand of dysphoria, though. I've never said I'm not queer. But it's still a lifetime of coming out, again and again.

No mud, no lotus.

The warm vitamin-gold fuzz of euphoria touched me in my bad place when my local bookshop launched an LGBTQIA+ book group in the autumn of 2019. The bookshop sits at the top of the high street, one point of a pentacle whose other prongs variously include a pub, a church, a railway station, a former cinema. The shop, with its pale-green exterior and three arch-framed windows populated by tic-tac-toe displays of recent releases, is one of the reasons I moved to this small pocket of southeast London. When the newly launched group announced its first read – James Baldwin's *Giovanni's Room* – that quiver of familiar-new and familiar-old coincided. A bookish place to be a bookish queer.

After an hour or two's back and forth about decaying rooms, Paris in the 1950s and the portrait of queer European whiteness that only a Black gay American intellectual could have drawn, I remember standing in the doorway. My wine-loosened bad queer confession tumbled out. My life in the half-light. And then: acceptance. Radiant, reassuringly undramatic.

Many of us live in the messy blur between hetero and homo, between boy and girl. In the both, and. *Queer* holds the space for what lies in between. Plenty of room for bad queers in communities capacious enough to hold them.

Trees

During the brief summer of 2020, Britain's population edged cautiously then riotously out of lockdown. They filled the parks of south London with sound systems, frisbee games, blankets, bunting and balloons, singing, football, shuttlecocks, dogs born to feed a hunger for love. Late-night bars allowed late-night drinkers. Groups danced in the last sun's last rays.

On one night like this, warm on the baked earth, a small group of queer folks gathered. We brought once-cold wine and wine gums and copies of another book: *Guapa* by Saleem Haddad. The evening light drew itself across the park. The shade of the wide oaks and limes left long outlines that we observed from a discreet distance. With toilet facilities inadequate to host the hundreds of people, trees had become urinals.

Animals of all kinds do it to mark territory. But a tree is not human-owned. Pissing upright feels gendered, qualified by the wanton brandishing of an instrument that only straight white cis-gendered men – and even then, only some – feel confident enough to wield in public. Without a penis, squatting by a tree is vulnerable. With the full package of patriarchal privilege, it's an act of scorn. But when I speak to queer dick-owning friends (attached, not detachable) they tell me that urinals are a nightmare, that the vulnerability of urinating next to someone whose homophobia might kill you is one of the daily burdens to be carried.

That was prior to the new nightmare era of bathroom policing, in which trans and intersex people have been deprived of the right to public sanitation. This is alarmingly analogous to the nineteenth-century exclusion of women from public spaces in Britain, when public conveniences were designed exclusively for dick-owners. Public pissing is political. But then, the trees know that.

Haddad's book has nothing to do with pissing or parks. In the world of the protagonist, everything is dust and urban sprawl in an unnamed Arab city, reeling in the aftermath of soft revolutions that promised so much and yet delivered only a tightening of military and authoritarian diktats. And yet, we absorb the book's thin sheaves of tree pulp into our sweating skins. Gulping piss-warm wine from plastic cups, we talk about pan-Arabism. We talk about sentimentality and its wildly different affiliations in British or North African or South Asian or Middle Eastern contexts. We talk about queer cultures of the night – how the twenty-first century bars in *Guapa* resemble the twentieth-century Parisian dives of *Giovanni's Room*, and how even there, in queer clubs hidden from sight, others are shrouded further still. The butches and lesbians, present but offstage, for Haddad and Baldwin alike.

We do all this in the deepening shadows of lindens and London planes. Then we pull out our phone torches and begin to tell the real stories. As alcohol grips our bladders, we slip past one another into bushes to gasp sweet relief. Back in the circle the stories come, about the subaltern of Britain, about the landlords who extort money from their migrant HMO tenants, threatening eviction on a whim, using unfamiliarity with the law and difficulties with spoken English as tools to exploit and manipulate. That was then, of course. Five years on and anti-migrant cruelty has risen so much higher above the waterline.

Listeners and speakers, our ring of bodies draw closer in the indigo darkness. We aren't the only ones in the park, but in our small, closed group there is enough safety, enough for now. We witness the stories as the trees witness us in their shadows.

So do the mosquitoes. Wrapped in a cloak of booze and testimonies, we forget our bare skins. The next day we are itching and red raw, welts of flesh bloody from scratching.

We gather up our stories, our dicks, our bushes, our full bladders, our tingling flesh. We hold them, we let them go. The trees witness all of us.

Speech

The full hit of the Sharpie doesn't come till I'm halfway through my task. Ink fumes diffuse over the quiet chatter, muffled by occasional laughter. Cool sunlight slants through the high windows on the second floor of this community space on the Greenwich peninsular, close to the river. The LGBTQ+ charity Queercircle has been running the venue since 2022, hosting events and gatherings across the arts, health and social action. It is spring 2025: a season of dashed hope, of unbridled transphobia and the UK government's persecution of the disabled and chronically ill.

The elliptical shapes strewn across the long table are cutouts from discarded cardboard boxes, painted over in white. More tree pulp, corrugated and glued, but this time refashioned from trash, for making, for shouting. Each cutout is a speech bubble, ready to adorn with a border in coloured marker, for letters to form in the wide oval at its centre. As we hunch over our designs, our felt-tips give voice to the rage, hope and joy of speaking out.

Anyone who has spent time in queer communities will recognise the overlap between queerness, disability and neurodivergence. There's quite a convergence of us in queer circles. When norms don't make sense – neither compulsory able-bodiedness nor neurotypical visions of the world – the same goes for binary codes of gender and sexuality. Inversely, it is hard to live in a world full of norms that oppose you without sustaining some collateral damage in the form of illness and pain.

In other words, queer worlds run slantwise, deviating from unspoken custom. Those worlds are also more expansive than the word *queer* alone suggests. I knew my own unnamed difference marked me from a young age: I just didn't know how. It's not surprising that I felt at odds with humanity. Late diagnosis in my forties has upended my bag of queer stories. I am not *just* queer. I am queer *and* autistic *and* ADHD.

Like Roxane Gay's bad feminist, I am an impure queer of conflicting parts. I am not collecting labels, though badges are a perfectly queer act of DIY protest-in-the-making. I use words to make sense of the world, but sometimes they don't hold. The queer craft of the speech bubble, for protests and demos, for photographs, for a place of joy and rage and hope, reminds me of the *and* in between each term. Queer and. Autistic and. ADHD and.

While gathering my thoughts in visible form, speech bubbles up from old places.

As a child, I rolled words round my jaw like boiled sweets. Words fell apart in my mouth because they were hard work. I repeated them out loud, over and over, a masticated word world that broke down on my palate, became songs, exhalations, drawn-out macaque squalls. The urge to speak fluently came at eight or nine months. By the age of three I'd taught myself to read. Language was hard to utter, but silence was harder. So I talked. I talked *a lot.*

The family myths about my cheerful monologues and bibliophilia I believed to be fabulations until my friends started having children. Then I noticed the one or two who spoke in sentences before they could walk. As tiny toddlers they sat quietly reading book after book – really reading, not just turning the pages. When excited they told me long strings of facts in anecdotal form. *And and and.* According to a 2017 systematic review that assembled existing studies on the subject, hyperlexia, the precocious ability to decode written language, is found in about six to twenty percent of autistic children, and sometimes neurotypical children too.[1]

The common assumption is that autism causes developmental delays, but sometimes the opposite is true. According to charities like the National Autistic Society, and in testimonies collected by the US-based Autistic Women and Non-Binary Network, early language acquisition, especially advanced vocabulary and grammar with a more limited understanding of reciprocal conversation and non-verbal cues, is an atypical but nonetheless real presentation of autism.[2] It's a perplexing condition. Spiky profiles and colour wheels describe complexly different spectrums of thinking, sensing, learning, yearning to be understood.

Speech bubbles up, repeats, sinks down into thought. Returns, ululates, rotates in the mouth. Sharp-sour one side, cloying-sweet the other.

At school no one else spoke to themselves. I was shocked by the quiet in the classroom during work times, but equally the erratic screams of children together at breaktimes left me confused and overwhelmed. When I got my words out fast or loud or clear enough my schoolmates mocked me. Vowels too short. Words too long. Too much copying. So I lengthened my estuary twang and shortened my glottal stop. When I wanted to repeat, I held my breath. For a while I lisped from braces buttressed against crowded teeth.

Speech bubbled up; I pressed it down tight. In case the wrong thing came out.

My northern parents loathed the estuarine accents rising through the walls of their suburban home. The voices of their children, the estate they lived on, the small outer-suburban sprawl just within London's biggest peripheral motorway: too many reminders of social difference. Deriding their children was a flood defence. They sneered when I dropped my Ts, refused to speak to me till I sounded every last syllable.

So I held my breath. I dropped sounds at school, picked them up at home. When speech bubbled up, I erected barriers to the flow.

Dammed without outlet, words went back inside again: a familiarity in a bewilderingly hostile place. Internal echolalia is commonly reported in autistic people, but when I turn to peer-reviewed research there is vanishingly little to describe it. How exactly would you identify internal voices that strip words down and recombine them so many times that meaning pours through them like the pink rose of a child's watering can? Lexical rhythms, *la-la* syllables store music for the future. Scores, chords, time signatures, hosts of vocal variations transform speech into song. Composition is made of repetitions and alternations. You could say that echolalia is music's first rhythm, its first lyric.

My friend A has a theory that all the paradigmatic shifts in culture and science are largely down to neurodivergent people of one form or another. Expert pattern recognisers, precociously talented at an early age, we struggle to adapt to the world around us, yet many of us create wondrous artefacts or polyphonic harmonies or extraordinary concepts.

Not all neurodivergent people. Let's not digress into the alienating territory of *the supercrip*, the disabled person imbued with superpowers that are somehow supposed to compensate for the cruelty of the ableist world around them. But still: neurodivergence and creativity are more than passing bedfellows. Queer neurodivergence and creativity make beautiful music together.

Speech bubbles, but instead of rising to the surface it becomes underwater patterns. I wish I had known sooner about echolalia and speech processing, how this is an important component of experience for many autistic people, how repetition leads to meaning.

Because it does, doesn't it?

Speech bubbles.

Speech *bubbles*.

You could say communication is my special subject: for four decades I have studied how others express themselves without falling into silence or its opposite, noise. I've observed stammers, stutters, tics and involuntary English fillers such as *er*, *like*, *you know*. In French: *bah*, *bref*, *fin*, *euh*; in German: *doch*, *naja*, *also*. I've learned to perfect volume, rhythm and speed to brake and accelerate over emotions big and small. Every word is orchestrated for the benefit of those with whom I am conversing. I learned how to mask as neurotypical years before I learned how to pass as straight. But then of course, passing only serves until it breaks you.

I watch how tales are told: how the impresario teller draws the audience into their world, puncturing the tension to catch a laugh. I don't tell stories that way, with a beginning and a hero's journey and a final climax. I wish I could. But I have learned the value of shaping speech, holding words together in little bubbles and bags and carriers of all descriptions. *And and and.* The queer poet Emily Dickinson's invitation is to *Tell all the truth but tell it slant — / Success in Circuit lies.* The circuit is the repetition.

Now I know the slant of truth is more like a queer neurodivergent gradient.

This is what drives me as a writer. It is a skill honed out of necessity.

Speech no longer bubbles up the way it used to. Tension holds it down. My speech bubbles live in a vacuum, where a scream emits from the throat but fails to takes hold in the air. There is no oxygen in the laws of psychic life. But there is noise. So much noise.

Mildly intoxicated by the Sharpie's fumes, by the slanted light of the high windows, I carve a border of wheels and inclines around the edges of my speech bubble. I fill the margins with scarlet and blue. Inside I write slogans about access and respect. In silence, without the force of air, the crafting circle voices the queer feelings of speech.

Speech bubbles. Seen, but not heard.

Three stories. Three carriers of queer community and dysphoria and acceptance. Fear, safety, home. Noise and living slant.

Though it's tempting to suggest it, the opposite of queerphoria is not queer*phobia*. It is stasis. Apathy. A failure to hold. It is what happens when we stop telling our stories, and when they cease to move us. When we stop gathering and sharing them in our tiny spaces that, when joined up, aren't so small after all. When we stop giving voice to all of ourselves: queer, nonbinary, migrant, disabled, neurodivergent, chronically ill. All the places where queerness comes out loud, in the quiet, or not at all.

Queerphoria is a placeholder word. A place to carry stories, queer in the absence of any other name. Queer because we hold their place, and because they move us forward. Belly by belly. Bag by bag.

Note

1. Ostrolenk, A., Forgeot d'Arc, B., Jelenic, P., Samson, F., & Mottron, L. (2017). 'Hyperlexia: Systematic review, neurocognitive modelling, and outcome.' *Neuroscience & Biobehavioral Reviews*, 79, 134–149. https://doi.org/10.1016/j.neubiorev.2017.04.029
2. For example, see Bridge, CL (2018) '"Actually, It's Crooked": Autism and Precocious Speech' Autistic Women and Nonbinary Network, awnnetwork.org/actually-its-crooked-autism-and-precocious-speech; Neurolaunch (2024), 'Early Talkers and Autism: Connection and Misconceptions Explained', https://neurolaunch.com/early-talker-autism/; National Autistic Society (2025), 'Signs that a child or adult may be autistic', https://www.autism.org.uk/advice-and-guidance/topics/diagnosis/before-diagnosis/signs-that-a-child-or-adult-may-be-autistic

Gerardo Sámano Córdova (he/him) is a writer and artist from Mexico City living in Brooklyn. He's currently Writer in Residence at Fordham University. He got his MFA from the Helen Zell Writers' Program at the University of Michigan. He has studied at Bread Loaf as a work/study scholar (2019) and fellow (2023) and at the Tin House Summer Workshop (2019). His second novel *Imps!* Is coming out in 2027 from Tin House Books.

Gerardosamanocordova.com

@hello.samanito

Family Meal

When the first sheep came ambling down the street, among the halting, bewildered cars, past the people scrambling to get their phones out to capture it, we were eating burgers on one of those sidewalk-invading park-style picnic tables hip restaurants loved. The restaurant had opened only a month ago, farm-to-table style, and Elisa had wanted to try it, as she wanted to try every new foodery before it became popular, corralling J, Seb and me to join her. The sheep walked toward us, unbothered as if the pavement had been a meadow, its wool tinted cotton-candy blue. Except for pigeons and a squirrel or two (and without counting the gazillion pet dogs and cats), animals were not seen in this city, certainly not farm animals, certainly not alive, certainly not colored electric blue and easygoing as if the city were its playground. Maybe the city had indeed been its playground once, when the city wasn't a city and sheep were wild.

'Bananas!' J said and pointed at Elisa. J who had shed the

letters of their name one by one, molting like a soft cicada, letting their wings dry. 'You were just...'

J shut up. We all knew what Elisa 'was just', Elisa was just finishing a story about her great great great aunt. An aunt who having inherited a sheep farm from her parents maintained it throughout her whole life. The woman grew old, old enough that she remembered her past much better than her present. She remembered the days of the drought when she lost all but eight of her sheep, remembered each of their names, Lorenza, Catalina, Cassiopeia, and so on, the fanciest names she could think of, names she wished she could've given herself. She remembered how she almost lost the farm, how she couldn't pay her bills, how the ewes were so famished they couldn't bear babies, and the memory was so much more present and dear than what she had now, the abundance in which she lived with more than a hundred sheep managed by relatives whose names she could never remember. She called all of them Niece. And because she found herself missing the scarcity days, she knew she was well old, the age when she could romanticize those tough days, days she had to ration her food or not eat at all so the sheep could eat instead, and how it was still a miracle that she and her eight sheep survived, the worst of times leading to the best of times when all her efforts to tend her farm began to bloom, and the grass grew again, and the sheep grew their wool again, and the ewes had their babies, and how wonderful that had been, the one-two punch of misery and success. And now she missed those days when it was possible to count the sheep with her hands, a finger for each and two thumbs for herself, the days when her relatives had been content to let her be in her faraway farm, her name conjuring something lesser than a ghost. In their lush family tree, she was a single leaf in a short, lonely branch, her farm and no one else's, her struggle and no one else's, hers and the sheep's.

And now she had too much: too many sheep, too many relatives with too many squealing children. She wished all would drown, but she wasn't so lucky and also not a murderer. She knit them sweaters instead. At night, when the stars shone as fluffy as her sheep, and the farm smelled most farmy, shit and damp wood and grass and wind, she nicked wool from the stores reserved for selling. She dyed the wool blue with boiling red cabbage, a November-sky blue. She knit chunky blue pullovers for all the relatives she called nieces, and when they thanked her but didn't wear them because they were too itchy or too warm or too cumbersome, she smiled and said *Just once, wear them for me just once, all together and we'll take a picture, a big family portrait that we can hang above the fireplace*, the fireplace she used to enjoy alone, just her and the fire whose crackling replaced her thoughts, the most pleasant of feelings to have one's thoughts be nothing but cracks, snaps and pops. What a good idea, her relatives said. The nieces gathered each other, wives and husbands and children, and set a camera on a tripod in front of her farm, on those grasses that had once refused to feed her sheep, and after they had placed her in the very center amidst a sea of blue wool sweaters, she the only one not wearing one, and after the camera snapped several times and her relatives had clapped and cheered, their sweaters began to untwine. Wool strands grew like tentacles, wrapping each of the nieces in blue wool cocoons, and after all the relatives ceased squirming, fighting, trying to survive, she sat down on the porch and drank coffee. Thirty wool cocoons lay on her lawn, now immobile, all human sizes and shapes, her nieces: wives and husbands and children. It took a week before the sweaters unraveled again, a week she diligently kept watch over the wool cocoons while crows crowed and thrushes sang, the days rose and set, and the mites and dust of the wind danced above them, sparkling across the moonlight. It was a peaceful week. But now the sweaters unraveled, their wool tentacles opening up like blooms to reveal, at the center of the cocoon, a moth for each of her relatives. The nieces had transformed into blue-hued moths that shook and, once accustomed to their new bodies, small and lithe, spread their wings and flew.

She kept eight of her sheep, her true family, the rest she drove away from the farm into a wooded area she imagined was the closest the county had to untouched nature. She hoped that in a few generations the offspring of these sheep might turn wild again, brutish and glorious, that is, of course, if any of them survived.

'Bananas,' J repeated as the blue-tinted sheep kept walking toward us, the impossible embodiment of Elisa's story.

'Totally bonkers,' the rest of us said.

Seb suggested it was a prank. 'How did you do it, Elisa?'

But Elisa had donc nothing, she swore. And how could she even if she had wanted to, how could Elisa have access to a sheep? Who of us had access to sheep? We were cityfolk. Devotees of this city where we'd found each other.

'What day is it?' Seb asked. 'Maybe it's a holiday where a sheep is let loose.' But we couldn't come up with a holiday that let a blue-tinted sheep loose in the city.

'Maybe you conjured it, Elisa,' J said. And though they were joking, we all thought it was possible. Why not? It was a Sunday lunch and together the four of us could conjure up anything.

A bike almost ran over the sheep. The rider cursed it, as if the sheep had planned to block him, as if the whole reason for the sheep's existence was to annoy him. We scoffed, as if we hadn't thought the sheep existed solely because of us too, because of Elisa's story.

'Poor sheep,' Seb said, taking a giant bite out of his burger.

'Seems good,' J said. 'Like it doesn't care.'

The sheep was just then passing by our sidewalk-blocking picnic table. 'Baa,' it said as if agreeing with J.

'See, it agrees,' J said.

Elisa squeezed out of her seat to pet it, but the sheep dodged her touch and continued on its way down the street. Down, down, until we couldn't see it anymore. The street quieted back into the rustling of trees, the zip of the cyclists, and the occasional hum of a car, not a roar, as if even the cars knew to keep it easy. We sipped our beers. It was the end of summer, the heat and humidity finally letting us breathe, a brief season of perfect weather before the cold, a season so brief we knew we wouldn't have another Sunday like this. We ate. Two more blue sheep trotted down the street. Unlike the other one, these ones seemed to be in a hurry, as if these two had lollygagged somewhere up the street and were now trying to catch their friend.

'So weird,' Seb said.

We nodded, watching the sheep shrink to blue dots down the street, listening to them baa, a string of baas so joyous we assumed they'd found their third, reunited. We had been lonely too, the four of us, before we found each other in this city.

'I have a story,' J said.

We leaned in. We had finished our burgers and were now picking at the last of our fries, those oddball overfried bits that pack the most flavor. We ordered another round of beers. Our lunch would end, Sunday would turn into Monday, soon Elisa's wife would have their baby and they'd move to their dream house in the country; J would finish their PhD, a star physicist recruited into faraway research centers, contributing to theories whose importance we understood only by the enthusiasm with which J tried to explain them; Seb would follow a man out of the city and continue chasing men all over the country, the way they made him feel gorgeous, a demi god playing at being human; and I would leave the next morning, a flight crossing oceans to start a new job, suitcases already packed. But we tried to pay no mind to the minutes ticking just out of earshot, a countdown that would scatter us away like sparkles flying out of a firework blast.

'Children from all over the city got an invitation to a birthday party,' J said.

'Is this a real story?' Seb asked.

'As real as any other story,' J said.

'I mean, did it really happen?'

'When I tell it, then it will have happened.'

'What does that even mean?'

'Just let them tell it,' Elisa said.

Seb stole a fry from my plate. J continued.

'So, children from all over the city got an invitation for a birthday party. It showed an address in a neighborhood with huge houses and said to meet at eleven in the morning. Because the invitation didn't say who the birthday party was for, some parents refused to bring their kids, but most parents did, assuming that once at the birthday party they would discover who they'd be celebrating. At eleven (some a bit early, others a bit late) kids and parents gathered outside the iron gate of a massive house. The kids were all about the same age, eight and nine, and some even knew each other, from school or their neighborhood, some were even relatives, cousins. A bouncy castle peeked above the high walls of the estate, and past the gates, on a sprawling lawn, they saw a row of carnival games with their lightbulbs already flashing. There were balloons all over, and delightful music, and a smell of treats so inviting, kids and parents alike shook in anticipation. Finally, once it seemed no more kids or parents would gather, a couple strode down from the house to the gate, all smiles and tidy hair. "Welcome," the couple said and opened the gates, but when the first parents tried to go in, the couple stopped them. "Sorry," they said, "the party is only for the kids." The parents were bewildered, disappointed, but their kids had already run inside, and they seemed so happy, and the couple so very respectable, the parents acquiesced and left, shouting after their kids they'd be back at nine, the time the invitation said the party ended.

'The kids ran, they screamed, they bounced, they played. Some banded together and roamed in packs, some enjoyed the birthday wonderland solo, careening from one unfinished game to the next, some stayed bouncing in the castle, believing that if they bounced high enough they would learn to fly, some sat in shaded spots to count grass blades and let ladybugs crawl on their arms. But no matter what they did, or however many times they changed distractions, they eventually tired, and like all tired, thirsty, hungry children they gathered at a long table laid out with plastic plates and cups and a birthday hat for each to wear. The kids sat down. They were exhausted. It seemed as if they had been playing for hours, days! But the sun was still high as if it were noon still. They waited and wondered when the grown-ups were going to start serving food. Where was the cake? And who was the birthday kid?

'"Is it you?" "Is it you?" "Is it you?" the kids asked each other. No one seemed to be the birthday kid. They just wanted to know who the kid was so that the kid could go fetch a grown-up and feed them, give them soda, some juice. They'd settle for water! Still they all kept themselves in their seats and wore the birthday hats because one of them had suggested that if they sat and wore the hats and behaved like good little children the grown-ups would come. They had to come. One of the kids started crying, the kid was so hungry. Another followed, and then another until the long table shaded by monumental trees shook with a wailing louder than any city siren. The kids cried for so long that when their tears dried and their snot was slurped and wiped on skirts, t-shirts and pants they all seemed a bit older, a bit taller, a bit more weathered. Still the sun had barely moved in the sky. '"I'm going inside" a kid said, and ran toward the house. The rest of the kids followed. The house was massive, with old rooms filled with wood and glass and leather books, and other rooms so modern they were blindingly white, with white fluffy couches and screens all over. But the kids were so hungry they bypassed all the video games and TVs and air hockey tables and board games and found the kitchen. There they found every kind of snack and soda, and the more they ate the more food they seemed to find, as if as soon as they closed a cupboard or one of the fridges (there were three!) they replenished. They stuffed themselves. A few puked. Then they napped.

'When they woke up, the sun was still out, still afternoon strong. Or had they napped so long it was already the next day? That couldn't be true, their parents would've picked them up. What was true was that they were all teenagers now, in varying degrees taller, lankier, plumper, zittier, and much more annoyed. "Who is the birthday kid?" they demanded, believing the birthday kid would know what was happening. But no one admitted to being the birthday kid. And so as teenagers they spread throughout the house to watch movies, to read, to make out, to hang out with friends, the pleasure of doing nothing together. They forgot they'd been kids a few hours ago.

'And when their t-shirts became too snug, and their waistbands cut circulation to the lower half of their bodies, the teenagers climbed the stairs of the house and in its upper floors found new clothes. Some favored dresses, others pants and shirts, others soft blouses, others skirts and boots, others fancy shoes and others sneakers, others tried them all and liked them all and tried a style for one minute and changed the next. Some stuck to what they'd chosen, their style, they said. And like that, in trying the many versions of themselves for what seemed like days, like months, like years(!), they grew longer hair, and some grew beards, and some grew even taller, and some grew larger breasts, and some plumper hips, and some bigger muscles and rounder bellies, and some their voice had changed so much it reminded them of their parents. And now it was dusk (finally!) and they were still in this house, and they hadn't eaten cake yet.

'They gathered back in the kitchen, pissed off that they had spent the whole day in this party and the birthday kid had not appeared yet. "Who is it? Who is it? Who is it?" they demanded, but no one admitted it was their party. They sang *Happy Birthday* anyways. Maybe with the song the birthday kid (now a twentysomething) would finally reveal themselves, and then they could cut the damned cake, have their piece, and leave. No one came forward. "Come on!" one of the twentysomethings screamed. "Just let us celebrate you, please." Everyone else agreed. "Please," they said. "This is idiotic," they said. "Fuck you," they said.

'"It's me," a twentysomething said.

'"Shut up," another one said, "it's not you, it's obviously me."

'"No way. It's actually me."

'And they fought, because now everyone wanted to be the birthday kid, whether they wanted to be celebrated or just get the party over with didn't matter, they fought with the same fervor, and they punched and pulled their hair and scratched and kicked, and once everyone was bruised and bleeding, they stopped, crumpled in the couches and armchairs of the coziest room in the house, with a fireplace and rugs and a stereo connected to huge speakers. "What if no one is the birthday kid?" a twentysomething suggested.

'"Someone has to be," another said. "Someone has to have a cake and blow the candles, otherwise why are we still here?"

'"To dance!" someone said. And the music was amazing. And they danced, and many drank, and many fucked, and some found cigarettes and lit each other up in piles of sweaty nakedness. The grandfather clock in the foyer chimed seven and their faces were now older, and they scrambled to dance more and fuck more and drink more and shout more, and some that had fallen in love found nooks to cuddle each other and others stayed in groups playing cards and laughing and a few others found comfortable armchairs to read in, happy to be alone with the voices of their party-mates echoing, happy to exist close to each other. And when the clock chimed eight, the partygoers left the house bringing blankets with them, and in the darkest part of the lawn they spread them, and they sat and propped each other back to back to watch the sky. The stars blinked into existence, one by one, and then in clusters, filling the sky with the constellations and the Milky Way and all those other stars who burn brighter pleased to have no name to call themselves. And like that, some fell asleep holding hands, against each others shoulders, or cuddled in someone else's lap, and those who stayed awake combed their friends' hair, white now, almost non-existent now, and like that, in spectacular silence, the party ended.'

J smiled. An ant crawled on the table. We watched it make its way across from one side to the next, past J and Elisa, past Seb and me.

'That's it?' Seb said.

'Well, yeah,' J said. 'What more do you want?'

'Did they die?' Elisa asked.

'No. The parents came and picked them up. At nine, like they said.'

'But they're old now!' Seb said.

'I guess,' J said. 'Or maybe they were just lucky to have a day with each other.'

'A whole life,' Elisa said and lifted her beer. We raised our own and clinked.

'Help!' We heard his shout before we saw the man in black jeans and black t-shirt running down the street toward us. 'Help!' A sheep, also blue, chased him. A car screeched, almost ran him and the sheep down. 'Help!' He slammed into the side of our table. Elisa snapped right up, but the bench made it difficult to stand and she folded back down. J held the man's wrist as if they were trying to pull him up from a sinking ship. Encouraged, the man tried to get on the table. We moved plates and glasses and ketchup and mayonnaise out of the way.

The man, breathless and half atop the table, looked back to see the sheep had abandoned the chase and now sauntered down the street, down where the other sheep had gone. 'I'm sorry,' he said.

'Are you okay?' Elisa asked.

'I'm okay,' he said. 'I'm sorry.'

'No worries,' J said.

'May I sit?' the man asked.

Seb and J scooted over, and we all took back our empty plates and half-full beers.

'I'm not sure how to… do you know the end of times is coming?'

'Oh,' Seb said. 'You're one of those. Will you try to sell us god?'

'Oh no,' the man said. 'I just want to make sure you have a plan. See there?' He pointed up the street where three more sheep were walking down. 'More are coming.'

Behind those three, seven sheep followed. The cars stopped. Drivers and passengers got out. People once again took their phones out to film them, letting them pass.

'What are they?' J asked.

'Sheep,' the man said.

'We know they're sheep,' Elisa said. 'But what else are they?'

'Blue, I guess.'

'I mean, are they here to destroy us?'

'Sheep? No. Why would they?'

'You just said it was the end of times!' Seb said, his voice pitchy with amusement.

'Yes,' the man said. He looked at each of us. His bushy mustache twitching. 'What are you going to do about it?'

'Us? What can we do?' Seb asked.

'Have a plan.'

'What kind of plan?'

'Of how you want to spend your last days on Earth.'

'I thought,' Seb said, 'you meant a plan to stop the end.'

'Oh no, there's no stopping that.'

'How soon is this end?' J asked with their quiet smile that could soothe even the most frazzled of fears. We smiled with J, our own kind of smiles, loud and showy, toothy and joyous, always complicit.

'So near,' the man said. 'The end is so so near. But now, will you excuse me?' The man stood, lanky in all black.

'A kiss,' Seb said.

'Pardon?'

'Will you kiss me? If this is really the end, I want a kiss.'

'Oh yes. Of course.' The man bent down and found Seb's lips with his own. Seb clasped the back of his neck, the man leaned down further, a whole show of tongues and desire. Done, Seb brushed the man's mustache with his thumb.

'If you want,' the man said, 'my place is not far, we could fool around.'

'And leave them?' Seb said. 'Not right now. Not when the end of times is so near!'

'Some other time then,' the man said. 'Or some other existence.'

Seb nodded, and the man ran away. More blue sheep filled the street, hundreds and hundreds. People moved away, cars disappeared, until there was nothing but a slow river of blue sheep moving among the four of us: Elisa, J, Seb and me. Soon enough, the flow of sheep would ebb and the last one, a young sprightly blue, would run behind its elders, enthused for the adventures that lay ahead, and we would have our last beer, our last cheers. But for now, while there was nothing in the city but an ocean of sheep and our table stood as the one thing not covered by the herd, us an island in a wooly river, unable to move, we were happy that amidst one of the most wonderful things we would ever experience, we were stranded together.

Joelle Taylor (she/her) is the author of 4 poetry collections and one novel. *C+NTO & Othered Poems* won the 2021 TS Eliot Prize and Polari Prize. She was awarded the Outstanding Contribution to Literature by *DIVA* in 2024. Her novel *The Night Alphabet* was Book of the Year in both *The Guardian* and *The Spectator.*

Joelletaylor.co.uk

@jtaylortrash

The below works contain discussion of homophobia and misogyny.

Psalm

o Maryville / song of loose shirt / you button down boi / you thick rod of irony / o Maryville / you sawn-off mini skirt / you tights torn into choir / o Maryville / o swagger / o keychain & denim / I am plural / o Maryville / we dress as our greatest fears / we dress as ourselves / o Maryville / the etymology of dyke / so many holes to fill / I knew your mother / saw them / lower her body / into her body / saw how she became cenotaph / the neighbourhood children left flowers at / o Maryville / I remember your sister / how antelope she was / how she froze when she heard the first roar / how she fell into the o of the roar / o Maryville / the antelopes are eating the antelopes / o my Maryville / forgive us / their trespasses.

o Maryville / let us walk alone at night / & let the night not follow us / let us drink too much / & awaken in each other's mouths / o Maryville / let us be ugly / let us unwash / let us language / our mouths are filled with men / line dancing / let us pass the half-smoked cigarette / o Maryville / let us fatten / let us leave our faces / on the back seat of night buses / let someone take a photograph not of us / but because of us / let our limbs grow wild / our hair retreat / our hormonal seas / let our breasts // let them // let us inherit each other's teeth / o Maryville / keep us alive this death / keep us from prayer / deliver us from ego / for thine are the body / the birthing & the burning / forever & ever // *are you a man*?

Valentine – snow globe

& then there was the time
Valentine squatted a snow
globe, used a communal crow
bar to prise open its legs
& shifted herself & every friend
from the club that night
into it. By morning we had blankets
as curtains & sleet fainted like silk
nightgowns across the beds
dark circuses Wurlitzed
our eyes & we shared
a mirror full of starting lines
knowing that at any moment
we were going to begin.
But the floor kept falling
to the sky. But we kept forgetting
our lines. In the living room
snow dropped like dot to dot
connect them to make a family
names tore free of their moorings
& we were all coloured
outside the lines, all
blizzard. I'll be mother
Valentine growls
her mouth an exhaust
pipe we press our lips
to.

The Battle of Maryville

//

Valentine

the men outside
are men outside.
Valentine wonders
if it is always
the same men outside
if they   want
the same thing.
They want to come
in   the locked room.
The occupied body.
She muses   it is the long road
back to a mother, the baby
who turns at birth, who knocks.
There is a crack in the display
case's idea of itself   outside
naked knuckles shiver together
their towels half-slung around waists
or flicking like tongues
at the backs of legs.
Valentine understands
that to some boys
no is an act of aggression.
Voices are thrown   but miss.
The first bottle that spins
into the bar   lands
with its neck pointing

toward her   the bar dilates
& we are film noir.
Valentine cracks open a grin
picks up the bottle   considers
glass: atoms coming together
in short order   inside the bottle
is a bar   its lights blinking
bewilderment its tiny women
gazing up at her. When the
bottle breaks the world pours
out & the flood rises
from our swivel backs
arms link like chromosomes
& Maryville is nation
facing the door that leads
to every door & what is a door
but the only way home.

//

Angel

what circus, what zoo.
Dudz wonders how war
can be civil, while Jack
contemplates the quantum
physics of fighting
if on a molecular level
every woman here is
inside the ring of her
blood cell waiting
for the bell, but Angel
o Angel, her white
fire kindling, walks forward

knowing her fear is
a dress she can no longer
fit into. Around her
the bar convulses. Angel
knows when fists fly
they do not return
not even for seeds
on windowsills.
She holds her whole
self against the door
the weight of
expectation
& for a moment
she is a child
telling the wind
to go home
a girl
punching water
but fists startle
easily, flock,
their murmuration
making the shape
of men pushing
into a room.

//

the men bring the forest
in with them & in their dark
thinkings, animals hunt
themselves & girls in red
hoods turn to thank them
there is something wild
in their civility.

Ladies, they say, ladies
their faces red, white
& blue, *ladies.*

//

Jack Catch

Jack Catch rolls back her sleeves
then the skin on her forearms,
cartilage, the muscle, throws a
femur at the men
throws early adolescence
throws a girl at the men
who catch everything
& understand nothing.
She stands her ground
throwing air
handful after handful
until the night blues
& gasps.

//

Dudizile

Dudizile is tired
of stories that end
like this. What is free
is given a high rise,
what is other is given
a new dress,
the gentrification
of fucking.

The men who break
into the bar are men
she has known
all her life. Is that a
father over there, an elder
brother? Is that the boy
who sat behind her
in school, on the bus,
who walks beside her
each night –
are these the men
who are always behind her?
Dudizile shrugs
picks up her pint
slowly sips
wipes her lips
on her sleeve
whispers to the glass
& sets it free.

//

here we are again
women pushing men
out of their bodies
how many women
does it take
to make a mother.

//

poor men
they had forgotten

that if you
punch a woman

six more grow
from the wound.

//

SCENE ELEVEN

DOWNSTAGE Right. Interior Maryville bar.

LX1: the yellow of teeth, of fingertips.

FX1: a roaring smile. Boystown CD, *You're Just Too Good to be True.*

LX2: follow spot on a chorus line of high kicking butches moving forward in a tidal wave, pushing men back onto the street. The door closes and is bolted. The room erupts into women not moving away from one another. White petals slouch from the ceiling but when they land, they become femme ingénues, each a brunette with a cigarette holder raised to her lips & as the cigarette is lit the smoke that dances from its end becomes a glass bead curtain & through it you are sat, quietly, reading this book.

James Cahill (he/him) is a writer, critic and art historian based between London and Los Angeles. His debut novel, *Tiepolo Blue* (2022), was shortlisted for the Author's Club Best First Novel Award and selected for H.M. the Queen's Reading Room. His second novel, *The Violet Hour*, was published in 2025. He was the lead author of *Flying Too Close to the Sun* (2018), a survey of classical myth in art from antiquity to the present day, and contributes to publications including *Artforum*, the *Burlington Magazine*, the *Financial Times*, the *Los Angeles Review of Books*, the *Spectator* and the *Times Literary Supplement*. His latest book, *The Beverly Hills Housewife* – a biographical study of David Hockney and his first Californian muse – is published by Thames & Hudson in 2026.

@jamesmcahill

Gadfly

The time had never been right for a journey south.

'Go to Monte Carlo,' his sister used to say. 'The house is empty.'

'I don't have time to globetrot,' he would reply.

London was Eddy Day's world, and he was always on the go. There were private views, literary parties, soirées at the home of this or that society person; the invitations were unceasing. Once, in the social diary of *Tatler*, they had called him a 'gay gadfly'. He repeated the phrase often – laughed about it even as it made him uncomfortable. He was a man of ideas, after all, but since when had *Tatler* cared about that?

Talking about himself was a dance of the seven veils. 'I have many selves,' Eddy liked to say. Podcaster, provocateur, author of caustic book reviews for the *Spectator*... He'd made a few enemies along the way, but that was the price of being fearless. There was his photography too, but he didn't talk much about that. Even a gadfly has an interior life.

One day, as if by black magic, the carousel stalled. Eddy spoke on his podcast about the national crisis. He spoke robustly, just as he always did – without the petty, self-protective caution that he despised in other journalists. *Say it like it is!* But his enemies, for so long a dumb invisible mass, seemed to have been lying in wait. His words were twisted. His podcast was cancelled by the TV station that had sponsored it. ('We have to take a hard line,' the chief executive said, with robotic resolve.) Eddy's name was everywhere – on Fox News, on X, on the lips of his partygoing friends. A death threat arrived in the post, scrawled over one of his own essays for the *Salisbury Review.*

Eddy came to realise that the mob speaks with an inarticulate roar, and yet the roar has a way of disguising itself as clever, as *individual*. He would have written a defence of himself, laid out his theories in full, if any editors had been willing to listen. But in the space of a week, he had become a leper. Friends made excuses; colleagues ghosted him. He went from being angrily amused to bewildered. Was this how it all ended, a career – an entire *life* in the public eye? Could cowards be so powerful simply by closing ranks? He lay in his one-room flat with the curtains closed until Ella turned up, allowing herself in with a key he'd forgotten she had.

'I have no life,' he told her, staring at the stains on the ceiling. 'I have nowhere to go – nothing to live for.'

'Go to Monte Carlo,' she said. 'Wait till this blows over. It will, in the end.'

Eddy sat in front of his sister, leaning forward, holding his head in his hands. A headful of *himself*. All those ideas, suspended in his two palms like a dead weight – they couldn't help him for now. In silence, he repeated the words in his head. *Monte Carlo.* Charles's mount. The playground of the idle rich. Had it come to this?

At Nice airport, a young man observed him from behind a glass screen – glanced at Eddy's passport, then back at the sweating reality. The photo had been taken eight years earlier: a forty-year-old face, fuller than it might have been, but spry in middle age, like Truman Capote before the dissipation really set in. Eddy tried to discern a reaction, but the man just handed back the passport and looked straight past him.

A taxi driver was waiting in the arrivals hall. Beyond the sliding doors, the heat of the day was like a laying on of hands.

'You've had some dreadful incidents here,' said Eddy from the back seat, as the driver – a young Arab man in a polyester suit – steered them out of the airport. 'Attacks.' Eddy repeated the words in French.

The driver didn't seem to have heard. They coursed onto a motorway. Vehicles flew by like missiles in the afternoon sunlight.

On the far side of a tunnel, the landscape became mountainous. Eddy thought of ancient Greece: that timeless collocation of sea, sky and headlands. The birthplace of democracy, the only proper democracy there had ever been. Everything else was a travesty. They turned off the motorway and climbed a winding road. Pine trees cast a mesh of shadows. After twenty minutes or so, the driver nosed the car up a narrow incline. From behind a row of cypresses, the house edged into view. Eddy held his breath. He'd never seen the place, not even in photographs. It was like an eagle's nest, angled towards the city from a high promontory. The design was sharp-edged and geometric. Each level extended into a balconied terrace. Two giant slabs projected from the hillside like drawers, scattered with creepers.

Ella had bought it from an elderly American heiress. She called it a period piece, whatever that meant.

A woman was waiting for him at the top of the steps.

'Monsieur is tired after the journey?'

She was silhouetted by the open front door. Behind her, through the house, were giant windows. Eddy struggled for a moment to make her out. Her eyes were large and brown inside tortoiseshell frames. They remained on him, unblinking. Answering in French, he said that he felt very well. Never better. There was a pang of annoyance that he kept well hidden; he had never been good with the heat.

Inside, he followed behind the housekeeper, maintaining an ambling pace that he sensed she slightly resented. With a leisurely air, he looked around the open-plan space: the kitchen of black quartz, the leather and chromium sofas, the black-and-white photographs of Monaco and its beautiful ghouls.

'Ah, yes, *Helmut Newton*,' he said, as Mathilde began to descend the stairs.

'Your bedroom is this way, down below.'

Eddy grinned and followed. To think that Ella barely ever came to this place, and yet here it was, immaculate and staffed and ready for him. He noted with a certain satisfaction that there were no books.

When the housekeeper – her name was Mathilde – had left, he stood alone before the glass doors to the terrace. The town glittered in the distance, its towers bristling against the blue. He *was* tired, despite his earlier denial, but the tiredness was manifesting as a strange, jittery aliveness. He felt amused and close to tears and suddenly *heroic* (it was the view that did it, dazzling and elating him). He might have been looking at a magnificent painting, he thought, for the effect the vista was having on him. He removed his tie and undid the buttons of his shirt. Drawing the shirt off, discarding it on the shining parquet, he savoured the warm touch of the air on his chest. Then he removed the remainder of his clothes, piece by piece, and left them in a pile.

Out on the terrace, the sun was still hot. With his hands planted on the parapet, he took in the view, steadying himself against a spasm of vertigo. The hills were scattered with houses that shrank with sham modesty behind crops of palm trees. He was higher than all of them, too high to be seen. In the mid-distance, on the opposite site of the valley, was a white building with a golden dome.

The idea of sin still fascinated him, frightened him. He knew he should have freed himself from it, the way Ella had. But not everyone wants to be free. He dreamed sometimes of other realities, and woke with the sinking belief that his many selves were really just deflections. Ways of not living a different life.

Ella was rich. Eddy was poor. It had been that way since they were young. Two years older, Ella had gone into corporate law. While still at university, Eddy had accepted the role of art critic for a political magazine. He had begun to contribute to the magazine's diary column (short acerbic notes from his gadfly life), and he had become a commentator – a voice, a figure. A *force* in the British media. Ella had worked eighty-hour weeks in Canary Wharf, marrying and reproducing in the meantime. Eddy had thought hard and felt deeply. Didn't that count for something? The events of his life were not events in the normal sense, he sometimes felt, but flashes of insight, coordinates in a larger totality – like photographs. Not that he always intuited the significance at first. Meaning came later, as with art.

In the distance, the Mediterranean was a seething play of light. He felt intrepid to be standing there. But with a shift in the breeze, he felt exposed – like a fool for taking such a risk. He went inside and knelt down to gather his clothes.

Mathilde was standing in the kitchen, watching him with calm intrigue. He gasped, and the sound came out as a mewling cry.

She averted her eyes and indicated an envelope on the countertop.

'Your sister – she asked me to leave this for you.'

'Get out,' he said, in a wheezy voice, half rising on his knees. '*Begone.*'

In the morning, he walked to Monte Carlo. He bought a copy of *The Times* at a tabac, then sat outside a cafe near the harbour. It was only ten o'clock, but the sunlight and heat were strong. The discovery of what the envelope contained, a wad of cash totalling five thousand euros, had alleviated the horror of finding the maid spying on him. He'd even begun to see the funny side, as he sipped a whiskey sour the previous evening. It had been like one of those ancient myths of a mortal spying on a god. Things never went well for the mortal. Well, perhaps she would receive her just deserts, that Mathilde.

The envelope of cash made an impression in his jacket. He stroked it absent-mindedly as he perused the news. The United Kingdom was finished, he told himself. Everything he'd said had been correct. Surely that was why he had been ostracised. People couldn't bear to hear the truth, and they were punishing him for saying out loud what everybody knew.

He felt his mood darkening, and by an act of will he turned his mind to other things. The town would be worth exploring, he supposed, although he more or less knew what to expect. He might write about what he found. *Despatches from Monte Carlo.* He began to smile. Yes, a mordant travel journal crossed with a defiant retrenchment of his world view. Local observations offset by global analyses. It would sell, he was sure of it. The book would be his redemption.

A spectacular return to form.

Searingly defiant – irresistibly funny.

A small masterpiece of observation and a trenchant political memoir. Day is less a polemicist than a prophet for our benighted times.

He played in his head with the cover quotes he could imagine receiving. *Memoir* wasn't quite right; it suggested something softer and more self-absorbed than he had in mind. *Tract*, maybe. He folded the newspaper and fingered his bundle of cash. Out of nowhere, an idea came to him. He should visit the casino. He disliked gambling and had no respect for those who practised it, but this *was* Monte Carlo. (Years ago, in Madrid, he had forced himself to go to a bullfight: a repulsive spectacle, and yet hadn't he watched every second, spellbound, and cheered with the worst of them when the beast was finally slaughtered on the sand?) He could observe with an artist's eye – garner some local colour.

His concentration drifted; his smile faded. Exile in a strange southern town, the seat of glamour – could he have predicted all of this, when he recorded that fatal edition of his podcast?

The western tradition was imperilled, he had said. The glorious work of the Enlightenment, the order and rationality that were the gifts of the ancients, were being destroyed. A creature with a black heart was stealing through the nations of the world. Educated liberals were aiding its passage, abetting its evil.

He ordered a second coffee. Perhaps some of his phrases had been a little sharper, a touch more direct. But critics were apt to seize hold of a resonant line, a mere word, and make great play of it. He commanded himself, here in the stillness and heat, to think no more about it.

A group of young men and women had arrived at the next table. They were in high spirits. Their conversation was noisy and unselfconscious, slipping from French into accented

English. Everything about them spoke of affluence and leisure – their clothes, their complexions, their expressive motions. Eddy watched them with a mixture of interest and distaste. One of the men was deeply tanned. His black hair was combed back as if he'd been swimming. He laughed in response to a comment his girlfriend had made, and for just a second his eyes met Eddy's.

They had met on Clapham Common the previous summer. Malik had been sunbathing. Eddy had been strolling with his Pentax 110.

That was how Eddy had spent most of his weekend afternoons – roaming in one park or another. His eye picked out solitary men. He would watch from a distance, then make an approach. 'All you have to do is stay lying there – I'll photograph you.'

Some of the men were hostile. More often, they were vaguely amused and willing. They would lie in the sun and allow him to crouch around them, one eye screwed shut as he pointed the camera. He liked olive-skinned men the best. Their bodies looked good on black-and-white film. As the weeks went by, he invited some of them back to his flat, offering them a banknote or two for the bus fare. In a corner of the room he set up a studio, draping bedsheets from the curtain rails. The men would remove their clothes, down to their underwear. They would recline on the sofa. Eddy photographed them in near silence, ignoring the beads of sweat on his face and neck. Occasionally he gave instructions – the leg a little higher, the head more tilted, *just like that…*

Malik had been a promising subject. Barely out of his teens, but tall and as muscular as a man in his prime. On his first visit, he lay motionless on the sofa, returning a solemn stare. On his second visit, Eddy directed him into the pose of the Barberini Faun.

But the next time Malik came, something had changed. He seemed bored. He couldn't keep still. There was something arch about the way he threw himself back on the sofa, tucking his hands behind his head. He kept fingering the waistband of his briefs. Eddy turned round to change a roll of film. When he looked back, Malik was watching him with dark amusement. He had pulled off his underpants and flung them to the floor. His legs were spread as wide as a gymnast's, his feet high in the air. Slowly, without breaking his gaze, he brough his ankles together and then opened his legs again in a languid scissoring motion. Eddy was unable to look away before he saw Malik's erection, swelling and lolling like a drunkard in bed.

He walked along the promenade, recalling how the camera had trembled in his hand as he ordered Malik out of the flat. How he had destroyed the rolls of film and thrown away all his earlier pictures of Malik. There had been no more studio sessions after that.

Monte Carlo was a town of dissembling appearances, he told himself. Just here, on this stretch of the coastline, if he ignored certain details, he could be in Spain or Morocco. He felt dizzy in the rising heat. This was how the bull must feel in the ring, on the heat of the sand.

On the Avenue de Monte Carlo, the twin cupolas of the casino rose into view. The building was like an antique toy, a wind-up contraption. He walked round to the main entrance on the Place de Casino. Inside, the lobby was blissfully cool. His leather soles clacked on the marble. He changed a handful of banknotes into chips and dropped the plastic discs into his trouser pocket. Wandering into the nearest gambling chamber, he passed close to a table where a roulette wheel was turning. Two men and a woman sat around the table, blank but attuned. The ball rolled in the opposite direction with a glassy whirr.

It was like moving through the staged reality of a film, a play, an opera… Eddy felt his own motions becoming slower, lighter. The carpet was so deep and cushioning that he felt weightless. The croupier shot him a glance. Sinking his hand in his pocket, he clutched the chips. The ball rebounded off the metal deflectors. He thought of Gospel Oak Methodist Church – all those Sundays, long ago. The coolness of his mother's hand gripping his own.

He looked away, into the burnished dimness of the room. The ball dropped into the numbered pockets. He heard it staggering to a halt. The croupier called out the winning number, but his voice was interrupted by a gasp. It was the woman's voice, close to a cry of pain.

'Yes! Yes, oh yes, oh my God, YES.'

He kept the chips in his pocket as he passed back through the atrium. They were smooth and shapely – little platelets that knocked together like castanets.

'What's that building, Mathilde?'

Eddy was sitting on the terrace, finishing lunch. He had given up reading Gide's *The Immoralist* and was scanning the hillsides.

'Which one, monsieur?' Mathilde came to stand beside him.

He took a final mouthful of watermelon and discarded the rind. 'On that hilltop directly below Mont Agel. With the gold dome.'

'Ah. The Bacon Museum.' She began to clear his lunch things.

'Bacon?'

'François Bacon.'

Was Mathilde's French accent thickening?

'Bacon – my goodness. Here, of all places?'

'Monaco was his favourite place to gamble. They made a museum for him.'

'A dissolute man,' Eddy said. 'But he knew something of the horror of life, the lurking obscenity…' He laughed uneasily, surprised by his own earnestness.

'He was unlike anyone I ever met.' Mathilde's eyes were bright with feeling. 'He never cared if he lost.'

'You knew him?'

'I met him many times, when I worked at the casino.'

Eddy ran his fingers over the chips inside his trousers.

'I was a croupier for twenty years,' she went on, lifting the tray containing his plate and wineglass. She stood still and looked out at the view. 'I knew all of them.'

That evening, he mixed a whiskey sour and telephoned Ella.

'How can it be,' he said, adopting the easy tone he had used in his podcast, 'that Monaco – this cultural desert – boasts a museum devoted to Britain's greatest post-war painter?'

'Oh, that,' said Ella. 'It sprung up a year ago. A Lebanese billionaire owns it.'

'I'll go and have a look tomorrow.'

'Shouldn't you rest for a while? You've got plenty of time to explore.'

'You make it sound like I'm a patient in a sanitorium.'

'Ha. Well, there is a sanitorium somewhere there in the hills. Or the modern equivalent. A wellness clinic, I guess you'd call it. Olivier de Botton used to go there when the living became too hard for him.'

'Oliver *who*?' Eddy's shrill laugh rang through the empty room.

'The old queen who I bought the house from. The fashion designer. *You* remember.'

Eddy didn't answer for a number of seconds. When had Ella begun to speak like this? There was something coarse and overfamiliar in her tone. He felt as if he barely knew her anymore.

'You bought that house from an *heiress*,' he said, aware of the icy amazement in his words. 'You told me so at the time.'

Ella gave a throaty laugh. 'Oh Eddy. That was the guy's nickname. The heiress. Everybody called him that. He was the wildest old bohemian in Monte Carlo. If the walls of that house could talk!' She paused, as though to take a drink or a puff from her cigarette. 'Still, I don't think things ended well for him.'

Eddy drained his own glass in a single burning gulp. The alcohol numbed and soothed him. He ceased to listen as Ella switched to complaining about her husband. His focus shifted to the window. The Bacon Museum was floodlit against the night. It looked like a lamp, resting on its pedestal of hill, one of those domed lanterns crafted from metal and perforated with eyelets. He fancied he could reach out and pluck it from its pinnacle, turn it around in his hands like a beautiful toy. The pleasure of the idea was tempered by a feeling of unease. What was it? He stared out into the night. That thing Ella had said, and the way she had said it… He studied the open-plan room, but it gave up no secrets.

It didn't seem as hot as the previous day. He decided to walk. He wore a light-blue shirt beneath a linen suit, and brushed suede shoes. As he set out along the road, his eyes danced over cacti and bougainvillea. The roads were deserted – silent except for the rush of the cicadas.

The Bacon Museum! He laughed as he descended, thinking how strange it was that the place had arisen from nowhere. Money could magic things into existence.

The route had looked simple from the house. Down, then across, then up. But as he reached the trough of the valley and looked for a way up the opposite hill – even as the gold dome glimmered in and out of view, over the tops of trees – he took a wrong turn, into a cul-de-sac, then another wrong turn as he tried to retrace his steps. The heat was building.

Soon he was trapped in a maze of sunny, directionless roads. They all looked the same, winding this way and that, up and down, terminating in closed gates or a sudden vacant plot where a house had been razed. He came to an uphill route where the ground was uneven. Embankments rose on either side, thick with shrubs. His breaths turned into groans. There was a maddening, tickling wetness in his crotch.

He tripped and fell, bashing his shoulder and slicing his hand on a stone. Blood trickled down his wrist. It was startlingly red in the sunlight. He sucked it away, waiting for the pain. In the few seconds that he lay on the ground, the day seemed surreally still, almost as though time had fixed itself in the deep blue of the sky, the green of the hills, in the shining blades of the palm fronds high above. As he climbed to his feet, he saw something he hadn't noticed before: a wooden gate set into a wall of red and green vines. There was an intercom panel. Someone would be able to assist – give directions. With a quivering finger, he pressed the button. No answer. No sound except the cicadas' endless roaring.

When at last he reached the top of the hill, he found himself in a dusty clearing. At once he saw the museum, giant and gleaming, only fifty yards away. The building was bigger, up close, than he had expected. Grandiose and overtly new. Beneath the gold dome, the structure was faced in white render. The effect was of a Russian church or a mosque. It was an elaborate imitation of nothing specific, verging on grotesque – and yet, he couldn't help admitting, rather lovely.

All this time he had been climbing the right promontory. He clasped his knees. His trouser leg was torn from the fall; his shoes were caked in dust. The blood from his cut had trickled onto the cuff of his jacket. It was drying in a wriggling shape like the shadow of a tree.

Tentatively, unsure now if the place was open, he pushed on the oak door. It opened with a whine, admitting him to a lobby that was high and square and airconditioned to a harsh chillness. There was a faint, not unpleasant smell of must, similar to the odour of a church, although the décor was sparse and modern. A three-sided desk stood beneath the dome, like a giant snooker rack on the sandstone floor.

A young woman sold him a two-day pass.

'In case you want to return,' she said.

Eddy crossed into an empty gallery where a glass ceiling admitted broken stripes of daylight. Three of Francis Bacon's triptychs were stationed around the walls – three groups of three canvases. The fourth wall had been left empty.

With deliberate motions, Eddy walked to the centre of the room. The openness of the space made him feel ceremonial, and wincingly aware of his body. He glanced down at the ragged mess of his clothes, his bloody cuff and exposed knee.

He looked up and recognised the triptych straight ahead of him. How strange to find it here, when he had been sure it belonged to a museum in Germany. It was the three-part *Crucifixion* from the mid-1960s – he remembered it from a TV documentary. In the central painting, a carcass hung from the ceiling, descending in front of an orange wall, trailing its bandaged hooves onto a red carpet. The other two panels, on either side, were scenes in the same orange parlour. On the left, a nude woman stepped across the black void of a doorway, tiptoeing away from a body pulverised against a mattress. On the right, two men in jackets and Panama hats leaned together on an altar rail. Beside them was another dissolving body – this one erected on a stake. The hunched figure wore a swastika armband.

Eddy wasn't sure how long he had been staring at this last detail before his mind snapped free. He clenched his eyes shut.

He had the whole museum to explore, but he wanted to leave.

As he passed the desk in the lobby, the woman handed him a large softback book: the illustrated catalogue of the Bacon Museum.

'It's free,' she said, in response to his silence.

Clutching the book in both hands, Eddy returned to the clearing outside. The midday heat struck him like a blunt object. He began his descent, reminding himself that he knew the way now, and that it was downhill for the first half. The day was hot and bright, but the weird inertia he'd noticed before had gone. A gentle breeze was sifting through the foliage. Time was back on its normal course. Slowing his step, he held out the book and flicked through the pages. The images made him nod and hum. He thought vaguely of the twentieth century, and the violence that lies dormant in the mildest of impulses. He tripped, recovered his balance and flicked on as he walked. At the centre of the book was a fold-out. The right-hand page opened into a separate leaf. The sun blinded out the images. He re-angled the book. It was the *Crucifixion* triptych, displayed across a three-part centrefold.

He brought the book closer to his face. Somehow, the reproductions were more gruesome than the paintings in the museum. His eyes stalled on the two men, praying in their Panama hats, smirking as they turned their eyes from the monster. The realisation hit like a fragment of a forgotten dream: the men were smiling at him, right now in this place, as if they *knew*. He met their shadowed gazes and saw the people – the hypocrites – who had driven him to Monte Carlo, lost him his podcast, destroyed his reputation.

He cursed out loud – a word he'd never spoken. The utterance rose through the air, into the treetops. The book flew up. He felt dry earth against his forehead. Opening his eyes, he saw pink flowers, pale dust, and the book – sprawling at the base of a tree. He rolled onto his back. His head was pulsing. The sky was pink behind spiked fronds. His shoulder ached horribly. In a surge of energy, he rolled onto his front and thrust his arm towards the book. He grasped the pages and tore the centrefold from the binding. Rising unsteadily, leaving the remainder of the book on the ground, he walked – half-ran – towards a plastic bin on wheels that stood in front of a wooden gate. It was the same gate, set into a wall of creepers, where he had tried the intercom before.

He flipped open the lid, releasing an acrid scent, and hurled the torn-out picture on top of a rubbish sack.

He froze. The wooden gate was ajar. A man was standing in front of it.

'I saw you on the camera.'

A tall man, aged in his sixties – Middle Eastern, maybe, with cropped hair and a broad, handsome face. He wore a short-sleeved linen shirt with matching trousers.

Eddy finally understood. All the houses had video cameras. This was Monte Carlo. Nothing was left to chance, at least where security was concerned.

'What are you looking for?' The man stroked his forearm with his fingertips. His accent was hard to place.

'I was throwing something away.' Eddy opened the bin and snatched the centrefold back.

The man extended a hand. Eddy passed him the torn-out pages.

'You like art,' the man said. It didn't seem like a question.

'I was at the Bacon Museum, up the hill. I fell, just here, a moment ago – and before…' He struggled to control the flow of words.

The man stood there, running his fingers along the edge of the page. 'Do you want to come inside? For a drink of water?'

Behind the gate, a flight of stone steps rose through a tunnel of vegetation. Water had recently been hosed on the stone and a floral aroma hung in the air. The steps led to a screen door.

Eddy followed the man into a room paved in dark wood. The light was dim. The furniture was sparse but solid – sculptured mahogany chests, low couches, a geometric tapestry on the wall. At the far end, gauze curtains swayed before an oblong of light.

The man held out a tumbler filled with water. 'Here.'

Eddy took the glass and drank. His teeth chattered against it. Water ran down his chin, onto his shirt.

The man's green eyes were unwavering. Eddy tried to quell the trembling that had broken out all over him.

The man took the glass. 'Better?'

Eddy nodded. His senses were acclimatising. Doorways led off from either side of the room. At the centre was a low table containing two piles of books – dictionaries or encyclopaedias with gold lettering. Alongside them was a dried corn cob, parched as a piece of bone. Music was playing from somewhere deeper in the house, so faint that it could have been Eddy's tinnitus.

'I'm Iskandar,' said the man. 'And this,' – he extended one hand – 'is Sam.'

A younger man was standing now in one of the doorways, scarcely visible in the gloom. He was dressed in similar linen clothes. He took a brown-papered cigarette out of a packet and twiddled it between his fingers.

'Man, you look like hell.'

'I found him out by the bins,' said Iskandar. 'Digging up something he'd buried.' He held out the picture of Bacon's *Crucifixion*.

There seemed to be a current of subtle humour between them, an ironic sort of understanding, although both remained serious – almost formal.

'You must forgive my appearance,' Eddy stammered. 'I haven't been myself.'

'Sam's a filmmaker,' said Iskandar. 'He'll show you his work.'

The younger man sighed, then tucked the cigarette between his teeth.

'Don't be shy,' said Iskandar. 'Show the man your studio. You are both admirers of the English painter–'

'Irish,' Sam interrupted. 'Anglo-Irish.'

Across the room, the curtains were like the mouth of a tunnel. They billowed inwards to reveal a view of the shimmering sea.

Sam led Eddy through one of the doors. They left Iskandar in the room with the piles of books. At the end of a passageway, Sam flung aside a curtain to admit a blaze of light. They were in an open courtyard surrounded by stuccoed arches. Flowering vines spilled over the walls.

'We call it the Garden of Allah,' he said, as though sensing Eddy's wonderment. 'Like in Hollywood.'

'Ah yes,' Eddy said, and cleared his throat. 'The hotel where Stravinsky stayed.'

Sam stopped and turned. 'Dorothy Parker, too. She practically lived there, for a while.' For the first time, a flicker of amusement entered his eyes. 'Men weren't allowed into the hotel without female company – the place was getting a *reputation*, see. So if you wanted to get into the bar, you said you were a friend of Dorothy.'

Eddy nodded and pressed his lips together. Any minute now, and he would feel strong enough to thank these men and leave. A glass of water had been all he needed. But he shouldn't be impolite.

'Iskandar created all this from nothing,' Sam said, leading him on and waving a hand around the courtyard.

At the far side was a whitewashed room with a stone floor. Arched windows allowed a clear view of the sea. The space was empty apart from three vast rolls of crimson wallpaper that had been propped endways and partly unravelled like giant scrolls, to create three separate parabolas of red. The exposed sections of paper sagged and swayed in the breeze from the open door.

In front of one of the paper convexities, Eddy now saw, was an iron-framed bed. It was covered in a grimy mattress. He turned and caught sight of himself in a free-standing mirror, close to the door they had entered by. A large flap hung away from his trousers, exposing his grazed knee and a section of his thigh. His face was bleeding and wet around the chin. His shirt had lost its buttons and come undone. It hung in two sweat-drenched flaps.

Sam came towards him. In his hand was a black box with an extending handle. In another moment, Eddy recognised it as an old-style video camera, one of those Super 8 models from years ago. Sam passed it from one hand to the other, then held it up and tracked the room through the lens.

'I'm recreating Bacon's *Crucifixion*,' he said. 'A film version. The same picture you tore from the book…' He looked back at Eddy and smiled. 'What are the chances?'

His smile broadened into a toothy grin as he kept the camera poised midair.

'Kneel there.'

The instruction was so simple, so calmly delivered, the man's intention so precise and determined, that Eddy gave in. The headful of thoughts had gone, lost outside on the sunbaked road. Memory, anger, fear, all of it could wait. Here, just for a moment, was another possibility, with a logic all of its own. He was a shell – a vessel – or *could* be. Conscious only of the thudding of his heart, he lifted his knee onto the mattress. He heard the camera whirring behind him. He planted his hands further up and felt the bareness of his exposed thigh in the breeze. He crawled forward on the bed and fought off his jacket. The camera whirred on like an infernal insect.

His head dropped. Looking back through his parted legs, he saw the glass eye of the lens, the head of the young man behind it, and to one side – in the mirror – his own body, reconstituted as an amalgam of shapes: the outstretched buttress of his shirtsleeve, a broken column of pale leg, the dusty sole of his shoe.

He prised off his shoes, then unbuckled his belt and let it drop to the floor. The buckle clanked like a manacle. As he kicked off his trousers, the chips from the casino fell over the floor. He heard his shirt tear as he pulled it off. He was aware of Sam circling the bed, gliding this way and that, guiding the camera over every detail. Eddy gave the waistband of his briefs a hard downward tug.

The whirring seemed to intensify, growing close to a whine. Eddy turned onto his back, feeling the mattress creak and bounce beneath him, and flung out his arms. A light somewhere overhead blinded him. He screwed his eyes shut, but the light was still there. He turned back on his front and drove his head into the mattress.

The whirring stopped. In the silence that followed, the breeze stroked his naked shoulders. He shivered. A moment later, he heard footsteps and the faintest murmuring, and perceived that Iskandar had come into the room.

Beyond the gauze curtains was a terrace. Far below, the town was concealed by umbrella pines. Only the sea and hillsides were visible.

'You'll come again,' said Iskandar. He waved Eddy to a wicker chair and sat down in another. 'At four o'clock, the day after tomorrow.'

Not a question but a statement of fact.

Eddy was wearing a fresh shirt and trousers, lent by Iskandar. The linen felt coarse but not unpleasant against his skin.

Sam appeared from behind the curtain. He was wheeling a pewter bar cart, set with glasses of tea.

'Have you got anything stronger?'

'We don't drink,' Sam replied, with a shrug.

'People think we're father and son,' said Iskandar, whose

thoughts seemed to be on a different plane. His smooth forearms were spread along the arms of his chair.

'They pretend to think that,' said Sam. 'They tell themselves that's what we are.'

Eddy took a large gulp of tea. It was hot, but not enough to burn. 'Welcome to Monte Carlo,' he joked. 'The unreal city.' He found that his amusement was straining against some other emotion. A delirious, sun-stroked grief.

'Nowhere more than the Bacon Museum,' replied Sam. 'A whole museum of fakes.'

'Fakes?'

'Every painting there is a replica. The owner wanted a gallery of Bacon masterpieces – and since he couldn't buy them…'

'Impossible,' said Eddy. The word came out as a dry whisper.

'It's all very high-tech. Photogrammetric printing, they call it.'

'I prefer things that are handmade,' said Iskandar, who had been listening in pensive silence. 'Like that wallpaper you saw. Sam made it all.'

The heat of the afternoon was subsiding. The sun was low in the sky. A cruise ship had appeared in the bay, a little white rhombus on the water, dispelling the illusion of an unpeopled wilderness.

'Tell us about yourself,' Sam said. 'Tell us who you are.' And once again, there was a terrible gentleness to the instruction.

William Rayfet Hunter (he/they) is a British-Jamaican writer based in East London. Their fiction, poetry and non-fiction explore queerness, race, desire and displacement. Their acclaimed debut novel, *Sunstruck*, showcases their focus on morally complex characters and the contradictions shaping queer and diasporic life across contemporary British culture.

Williamrayfethunter.substack.com

@willhunterr

The below work contains depictions of sex and drug usage.

Stained Glass

I

Christmas Day, 1998. There is a mix up. You tear the brightly snowmanned paper off a squishy, oddly shaped parcel bearing your name. Inside is the most beautiful thing you have ever seen in your entire life – all five years and one month of it. The parcel contains a teddy. No, can't be, it has no head. Or arms. Or legs. Not a teddy, then. It is soft to the touch. Furry. Round. Spotted, like the leopard who got his spots from the Ethiopian's fingers dipped in coal ash. Spotted. Soft. *What are you?* You hug the thing close to your little chest. Soft, yes, but also something hard. A cold-light metal feel through *The-Tiger-Who-Came-To-Tea* pyjamas. Little fingers work the gold. Two orbs that click apart then together again. Inside, soft again, but different. Vivid burning pink satin-silk. Snake of smooth, cool gold. Chain. A bag, then. Purse. *Your* purse. Sling it over your shoulder. Prized possession. Mummy has opened an Action Man. You laugh. Silly gift. Not for girls. She wants to swap. Hot sting of wet behind your eyes. Your purse. You are smart enough to realise this was a mistake but young enough to insist it was the right one. Months from now, your mother will slip the purse from a pile of your other discarded toys and you will find yourself playing with the Action Man. But for now, the purse is yours. You fill it with your most important things: Troll doll (hair cut off), shiny screw, rock with half a face, stolen key. You sling it over your shoulder and for the first time feel something you cannot yet name.

II

Saturday afternoon. You are six years old. Best friend stands opposite you. Knobbly kneed in red shorts. Unbearable sadness. Your tiny mind cannot comprehend the bigness of forever. You repeat the strange word he has said, rolling it around in your mouth, trying to taste it. *Oss-tray-lee-uh.* Only a day away, he says. Like school on a Sunday, then. No time at all. But somehow you know you will never see him again. Suddenly, all the games you have played seem silly. Pirates and princesses. Cops, robbers, mummies, daddies. All useless to you now. You hear, from somewhere inside the house, your names being called. Time to go. But he doesn't. You grasp his hand (sticky) tight in yours (jam-smelling) and run. You run to the end of the little garden and climb inside the rot-dried body of an old oak tree that the two of you made ship's hull, dungeon, race car, rabbit's den, spaceship. Safe inside this stolen extra moment, he puts his mouth on yours like you have seen men do to pretty ladies on TV. Grown-up magic you don't understand. Like *Oss-tray-lee-uh* and *hangover* and *because-I'm-the-mummy-and-I-say-so*. A kiss, it is called. And part of you knows you're not supposed to have done it and the rest of you is soaring into the sky as if this tree-trunk spaceship really could take you away from here. Later you will both be found and you won't be in trouble because the grown-ups know this must be hard for you and you promise you will practice your letters so you can write to each other but he was always bad with his letters so you don't know what will happen after he leaves. But right now, inside the tree, you know what it is to be loved.

III

Distracted at the table. Adults and siblings chatter about something you don't understand. Look across the restaurant and see a pair of men eating plates of curry and rice like the one in front of you. They have wine, though, and you are not allowed it. *When you're older*, that's what your dad says. There is a bunch of roses on the table between the men and, as you look closer, you see they are holding hands.

IV

A photograph. Taken in 2002. You are smiling next to your cousin. She is wearing your clothes. Baggy shorts, No Fear T-shirt hanging off her. From the brim of your backwards cap, her self-cut fringe tufts up defiantly. You are wrapped in blue satin. Feet crammed into plastic princess heels. Settled on top of your tight-cropped curls lies a shiny tiara. Your joy exposes the gap where your right canine should be.

V

You are in London. This in itself is exciting, new. It is spring and the pale sun keeps peeping out from behind swollen rainclouds. You were going to go on the Millennium Wheel. From up there you could have seen the whole of London town. You couldn't wait. But when you got there the man told your parents that it was fully booked up all day. You were disappointed for a moment, but then someone explained to you that it's because someone is getting married. Well, not someone, lots of people, actually. And not exactly marriage, but something close enough. And you were told this is important and you were told it has something to do with Elton John. And now, as you look at the queue, you can see rows and rows of smiling couples but the people in the couples are boys and boys and girls and girls and this pierces your chest with a shard of light and you aren't disappointed anymore. You are happy but you don't know why.

VI

Sun-washed, you lick the dribble of whiter-than-white ice cream from the back of your hand. And when you look up to follow your friends, you see two girls. They are a few years older than you. One has a thread of blue stars bursting up from the grass-stained cotton of her ankle sock. They are lying on a blanket, one propped up on elbows looking down at the other. They do not notice you watching. They do not notice anything at all except for each other. They are totally, fiercely focused. Neither says a word. The girl with the burst of blue stars reaches up a hand to tuck a strand of hair behind the other's ear. You pocket the moment and run after your friends across the dry grass.

VII

You have just smoked your first cigarette. You feel cooler than you've ever felt before in your life and also you feel sick. You are at a proper cool party. With proper cool kids. You wish you could think of a word to describe things other than 'cool' but every time you open your mouth it is the only word that wants to come out. The boy who gave you the cigarette is leaning against the corrugated iron side of a barn, inside which a Tinie Tempah song is whipping the assembled adolescents into a frenzied ecstasy. He is a friend-of-a-friend's big brother, a year older than you and taller by a couple of inches and so, leaning as he is against the wall, his eyes are now level with yours. Around them is a smudge of black eyeliner. He flicks his head in a way that makes his dark fringe swish across his forehead and you can't tell whether he is gesturing for you to join him in his leaning or if his hair was just in his eyes. You take a step towards him, brave because of your cigarette and the warm Bacardi Breezer you snuck from the bottom drawer of your older brother's dresser. The boy is asking you questions and you are answering but you can't really hear his words and you don't know what you're saying back because the drumbeat of your heart is filling all the space in your chest, your head, your ears. The boy stands straight and takes a step towards you. He asks you another question and you hear him this time and you nod and as you nod he dips his face towards yours. His mouth tastes like strawberries and smoke. His mouth is soft and wet and warm and you're not entirely sure what you thought this would feel like but it wasn't this and it isn't unpleasant exactly but it is surprising. He pulls back and asks if this is OK and you say that it is and he kisses you again. And then you kiss him back and you forget that all your friends are just on the other side of the waves of metal that now cool the skin on your back as you are gently pushed against the wall. He stands straight and grins at you, hair now out of place because hands, your hands, have been run through it. You grin back and open your mouth to say something but all that comes out is: 'Cool.'

VIII

The letter is on its way to your parents' house and now there is nothing that you can do about it. For all you know it has already reached the sorting office in your hometown, a hundred miles from the newfound freedom of university. This feeling thrills as much as it terrifies you. You try not to picture their faces as they open the letter. You sent it to avoid the shame you imagined seeing in their eyes. You are standing on a table in a nightclub, shouting over the music to tell your friends the truth. Some of them are expecting it, some of them will be surprised. One of them won't talk to you for a very long time and it will hurt but the way the rest of them hold you will make everything hurt less forever. You are standing on a table and someone is taking a picture of you. You have just said the words out loud for the third time in a row and one of your best friends, a girl with honey-coloured eyes, has opened her mouth in shock and joy and is showing off all her perfect teeth and those honey-coloured eyes are huge and wide. Someone is taking the picture and it fixes this shifting moment in time. Half in, half out. Behind you in the picture is a boy you haven't met yet. For some reason the light hits him perfectly. He has dark curls like fallen leaves and a lopsided, toothy smile. He is in the background of this important photo, the rotating light of the club rig picking him out for just a moment. Two months from now you will meet outside a different club and he will ask you for a lighter and you will end up falling in love with him almost immediately. You will spend nine months joined at the hip. One day, when he is still inside you, he will tell you that he loves and you will say it back. He will ask you if you really mean it and in that moment you really will. It won't last beyond the nine months for reasons you will come to forget and years later you will bump into each other on the street outside your house and you will be transported back to this exact moment and look back at all of this and recognise it for what it was. For now you decide it's probably easier to communicate what you have to say if you get down off the table and so you do. You get off the table and you tell your best friends in the world something that has been burning you up from inside for years and some of them aren't surprised and some of them are and it doesn't actually matter because you've said it now. All that matters is that you've said it and that the letter is on its way to your parents' house and you are speeding towards freedom, towards happiness, towards yourself.

IX

She is sitting on the steps in the alley behind the nightclub. You once found a dead rat here, as big as a cat, between the bins. Her wig and dress are in a Reebok sports bag next to her but her face is still on and her boy hair is stringy with sweat. She lights a second cigarette, puts the phone to her ear and says, *Yeah, yeah, babe, I know, that's so shit... No, no, of course... Yeah, it was alright, couple of hen dos but they behaved themselves... God, no, but I'll tell you about something when I get home... No, about Jamie... I know! And on a Thursday, can you imagine?... Can you put the oven on?... Nuggets, yeah... No, there are some... Yeah... The freezer, you dickhead... You're an angel... I love you... OK, I will... I love you, yes, OK, loveyoubye.*

X

The old towel around your shoulders is currently a murky grey colour but tomorrow you will notice pale splotches where the peroxide has burnt away the dye. You are not looking in a mirror, you are looking at the wall of the little kitchen in your first London flat. Your housemate is wearing marigolds and peering at the instructions on the box of bleach. You're asking him if it's supposed to burn this much. You're asking how long it says you should leave it on. You're thinking that maybe the break-up wasn't so bad that you needed to lean so hard into this particular cliché. You're privately wondering whether you should have done the patch test as the box told you to but it's too late for that now, so you decide to grit your teeth and bear it. This gives you an idea and you suddenly shout to your housemate to get the poppers. You figure that, given they help you relax through one painful experience, they might be useful here too. Your housemate hands you the little bottle with its plastic St George's flag wrapper and you use the currently grey towel to wipe away globs of blueish bleach mixture that your housemate has inadvertently smeared across the bottle and screw off the cap. You place the opening under your nose and inhale as deeply as you can. There is a moment where not much happens. You hand the bottle to your housemate, who takes his own huff of the amyl nitrite. You feel the poppers hit your bloodstream and your eyes go wide as you realise you've made a terrible mistake. The blood, let loose by the dilation of all your major capillaries, rushes to your head. It's as if you've opened a channel between the pain in your scalp and the inside of your skull and an agonising wave of heat rushes in. You scream and stand up, knocking over the rickety stool you were sitting on. You feel like your head has been set on fire. Your housemate finds this incredibly funny. He starts to laugh and cannot stop. He is bent double and then collapses onto the floor. The pain begins to subside as you too start to laugh and now you are both rolling around on the cheap lino tiles. It takes a long time for the laughter to subside and when it finally does the pain in your scalp has been joined by a dull throbbing at the back of your head and the satisfying, searing ache of laughter in your obliques. Still giggling, you allow your housemate to rinse the peroxide from your hair as you lean over a pink-ringed bathtub. When it's fully washed out, you rise to your feet and finally look in the mirror. Your hair is a shocking, unnatural orange and the skin around your hairline is hot, furious and pink. You start laughing again and this time neither of you can stop. Tears come and, every time you feel you might be able to control yourself, he catches sight of your hair again and you both crumple onto the bathroom floor. You have never been this happy.

XI

The pair are younger than you. Early twenties at most. The tube carriage is half-full and they decide to stand. As the train speeds up one of them wobbles slightly and leans into the other. They smile at each other sheepishly. You cannot tell if this is a first date or not. You have a feeling it might be the first time either of them has done anything like this. There is something naïve about the tension between them. They are talking in low voices and you cannot make out the words over the screech of the train. The taller of the two looks around cautiously, checking his level of safety. You want to catch his eye, urge him to do it, stand up and shout that they are safe here, that you will keep them safe. But that would be weird. Instead, you stare at them, willing them on with your eyes. Which is probably just as weird. But they either don't see you or take your attention as permission and the taller of the two brushes his fingers against the other man's hand, which opens up like a bloom, and their fingers find each other. They catch each other's eyes and look away then back again then laugh. And then they stop laughing and stand there, hand in hand, eye to eye, swaying as the gentle motion of the train rushes them onwards.

XII

I got us a bottle to split because it was cheaper.

Stunning. So, I think I'm gonna say yes…

Oh really…?

What?

Nothing.

No, don't be like that. What?

Well, I–

You've fucked him, haven't you?

Not exactly.

Not exactly?

We didn't *fuck*.

Right.

We hung out.

Like a date?

I guess.

You guess?

Like, two dates…

And you didn't fuck?

I don't like your tone.

My tone?

Yeah. Your tone.

Well, it's just not like you to not fuck someone–

Fuck you!

Exactly.

…

So…

What?

What's wrong with him?

Nothing's *wrong* with him…

You don't sound convinced.

Well, it's just that I'm pretty sure he's…

He's…?

You know...

No, I don't know. What is he?

A bottom.

Ah.

Probably.

Probably?

Yeah. As I said, we never fucked, so...

So, this assessment is–

More vibes-based, yeah.

Vibes based?

Sure.

He's got bottom vibes. And how, exactly, could you tell?

You can always tell.

You can?

Yeah. It's the voice.

The voice?

Yeah. And, like, the mannerisms.

Mmm...

Yeah, you could tell.

I don't know if I could.

...

...

...

...

So, are you still gonna see him?

Fuck you.

Hey, I'm just trying to help.

Well, you're not. And I'll have you know, I've been topping loads recently.

Oh, I'm sure!

Fuck you!

We tried that, remember? No dice.

Yeah, that was a bust.

Because...?

Because we weren't compatible.

Because…?

Because we were both…

Bottoms.

No, we weren't…

Tops.

I think you're being reductive, actually.

…

…

So… Are you still gonna–

Yes, I'm still gonna see him.

Cool. Good luck.

I hate you.

I know. I love you too.

XIII

He shudders and groans and you're glad you already came because the love-like feeling you get sometimes post-orgasm doubles and spreads through you like warm water as he collapses over you. He breathes in the salt of your neck, and you realise all at once that this is going to be the last time. You don't know how you know it. It's more like a premonition, half thought half felt. For a moment you panic. What if this doesn't have to be it, what if you're letting go too soon, what if you've misread everything? The possibility stings, and your chest goes hollow, desperate to cling to him, to pull the night back into permanence. But the wave passes. The certainty settles again, heavy and strange, like the sticky wetness pooling now in your belly button. You thought you had more time. But faced with this looming ending you welcome its strange finality. What you feel isn't sadness. Not even close. It's like an ember dying. Beautiful because you know it's almost gone. You focus your attention on the small mole on his right shoulder, the one you noticed on the beach the day you met. The one you have kissed a dozen times since. You see that it has been joined by a smattering of new freckles. You pour everything you have felt for him this summer – desire, tenderness, longing – into that little constellation and replace it with something else. A knowledge that you were both here. Fleeting but real. You watch the mole blur as tears begin to pool and you let this little spark of love burn out.

XIV

Now the music rises around you to an impossible height, columns of smoke, light cutting through, catching, swirling, fractured blues and pinks, beams of hymnal sound slanting down. Your friends are beside you. Mouths open wide in laughter that gets carried away in the surge of music. Every strobe-flash pins you in place, a living fragment in a window you can't quite step back from to see the whole. There are shapes inside it: hands joined, hair tucked gently behind an ear, a cherished letter found tucked away for safekeeping, laughter spilling onto kitchen tiles, corrugated kisses, tiara askew. They shift and blur as the bass surges, fleeting figures set in jewel-coloured glass, each pane cracked but not broken. Fixed together with solder and gold, they turn over each other in the dark. The congregation sways, arms rising as though in prayer, sweaty backs pressed against you. The song climbs and climbs, chorus without ceiling. He hooks his arm around your neck, pulls your head down until your foreheads bump, grinning wide as he shouts something you can't hear but feel anyway. Someone presses a drink into your palm, ice cold, and squeezes your hand before letting go. You turn and all of them are looking at you, eyes caught in the strobe, and for a flicker of a second you see yourself reflected back: coloured fragments now made whole, lit through and through and through.

Future Histories

You place the ring on my finger as halfway around the world, someone else is deciding whether it will mean something. We've already started the paperwork, the act of informing the archives and histories that may survive that we were together. And the diamonds that now adorn your left hand and mine, we're told, are forever. Our bodies aren't, and neither are the September nights on which we dance or the silly songs I sing for you or the braids you plait into my hair. But just as we look at names on park benches and imagine, we believe someone else will.

Nirali Sheth (she/her)
& @firewordsparkler

About the Editors

Jenna Gordon (she/her) is the Editorial Director at VERVE Books.

Demi Echezona (she/they) is an Assistant Editor at VERVE Books, contributor to *Nonchalant Magazine* and aspiring poet.

About Switchboard

For over 50 years, Switchboard has supported the LGBTQIA+ community through challenges and triumphs, offering a listening ear in difficult times and moments of joy.

Their support is completely free and available wherever you feel most comfortable, whether that's via phone (0800 0119 100), chat (switchboard.lgbt) or email (hello@switchboard.lgbt).

Switchboard's services are open from 10 am to 10 pm, every single day of the year. Their trained volunteers are available to discuss anything related to sexuality and gender identity; whether it's sexual health, relationships or just the way you're feeling.

For anyone, anywhere in the country, at any point in their journey.

switchboard.lgbt
@switchboardlgbt